YOU'VE GOT TO LOSE TO WIN

Will Simpson

ISBN-13: 979-8-9880928-0-3 (eBook)
ISBN-13: 979-8-9880928-2-7 (Paperback)
ISBN-13: 979-8-9880928-1-0 (Hardcover)

Cover design by: Emery George & Will Simpson
Library of Congress Control Number: 2023907664
Printed in the United States of America

This book is not possible without the support and patience of my wife, Caroline.

She is the one who said, "Go, it is about time," when I first brought the idea up.

As with everything, her support was immediate and complete.

I. Love. You. Caroline, always.

CHAPTER ONE

SHUFFLE UP AND DEAL

"What the fuck, Fatman? You steal this felt or what?" Arnold spouts off as he bursts in and sees his friend Slade crouched on the living room floor. Slade is sweating and aggressively laying out a sizeable piece of green pool table felt and carpet pad.

Arnold is a handsome man with a slight but firm build; his Italian features, dark hair, olive skin, and dark eyes are prominent. Even though he's a Texas native, he talks fast with the slightest accent picked up from his uncles and cousins, who mostly live in Jersey or Vegas. His wit and charm are seemingly on the edge of exploding as if contained in this "little Italian" firecracker!

By contrast, Slade is a more prominent fellow, but not what you would call fat, even though Arnold nicknamed him. Most would recognize him as "big-boned." Extremely fair-skinned, with bright steely blue eyes and long blond hair all one length past the middle of his back, usually in a ponytail. Most would pause before engaging in any kind of physical challenge. Slade is also a native of Texas and lacks any of the several Texas regional accents that land here in Central Texas. Many say he sounds like a Californian, but what does that sound like? Slade speaks almost in a rhythm you hear from a lawyer's disclaimer at the end of a car ad. Slade also doesn't hesitate to throw in a few big words now and again to remind folks that he is, in fact, the most intelligent person in the room.

He grabs his "sweat towel" and quips right back at his friend, as he has since junior high school. "Screw you fucko, be useful, and bring the table in. It's in the garage, and the door is open. Where the hell have you been anyway? How long does it take to whip up some fucking enchiladas? I'm sweating my ass off here."

"If you'd drop a couple of tons, you wouldn't sweat so much," Arnold snips back.

Slade starts to talk about genetics, but Arnold quickly heads out before Slade can drop words no one understands, especially him, into the mix. He grabs a three-by-six wooden folding table from the garage and takes it back inside.

They are setting up in the unoccupied "B-side" of the duplex that Slade owns. This side is nice but nothing special, especially compared with the "A-Side" that Slade lives in, with marble and wooden floors and a top-of-the-line security system.

"Here ya go, Fatman. Are you sure this shit's gonna work? I still think you should have bought a real table." Not waiting for an answer, Arnold continues. "Oh, I decided to go Italian: got a full pan of lasagna, some gnocchi, and salad. I snagged two cheesecakes too. I already put it all in your fridge next door."

The two lay the pad on the table, slowly stretching and stapling the felt. Before long, the poker table is felted and ready to test out. Everything seems to fall into place for Slade to kick off the game with "Shuffle up and Deal"[1]

Lewis wanders in as the table is about to be finished.

Lewis is a shorter heavy-set guy, a bit younger than Arnold and Slade, but appears to be ten years older. Primarily bald, in his early twenties, he speaks with a stereotypically West Texan slow drawl. His go-to catchphrase is, "Man, I'm getting too old for this shit." It's almost like listening to some slightly higher-pitched version of John Wayne.

He seems to take a minute before every sentence, pausing occasionally to spit due to a significant dip of snuff. Lewis is a man of

---

[1] It's the phrase used in most poker tournaments that signals the start of the tournament. It's also used in single table venues to signal the start of a long session of poker; it sets the mood.

few words, but his crystal blue eyes and genuine smile make him seem like a dear longtime friend from the first time you see him.

"Sup, Bird-man? The table's looking good," he says as he runs his hands up and down the straps on his overalls. "Y'all gonna get the game going tonight?"

"Hell ya, Lewis, you should come play. I know you got the cash after you stole it from those chumps last night," Slade says while jabbing Arnold with his elbow.

Arnold pipes in. "Hell, ya, c'mon on in, Lewis. The water's fine!"[2]

Lewis shakes his head from side to side. "Not a chance. I might sit a bit and help pass out food or something. I ain't giving you two sharks[3] none of my dough." He opens the door to spit again.

"Bird-man, you got a spitter[4] in here somewhere?" he asks.

"Umm-hum. You want to see Ramona. Slade and Arnold in unison - "rootin' around for Ramona," a line from the movie *Neighbors*. Arnold and Slade often do this, speaking as one, using one-liners from various movies or shows. Slade adds, "Look under the sink on my side of the duplex. There are some spitters under there."

Slade, of course, has his own "spitter." Still, as with most things, he's not prone to share. Dipping is a common activity among most people whom Slade's known since junior high school. Everyone is expected to have an extra "spitter" or two around somewhere.

Ramona's playing hostess at the game tonight, and Slade's let everyone know. She's a striking redhead dancer from the local strip club and Slade's longtime (three years) fuck-buddy. Fuck-buddy or not, this is business, and Slade's learned that when men with large egos are in the presence of super hot chicks, it tends to loosen their wallets just a tad.

---

[2] An ironic phrase meant to sound as if the "waters of gambling" were safe and not full of "sharks" who would surely take your money. It was used to push the ego and goad people into playing against you

[3] Referring to the predators of a given gambling situation; i.e. card shark, pool shark, etc.

[4] Slang for spittoon and can be any cup, can or bottle used to spit tobacco in.

The table is done, and it's time for a test. It's almost noon; plenty of time before the food is served for the game at seven pm sharp.

Arnold grabs a used deck of cards and some chips. He hands Slade and Lewis a stack and starts to deal. "Niiice! The cards slide good. This might work, Fatman," Arnold says.

"Ante up! Let's play a couple and see what we think," Arnold continues.

"FUCK!" Lewis says, somehow with two syllables and that drawl. "This shit's way too bouncy, Bird-Man; you'll have chips all over the place. Even if people don't try to splash the pot[5], this will be a damned mess."

"I told you: you should have bought a table," Arnold snaps at Slade. "Let's go snag one somewhere. Lewis, can we borrow your truck?

"Slow your roll, fucko! This ain't your show; it's mine. You don't see me telling you how to wash dishes, do you? I can fix this. Just chillax." Slade's tone is commanding and definitive.

"Shuffle up and Deal" is not the story going around in Slade's mind. It's more like "Shuffle up, and deal?" Slade feels the slightest bit of worry, and he quickly pushes it aside and gets back to the job at hand. He's popping staples from the table, and as he rolls back the felt, Lewis sees the problem.

"Damn Bird-man, you shoulda used one sheet of pad, not two. That thin one in there would be the nuts[6]," Lewis adds, taking sides with Slade over Arnold.

"Fine, whatever. I would have got a real table," Arnold continues, still feeling the sting of Slade's dishwasher comment.

"Help me pull the fat pad out, and let's re-stretch," orders Slade.

---

[5] Referring to throwing chips of yours into the pot in the middle of the poker table. This is against the rules because it can severely slow down a game. It's not always possible to know exactly what chips were put into the pot when this is done, so the correct way to bet is to slide your chips out in front of you without letting them touch the pot. The dealer will then pull the chips in once the count is verified

[6] This is a phrase that simply means; the absolute best. It also means an unbeatable hand for example if one had an Ace High straight flush, that hand would be "The Nuts."

Reluctantly, Arnold helps pull the table felt back into shape, and in short order, the table is back together. "Ok, Fatman, if this shit don't work, can you get fucking real table then?" says Arnold, still trying to hold on to some dignity.

Slade replies, but this time almost monotone, distinctly slower and quieter for effect. "Give me the cards; I got this." It's Slade's way of showing that he is, in fact, in charge. With that, he deals out the hand and stacks chips in front of each of them.

"Ante up, dill weed, let's see how it goes." Slade tries to lighten the mood by calling Arnold a friendlier nickname this time; it's good business to have everyone playing tonight in good spirits. And Slade still needs Arnold to come to fill a seat and potentially bring others to play. This is, as most things are with Slade, a calculated move.

"The Simonis[7] is good for card movement. Let's see the bounce," challenges Arnold. As the chips are placed or even tossed a bit, they land with a nice little "plunk" and no bounce to be of concern.

"Lucky," says Arnold. And the table is done. Slade lets the comment go as there's no real upside to putting Arnold in his place, but the defiant comment irritates Slade. Slade takes a quick inventory and notices a few drinks and a particular brand of cigarettes that must be picked up.

"Let's make the rounds and ensure we have a full house tonight. I'm gonna grab a shower and snag Ramona so she can finish setting shit up. I'll snag the rest of the supplies while I'm out." Slade continues, "Let's meet up at the Side Hole about two, two-thirty, ok?"

"Sweet Fatman, I'll be up there in a bit. Are we gonna chop it up fifty-fifty while we're both playing tonight? Set a limit or something, then chop winnings," Arnold inquires. Slade isn't particularly thrilled; he knows he's the far superior player but is stuck keeping Arnold happy. "Sure, fucko, whatever's good for you. Let's nail it down at The Side Hole." Slade replies flatly.

---

[7] high-end pool table felt that gives a more consistent and predictable roll

"That works." Arnold then piles on another request. "Have you thought about adding a bit of excitement to the game and not just boring-ass Hold 'em all night?"

"Dude, look, I've told you, I want to set up a structured and regular game. Tonight is a test, and if it goes well, I'll expand and have a night where we play mixed games and stuff." Slade says in a tone almost lecturing and undoubtedly definitive.

"Ok, ok, damn, don't be a dick about it. I was just saying," Arnold replies, feeling a little dismissed. With that, Arnold and Lewis head out, and Slade walks next door and notices Ramona is driving up.

"What the fuck! I thought I was picking you up?" snaps Slade.

'Well, Frank called me in when two girls called in sick," Ramona replied sheepishly. "I gotta work, and I wanted to come over and tell you I was sorry in person."

"Fuck me," Slade says aloud. "I need someone to do hostess shit."

"How about Becky?" Ramona offers. "She's not working tonight and is hot." She winks.

"Ya, she *IS* hot," Slade says, a bit too enthusiastically. Seeing Ramona's glare, he quickly adds, "For a skinny chick."

"Whatever, she plays on the other team anyway.[8] I'll call her," Ramona snaps. As she enters the duplex with Slade, she snags the wireless phone off the kitchen table to call Becky. Slade wasn't paying attention as his mind wandered, thinking about Becky. *I might put that to the test one of these days.*

Ramona hangs up to let Slade know Becky is set. And adds, "She is good with two hundred dollars plus all tips, same as I was getting. She'll head here around three-thirty, and I told her y'all start serving at seven. I also told her where you keep the spare key," with a clear note of finality.

As if she is reading Slade's thoughts, she turns to Slade as she heads out the door. "I won't be needing that key anymore anyway, I guess.

---

[8] This is slang for lesbian.

Good luck with your game or whatever tonight," she almost snarls, knowing as everyone in the rounder world does that wishing someone good luck is in and of itself bad luck.

Well, that's that, Slade thinks. Time for an upgrade anyway. I've been thinking I needed something new for a while. I Got the new place, car, and my game is on the upgrade path. I might as well round it out with a new piece of ass!

A quick shower later and Slade plops down into his hopped-up Honda. A CRX fully blacked out[9] with an aftermarket chip[10] and beefed-up suspension to the barely street-legal tires.

He revs the engine, rolls back the sunroof, pops in a CD, and cranks up Def Leppard. Of course, he has a top-of-the-line custom stereo, including dual fifteen-inch Cerwin Vega Woofers in the back. He quickly checks to ensure he has the "tools" of the gambling trade. Pool cue in the back. Wallet in the glove box. Pager on his hip. Glock under the front dash in its custom-made mounted holster (so it's not bouncing around when one hits a curve at ninety miles an hour).

All good, let's roll, Slade says to himself.

One last check for the "cash spots." Two short stacks of about twenty-five hundred dollars in each front pocket and a fat stack of thirty thousand dollars in the secret compartment Slade had built under the dash. *NOW I'm all good!*

Slade is ready!

As has become the usual method over the last six months, he knocks out the check box tasks early and leaves the action to flow as it does. He hits the liquor store first for the supplies to get that done. Slade has indeed transitioned to treating this as a business, not just another hustle. Today will not be spent wandering around, hoping to

---

[9] Car reference to all markings and emblems removed to give the car a smoother look, along with a dark tint on the windows. It's usually but not always done to a black or dark car.

[10] Car term for the computer control chip that controls gas flow, and other central things; It's assumed that this is an upgrade to make the car faster.

find another mark to take advantage of. Today there's an order to things, a structure. THIS is the beginning of how Slade wants things to be.

He's loading up the car with the supplies as his pager goes off. He recognizes the code[11] right away: It's Phil the bookie[12]. Slade's known "Wild Phil from Liberty Hill" for about three years, but Phil has become much more important to Slade over the last eighteen months. More than a mentor, Phil is a trusted person in his life. A father figure Slade never had.

Liberty Hill is nothing special, just one of the many little rural towns around the Austin Metro area. Most people, including Slade, couldn't even tell you their names or where they were located. No one knows if Phil is from Liberty Hill or if it's just a cheesy rhyming nickname that stuck. But it has, and everybody has a nickname.

Phil runs a tight ship. He has the reputation of always paying on time and supplying accurate and up-to-date lines[13]. It's generally accepted that Phil's your man if you want to make a sports bet locally. He's a great bookie but, like many rounders, good at one type of hustle; with other types, not so much! It's like a cycle for most. Make money on one end, blow it on the other. Most bookies are on the edge of being broke, similar to most hustlers. Phil's the exception to this rule, however. He has a successful sportsbook and has for a very long time. He has money and likes to throw it around. He would walk into a bar and buy the house a round, only to follow up with two more. Phil IS "that guy," and people love him for it.

Phil is a draw for poker games, and he and Slade both know it. Slade was pleased when Phil agreed to be a player in his inaugural game. Slade knows that having Phil is crucial to the first night's success.

Slade pops over to the payphone and calls Phil.

---

[11] In the gambling world, no one used phone numbers, only codes when paging. In case the authorities were to ever look at our pagers, it would be nonsense to them.

[12] A person who runs a sports betting establishment or sportsbook

[13] Lines refer to the odds given by a sportsbook for betting on a particular team in a sporting event matchup

"Sup man, you still comin' to give me your money tonight?" Slade jokes.

"Sorry little buddy, that's why I paged," Phil says. "Shit came up, and I gotta make a run to out-of-town. I know this is a big deal for you tonight, but I gotta handle this one in person. I can't say more, but I'll catch you up in the next day or so."

"All good," Slade says to Phil. And while Slade knows Phil would never let him down unless he had to, he can't hide the disappointment. Worry that he's feeling for the second time today is flooding his mind. For a brief moment, he lets that slip into his voice.

Phil hears it too. "Hey, little buddy, I'll make some calls, you'll fill it. Sorry to let you down."

Slade can detect in Phil's voice that he's honestly not happy to miss the game.

Before hanging up, Slade adds, "Hey Phil, I appreciate it. next dance is on me." Slade tries to lighten the mood, referring to table dances at the strip club. "Hit me up when you're back." He needs to scramble. At least three slots are open at the table now that Phil won't be there. At least two players were only coming because of Phil. They would either leave the game outright or leave early. Both scenarios were bad options.

Slade immediately pages Arnold with "-3" meaning three players were lost.

Slade proceeds from the liquor store to Eric's pool hall to see if he can spot any potential players. As his eyes adjust, he notices that there sits Danny the Drain. He's a union pipe-fitter[14]. The gang all tell him his nickname is based on his profession. The truth is that he'll drain his whole stack once he starts losing. He's one of those players you definitely want in a game. He isn't a terrible player but can't quit while

---

[14] Sometimes called a union plumber. This is a advanced level of plumbing of all kinds including industrial plumbing and fitting of high-pressure steam and ventilation pipes.

he's ahead. Constantly pressing the edge. He enjoys losing and getting mad about it. Such is one form of a gambler's addictive personality.

Danny's unremarkable features and medium build are of someone you pass by on the street every day and never notice. Almost always in jeans and a button-up, heavy-duty long-sleeve shirt that screams, "I work with my hands for a living." You would never know he makes over six figures in the union or has two kids in Ivy League schools.

"Hey, easy money, what are you doing off in the middle of the day?" Slade spouts off to Danny.

"Oh, the job got stalled. I think they found some rare fucking beetle or something. Shut the whole site down. Fuck it. I get paid either way," he grins.

"Hey, I'm gonna kick off my game tonight. You still thinking about comin' over? Ya know, we got good food and a hot Sugars chick servin'! Slade implores Danny.

"What the hell. I got time. When you startin' up?"

"Seven, we start the food and cards fly[15] by eight at the latest," Slade replies. "You don't want to miss the food. Arnold made up some lasagna and gnocchi, plus cheesecake for dessert. Full bar, of course.

"Now, Danny, you know the rules, right? Same as at Tex's game. It's a quarter[16] for a mucked[17] deck, and we all move on. Ya?" Slade checks in.

---

[15] When the game starts referring to a poker game
[16] In the gambling world, these terms all mean something other than their usual monetary value.
Nickel is five dollars
Dime is one thousand dollars
Quarter is twenty-five dollars
Dollar is one hundred dollars
Grocery Dollar is one dollar
[17] Mucked Hand or Deck is a Ruined Hand or Deck of cards
A mucked hand is when someone throws their discards into and mixes them with your live cards. Both hands are then dead. Throwing cards to cause this to happen is cause for removal from the game and repeated instances will get one permanently banned.
A mucked deck is one that is no longer usable typically because a card has become bent or marked in some way. Intentionally ruining a deck will have various penalties including paying for the deck and removal from the game.

"For sure, man, I got it. I'm chill tonight, though. It won't even be an issue."

Danny was also famous for getting pissed off when his luck is running bad. He routinely tears or folds, or even throws a deck of cards. Even at a discount, the full plastic decks are ten dollars in bulk. Slade, paying attention to other games, marks them up. Everything is to make a profit!

Well, this is good news, Slade is thinking. Danny is as big of a draw as Phil. And he sure likes to lose to show that he can! Slade quickly pages Arnold: "+1 ,+1" meaning they got one back, which will keep one at the table longer. Slade hangs out for a bit, shoots the shit with Danny, then exits without being too obvious.

Dropping a little white lie as he heads out, Slade says, "I need to get the supplies and such, make sure Becky has her shit right. See you at the game."

"Yep, see you in a bit to take your cash," Danny replies with a grin.

Slade hops back in the CRX, whips out of the parking lot, and heads to The Side Hole to meet Arnold. Suddenly he has the strangest feeling of nervousness. This is abnormal, and it's the third time today he's felt "strange." As soon as the weird sensation comes, it's gone. Slade knows this is a new turn, an inflection point. While Phil has said encouragingly that if tonight is a bust, you can give it a shot again later, Slade is unsure he has it in him. He wants, no, *needs* tonight to work well and get out of doing the hustle. He needs more.

As Slade walks into the Side Hole, he hears *Guns n' Roses* "Sweet Child of Mine" on the jukebox and is warmly greeted as the local royalty. Johnny, the bartender, asks, "You kickin' your game off tonight?

"For sure, man. You want a seat?" Slade beams.

"Of course, you know better! I ain't playing cards in shark-infested waters, but you know you got the eight[18] if you're itching to lose some cash." Johnny laughs as he says it.

Slade's mind wanders back to a few years before when he knew nothing of this pool hall lingo or lifestyle. It was like an echo chamber where he could hear the people in the pool hall talking, but their words and phrases were off and sounded muddled. To a naturally smart guy without context, this lingo sounded like an eerie foreign dialect of English. Yet he was intrigued. If he could learn this coded language they all spoke fluently, he would be part of them.

His hunches were correct. He'd mastered the lingo and was at home in this gritty life he'd been looking for.

Johnny is a well-built guy with a beaming smile and bright green eyes. He has a quick wit, which jives with Slade's own. It doesn't take long to notice how Johnny frequently looks at himself in the bar-length mirror behind him at The Side Pocket. In a word, Johnny is vain. Johnny is ten years older than Slade and is never seen without his ball cap. It took many months for Slade to realize that Johnny was going bald, and that's why he never takes off!

Johnny seems to have more money than a bartender's salary could afford: an old Porsche nine-eleven as his second car and (although most didn't know it) hair transplants. The truth is Johnny has the place wired. It's a beer and cash-only pool hall where Johnny regularly "supplements" the stock to take care of the skim. And an all-cash business makes this easy. He's also a decent pool player, not above hustling the occasional sucker.

There was a time when Johnny could have spotted Slade the eight-ball and made a winner out of it. These days though, Johnny and

---

[18] Got the eight (or any other pool ball number less than nine) Refers to a weighting system to balance a weaker player's chances of beating a stronger player. In the case of "getting the eight" the weaker player would win the game of nine-ball by sinking either the eight OR the nine while the stronger player must sink the nine to win

Slade wouldn't ever put this to the test. Everyone knows Slade has the upper hand even though he acts like he doesn't.

Arnold pops in right behind Slade and seems to be in good spirits. You can hear the excitement and pride in his voice as he announces, "Hey, Fatman, I snagged another player, so we're full plus one if they all stay."

Arnold would hit his usual local bars and places where players might hang out, while Slade used the pool halls as his base for recruiting players.

Slade seems a bit reflective, "You know I want to have a backup or two. You or I can rail[19] if the table is full. It makes the game go longer."

"You're such a downer," Arnold pops back. "Is that glass ever half fucking full? Plus, if all we're playing is boring ass Hold 'em[20] I'm happy to ride the rail!" Slade ignores the jab about the game being structured and shakes his head.

"Can I get a couple of beers, Johnny?" Arnold asks as the bartender walks away. Slade is no fan of the players Arnold brings. Arnold takes it as a slight as if Slade is getting "too big for his britches." In his mind, Slade should be thankful he's even in the game. He shouldn't make a big deal of playing any games people want.

---

[19] Outside of "the action" in some way. It can refer to someone waiting on an open seat or their turn at the action. This applies to both pool and poker. In some cases it can also mean that a person has been beaten and must move "to the rail" so another player can join.

[20] Hold 'em is a common poker game with a total of four betting rounds. Round one is when all players are dealt two cards in order going around the table, one card at a time. Round Two is after one card is turned face down or "burned" followed by three community cards being turned face up in the middle of the table, this is also referred to as the flop. Round three is when a single card is turned face down or burned followed by a single card being added to the other three community cards and is also referred to as fourth street. The fourth and final round of betting is when a single card is turned face down or burned followed by a single card being added to the other four and is also referred to as the river.

The players try to make the best possible poker hand they can using a total of five cards between the five face up community cards and the two in their own hand. Winning hands are as usual in all poker games as follows. High card, high pair, high two pair, high three of a kind, straight or five cards in counting sequence, high card flush or five cards of the same suit, full house or three of a kind AND a pair, four of a kind and the highest is high straight flush or five cards in counting order all of the same suit

Jimmy, aka Checkbook, walks in. Jimmy looks like a fish out of water. He's dressed cleanly in a neat button-down shirt freshly pressed. It matches perfectly with his earth-toned slacks with crisp creases down the middle. His thick blond hair looks like it has a fresh trim. Jimmy looks the very opposite of a pool hustler.

In fact, Checkbook isn't a great hustler, but he's good at pool and looks like such a straight-arrow that people couldn't help but try to beat him. Inevitably they'd lose.

Jimmy is also one of the few good pool players who's also a decent card player. Slade thinks, man, Jimmy could be the player we need to balance out whatever idiot Arnold rounded up. We're gonna make this a game, after all.

"Hey, what are you two up to?" Jimmy asks.

"Setting up for the game tonight. Wild Phil bailed on me, but we have a chair if you're up for losing a little of that gravy,[21]" provokes Slade.

"Who's coming? I gotta make sure there's at least one loose player at the table."

Again, Jimmy the anomaly. Everyone knows his tone of voice and the educated cadence from a top-tier school. With an MBA from Stanford, dropping an "f-bomb" is out of character for someone like Jimmy. Add to it the mismatch of his three-hundred-dollar pair of loafers touching this pool hall's dingy, dirty blue carpet. The anomaly is that Jimmy loves it here with the gritty people!

"I pulled in Danny the Drain," Slade says excitedly.

Jimmy jumps on it, "Oh, shit! In that case, what time? I'm in."

"Food at seven, cards fly at eight at the latest. I got Becky from Sugars serving up the food, and I'll have your Stoli in the freezer."

"I'm in for sure," he repeats, then adds. "I'll be there early to pick my seat." Pausing again, he continues, "Hey, you have another spot

---

[21] *Money that came easy without working hard for it.*

14

open? I think Lorenzo wants to play." Sam Lorenzo was a grinder[22], but he would hold a seat all night to expand the game. Slade understood that while he wouldn't make any money directly off Sam, he would help the rake.

"Hell, ya, tell him to come on. If we over-fill, I'll kick fucko out of his seat for the real players," Slade beams at Jimmy.

"Ya, you're a laugh a minute, Fatman," Arnold quips, still feeling a bit slighted; it dawns on him that people view Slade as the Alpha in this card game. This can't be easy, as Arnold's been in the alpha slot for the last ten-plus years, especially in the rounder side of life.

Arnold shakes off his jealousy and concludes that with Jimmy in, the room is filled and back on track. The game might be a little tougher than it would have been with Phil, but Checkbook can also be a draw. When he gets down and starts to lose, his mode is "go-off." In other words, fire back with more significant cash and more aggressive plays, which is better for the house and his cut.

Slade decides to push Jimmy a bit, taking advantage of his ego in case the night starts badly for him.

"Hey, Checkbook, you and Lorenzo should take separate rides so you don't have to sleep on the couch waiting for him to win your money back from the rest of us when you bust out early." Slade roars with laughter.

Arnold sees what Slade is up to and piles right in with the obvious fake laugh to poke at Jimmy.

"Keep it going! Remember: Buy two; they're small," Jimmy jabs back. While this one stings Slade's ego, and he congratulates himself for getting under Jimmy's skin as intended.

Slade flashes back a bit to a game not long ago where he was losing badly, and Jimmy kept goading him: "Buy two; they're small," he would say. Slade had to ask Arnold what that meant. He discovered it referred to Slade buying back in at double the initial buy-in rate. In

---

[22] A player who sits and sits and waits for perfect hands and is risk averse.

the end, if it hadn't been for that substantial loss, Slade would certainly not be here today about to embark on a new path: a business path.

Arnold and Slade wandered off to the side for last-minute planning. All signs of feeling insulted had vanished from Arnold as swiftly as they had come on.

Slade says, "Ok, we buy in for two dollars each and no deeper than a dime. We good?"

"A dime each, max." Arnold nods.

Then Slade adds, "And if either bails early, we square right then to get back to even. If we both go the night, It's fifty-fifty on the rake. If not, seventy-five / twenty-five. Good?"

"I like it," says Arnold. "I play my way, and if I want to bail if the table is still full, I can!" Then he pops out his fist for the bump and settles it.

Slade makes the rounds in the pool hall, asking if anyone else might like to join his card game. He knew the answer.

This was all a show!

Slade walks out of The Side Hole and hops into his clean CRX, heading for the duplex. His mind is racing; the drive home is a blur. The poker table is set, the food is ready and laid out on the kitchen bar, and Becky looks hot as hell! He's prepared, the room's ready, and the players are on the way.

One by one, people start knocking on the door. Some have signature knocks. Two short and two long: That's Checkbook. He's first.

Checkbook says hi to Becky as he walks in and quickly picks out where he wants to sit. "Can you get me a Stoli straight and a little bit of whatever Arnold cooked up? It smells great!"

Turning to Slade, "I'll get a dime stack." as he lays out ten hundred-dollar bills.

Slade is seated at the head of the table. Immediately behind him is one of the new custom wooden covered drop box safes he has just picked up from Vegas, along with fully customized sets of clay poker chips.

Slade slides the cash from the table into the slot in the cabinet in one smooth motion, then opens a large wooden box that contains the poker chips. They're pre-stacked in two-, three- and five-dollar sets so handing them out is efficient. Slade is proud of his chips, fully custom-made with "Bird–Man Poker" stamped into them. The custom box is emblazoned with the same on its outside lid.

Slade grabs a five-dollar stack, then adds five black chips to make it a full ten dollars.

"Here you go," Slade replies. "Let me know if you need anything chopped up[23]."

Becky interrupts as she brings Checkbook, his drink, and a plate of food. Slade isn't paying attention as they start to chatter back and forth. There's another knock on the door; one short, three long.

Arnold has arrived, along with Lorenzo and someone from the garage game. Right behind them are Danny the Drain, Tex O'Sullivan and t,wo of Phil's customers.

The table is full as it's set to hold eight people.

Slade pulls Arnold slightly aside and says, "You want to hit the rail first, or me? One of us should stay and rake."

"I got it, brother. You chill and host; we can swap every so often and see how shit goes."

With that, the players are seated and getting their orders to Becky for drinks and food. Arnold is collecting cash and handing out the chips.

Slade plops down on the black leather couch across the room from the poker table to look around and take it all in. It was happening. Slade is going to the next level and hosting his own game.

---

[23] Broken down into smaller denominations

The room fades. Slade's mind goes still and wanders back almost ten years ago to that little boy he was in eighth grade. Where this all began, and he was gambling with Arnold for the first time. That first loss would set up the possibility for the win today.

CHAPTER TWO

FLIPPIN QUARTERS

It's a crisp forty-five degrees, which in central Texas is an unusually cold morning for early October. The sky is clear blue, and the wind is all but gone as the cold front from the evening before has passed through.

Slade is a stocky kid with blond hair and steel-blue eyes. Even after a little over a month and a half into eighth grade, riding the bus seems odd and new for Slade. Until this year, his parents had chosen to drive him to school for "safety" reasons.

Consequently, he's had little interaction with other kids outside of classroom settings. The little cliques formed at bus stops and the ride itself before and after school haven't been part of Slade's life, and he's unaware of what he's missed.

His mom picks his clothes and makes Slade wear corrective shoes with a heel and arch support. These are the final touches to the "anything but cool" wardrobe, including off-brand patched jeans and slightly worn tee shirts. It's common for other parents that Slade knows to pick clothes for their kids, so Slade sees this as the norm. His father has always said, "fancy clothes worn outside of mornin' church are worn by people you can't trust." The thought of any other wardrobe was not a consideration at all.

Slade leads a sheltered and controlled life, unaware that the world outside his home and what his parents call "the church family" is not how things are in most places. Slade sees things that don't fit into his tiny world and assumes "those" people are the odd minority. Slade doesn't even have a view through TV that most kids his age have. His parents declare that the children will only be permitted one and a half hours of TV weekly. Slade's father rules the house with no room for questioning or disagreement.

Slade can remember the rare discussions when his mom would disagree. While there was never physical violence toward his mother, it seems there could have been. One of the most intense discussions he recalls involved him. He had been tested for a wide range of learning and intelligence abilities at his school (a progressive public grade school with accelerated learning programs.) With his estimated IQ of one hundred and forty, among other things, the school was recommending that Slade move directly from third grade to high school.

His mom loved the idea. She said it would be good for Slade to be around people who were on his mental level and would give him a leg up in the world. His father couldn't have disagreed any stronger. "School is a privilege, and I was already working to support the family when I was his age. He needs to toughen up and get to work, not keep his nose in books."

Slade's parents were strict disciplinarians following guidance from a combination of Evangelical and Baptist doctrines. Baptists and Evangelicals are both punitive Christian sects that do not allow drinking, dancing, or using swear words, for example. The sermons Slade remembers were of a mighty God who demanded obedience without question from his followers to be allowed into Heaven. These doctrines also deemed that the "Earthly Father" is in charge of the household without question. Slade's father followed this doctrine to the letter with the full support of his mother.

Children were expected to be seen and not heard and to always respect (really obey) their parents without question.

Corporal punishment was expected and doled out often immediately and in public. More often than not, the public spanking was followed up at home with a "real whippin'" of then to fifteen lashes which most often left large welts. Slade had been taught to walk the hall length where a belt was hanging without so much as a whimper less he would receive even more lashes. This all seemed perfectly normal to Slade: He was bad and deserved to be punished for it.

Slade's movements and interactions with people outside of the church are minimal. He's told and, of course, believes that it's "for safety." Still, as he would learn later in life, these were control mechanisms of a church that was (as with many American religious groups led by white men), in every definition, a cult.

One such restriction is in his own neighborhood.

Slade lives on the edge of the school district and outside of the Austin city limits. It's a small rural neighborhood with a horse ranch backing up to his yard. His street, to the South, only has ten houses until the dead-end, and to the North, has about thirty houses and also stops at a dead-end.

His little street is intersected by a small two-lane road that eventually takes a person to the interstate on the East end and a major four-lane highway West. It's what the locals refer to as "living out in the boonies."

Slade can't cross the two-lane road because "it's not safe." Slade also believed this without question. This was another way to control whom he could interact with and be influenced by.

Until Slade started to ride the bus, none of this had been a big deal. Most of Slade's non-school time was spent doing household chores like laundry and mowing the yard. Outside of that, he'd be found working in the family business packing boxes or doing the bookkeeping for the five retail plant stores and the warehouse. When he did get free time, he'd ride his bike on trails close to the house.

Now that he's riding the bus, Slade discovers that many kids live closer than he had known about, just on the other side of the two-lane road, and that they would mostly congregate over there to wait for the bus. Slade doesn't grasp that this separation also makes him seen as different in the same way he doesn't see his wardrobe as different.

Slade has little social understanding, so even seeing an entire school population dressing differently doesn't cause him to understand. To him, they're the different ones. The fear of being "in trouble" at school for talking in class, getting in a fight, or anything that might be reported to his parents has also made Slade self-isolate. Social interaction outside the church was taught as a bad thing from the start. Cognitive biases are set early in life and rarely get broken.

He thinks nothing of waiting alone for the bus as he makes his way up the short driveway with his slightly ripped, overloaded backpack hanging off his shoulder and his viola case in one hand with a couple of spirals and another book in the other.

Slade makes a slight misstep. His backpack slips from his shoulder, and all his papers hit the ground. As he reaches to grab them before they become wet from the dew, his viola hits the driveway with a loud clunk. Slade scrambles to pick up everything. The bus arrives and stops with the doors open waiting for him. Slade starts the day embarrassed, as he knows everyone saw him trip and fumble.

As Slade climbs on the bus, Arnold smiles and shouts: "Come on back, Fatboy! Let's get this bus a-movin'"!

Arnold is a wiry-framed kid with thick brown hair and hazel eyes. He has a larger-than-life personality. He moves with a noticeable grace and quickness. Arnold has a character that only adults are supposed to have. He tells people everything and is big and bold about it. Slade's been intrigued with him since seeing him on the bus on that first trip to Burnet Junior High.

Even though they'd gone to the same schools for the last two years, Slade didn't know Arnold or any of the other kids. Slade was in small accelerated learning classes, already doing high school level work, isolated. The neighborhood kids were all in regular classes together and bonding.

During the first three days of riding the bus, Slade learned that Arnold's dad drives a Ferrari and a Corvette. He found out that Arnold went to private school until sixth grade, knows karate, and was a runner-up for the Junior Olympic team. He even knew that Arnold's birthday was September eleventh, meaning that he had already turned fourteen and was one of the oldest in eighth grade.

Arnold often refers to the family restaurant as "authentic" since his family is first-generation Italian/American. In this mention, it seems Arnold is somehow also expressing that his family is well off. Even with his lack of fashion understanding, Slade can tell that Arnold never wears the same clothes daily and that others seem to comment on the various little alligators and horses stitched on his shirts.

Arnold is the leader on the bus. Slade finds himself drawn to the power Arnold seems to wield over the other kids and even the bus driver. Arnold can roam the bus freely instead of staying in his seat.

Slade also hears the other kids talk about Arnold: telling the story of Arnold beating up the neighborhood bully trying to steal a little kid's bike or something; in one story, it was a backpack, and in another, it was to protect a girl Arnold likes. Slade assumes this is why everyone seems to respect Arnold. Respect and fear hold the same meaning at this point in Slade's life, so being afraid of being beaten up was a reason for respect. At the same time, this held little weight for Slade as he was sure no kid could be as big and tough as his father. Slade feared his father in every way.

In comparison, Arnold was just another kid and was not afraid of kids.

Arnold is intrigued by Slade. He sees in him a curious attribute he does not understand. Slade seems calm and does not seem to want anything from Arnold. How is it that this uncool kid is not sucking up to him? He even gave him a nickname to drive an insult and a connection: Fatboy.

In truth, Arnold is isolated in many ways. He's on the other end of the "small classes" spectrum for kids needing extra help to make it through. While Arnold leads the neighborhood clique, he isn't quite as tight as he might appear. He, like Slade, was missing some of the classroom bonding and drama that started to emerge in Junior High School.

This is an odd but common thread for the two unlikely friends. Arnold would set himself as the Alpha in the relationship. Still, Arnold respected Slade even if Slade himself didn't see or feel that respect from Arnold.

As Slade finally makes it on the bus, Arnold grabs Slade's viola case and puts it on his shoulder like a bazooka or something. "We got to hunt us up some fun today, Fatboy! Let's get loaded!" The bus roars with laughter from the other kids, and even the driver chuckles. Slade is oblivious that he's the brunt of the joke, and he likes the attention he's getting from Arnold. Until today, all Arnold has done is talk about himself or call Slade by the nickname of Fatboy.

Arnold plops down beside Slade on the bus as they make their way to the school. He asks about the case and what is in it.

Slade explains what a viola is with a deeper tone and is slightly larger than a violin. He continues and explains that it also uses a particular music scale only used by a handful of other instruments. Arnold immediately makes a joke; "a FAT violin for Fatboy." And with this repeat of the offhand nickname created a few weeks earlier, the name will stick.

Arnold hops up and starts seat hopping as usual and Slade wanders off in thought. He knows there are three other instruments that use alto clef, but can only think of the trombone and the English horn. Lost in this thought, Slade is as usual not paying attention as the bus comes to a stop at the back of Burnet Junior High. As it does, his backpack and homework slide from his lap to the floor as the other kids laugh once again. The kids quickly exit the bus leaving Slade to scramble to gather all of his books and viola.

As he exits the bus, the others have already made it inside and the back door has closed. And, as happens from time to time, the door has auto locked. Slade will have to walk "the long way" around to the front of the school, then back to the lockers area.

Arnold has made more contact with Slade than usual this morning and Slade liked it. He wanted to hang out more. But, with only twenty minutes until the first bell, walking to the front of the school and all the way back to the lockers seems to take forever. He rushes to get his books, backpack and viola stowed in his locker so he can make his way to the basketball courts where he knows Arnold will be. With his delay at the bus and locked back door, Slade is the last to leave the locker area and walks to the courts alone. As he's walking up, he sees Arnold and heads his way.

"Hey Fatboy, want a dip?" At Burnet Junior High, you aren't cool if you're not dipping snuff.

Slade says no; paranoid that his father will pop out of a building and catch him in the presence of snuff. The fear is real and even if unrealistic it's justified. At thirteen, he still gets whipped for every transgression, big or small.

They're all sins and evil in the eyes of the Lord, his parents would say before doling out the punishments. They even had Slade trained to reply like a circus act in church when they would ask: "Slade, what makes a good boy?" "A whippin' does," Slade would reply on queue and with a smile as if he were thankful for being beaten. The cult brainwashing was thorough. Dipping snuff would certainly qualify as a transgression and even thinking about it drove Slade to panic.

Arnold is putting the can of Copenhagen back in his pocket as another kid walks up and says, "let's go Arnold, odd or even." He then pulls a quarter from his pocket, as does Arnold.

They proceed to flip coins in the air at the same time, catching them and slapping them on the back of their hands and showing them to each other. Arnold had loudly called odd during the flipping.

With the quarters shown, there was one head and one tail showing. Arnold snatched the quarter from the kid and said, "Again?"

And so it went, even was when both were heads or both were tails and odd was when they were different. Slade did the quick math and knew this was even odds. What he didn't understand was why they didn't simply flip one coin since the odds would be the same, but he quickly dismissed it as he was far more interested in the fact that money was being WON, not worked for.

Arnold then said, "Hey, you want in? We can do odd man out wins?" Observing the slightly confused look on Slade's face, Arnold explained, "Whoever has the odd quarter wins; if we all three have the same it's a draw."

Again, Slade quickly did the math, and saw the even odds of it. Pulling a quarter from his pocket and trying to sound cool, he says, "Hell ya, I'm in."

After a couple of flips or so, Arnold says, "Let's keep count. We can flip more if we don't keep digging out of our pocket, and we can settle up in the end." Slade knew he could keep track in his head and quickly agreed.

Over the next twenty minutes, Slade found himself down over ten dollars. Not only did he not have it with him, he wasn't entirely sure he had it, and he KNEW he could not get it from his dad. He was getting worried when he was literally saved by the double buzzer that signaled the start of the school day. Arnold quickly did the math and announced that Slade owed six dollars and fifty cents to him and four dollars and twenty-five cents to the other kid.

"Shit," Slade says, "I don't have it on me, but I'll get it to you first thing in the morning," patting his back pocket for a wallet he knew wasn't there.

The other kid is getting aggravated but Arnold steps in. Arnold pulls out his Velcro wallet (THE wallet in 1978) and says, "Here, here is your four and a quarter." He looks to Slade and says, "Now you owe me ten seventy-five."

While Slade is glad it's ended calmly, he's worried where he'll get the money. He sheepishly replies, "Cool man, we'll settle up tomorrow. I gotta get to class."

Slade is confused by how he lost so much in such a short amount of time. He knew the odds were even and can't make sense of it. But the real worry is how or even if he's gonna be able to pay Arnold the money he owes.

The rest of the day is a blur as Slade can think of nothing else.

Slade arrives home and does his chores and helps with the bookkeeping as usual for the family business. Again it's a blur as he heads to bed and waits for the family to fall asleep.

He creeps ever so quietly to his closet and digs in the bottom and finds his little chest of coins. To his relief, he sees that he has a good stack of fifty cent pieces and quickly rounds up the money he owes.

He comes up with a plan: He'll hide the money in his socks and shoes and be fully dressed before his father comes to his room to "wake him." He'll act like he's studying for a test or something.

Slade isn't able to sleep at all, fearful that his father will come in before he has his shoes on and somehow discover the money. Slade climbs into bed determined not to fall asleep, but his mind wanders. The thought of gambling has stirred a memory of his mother talking about his grandfather (her dad) and the fact that he was somewhat of a gambler.

"Your grandfather was a very wealthy man. He owned a construction company and would gamble with hundred-dollar bills." his mother had said. "He also ran moonshine and the police would call the house and say, "Francis, put away the good stuff. We need to put on a little show and we'll be out in about an hour or so." She would go on, "and this would irritate your grandmother because they'd all sit around drinking back at the jail and she knew it, not that she would ever say a thing. Women knew their place back then."

Until this precise moment, Slade had never given this story any deep thought of any kind, but, somehow, it was different and the hypocrisy of this story was confusing to say the least. How could a good man gamble, and when did he stop? How was his family so poor if his grandfather was rich? And what was this "back then" for women? Women never back talk to men, once you're an adult women just obey their husbands and do not talk back. This is the way it still is isn't it? Slade's mind is racing now and he can't think of one time that any woman has dared to talk back to a man and then he stops. He does remember a time in a grocery store parking lot. He was there with his mother and some employee lady getting cokes for the store. There was a woman screaming at a man as she got out of the car. He remembers the man grabbing her and throwing her back inside the car and his mother saying "I just do not understand why she did not shut her mouth. Everything would have been fine then". Slade remembers it clearly now including asking his mother what was wrong with the crying woman. Slade remembers the answer now and it made perfect sense. "She was sad because she realized she was a sinner, honey. She will need to pray for forgiveness, and then she can be happy again. God is good."

Slade's mind goes round and round on these topics, becoming more confused at the conflicting stories from his mother, but with a constant eye on the window.

As the sun starts to rise, Slade is up and out of bed, and dressed in a flash. He then starts to take notes (that he certainly does not need) from his high school level algebra book, as to appear to be studying when his father comes in.

As his father walks in his room to wake Slade, he says, "If you have so much energy, we can put you to work and you can start carrying your weight around here instead of wasting time in those books. Go get your breakfast and make sure the kitchen is cleaned."

Slade flies through breakfast and cleaning up the kitchen.

Just one more step, he thinks, as he's walking out the side door on his usual walk out to the bus. His shoe shifts a little and he can feel the change slide down his tube socks with the slightest clicking noise when his father shouts out "Slade, what are you doing?"

Slade stops dead, petrified that he'll surely get a whipping. As Slade turns, his father hands him his viola.

"I swear, boy, you need to get that head on straight and take care of your business. Hurry up and don't miss the bus!"

Slade gets on the bus without incident.

He sees Arnold and says, "We can settle in school. Meet you at the lockers."

This bus ride is a blur. Arnold is up to usual antics and seems to say something about Slade, but all Slade can think about is getting caught. He's aware of time as the bus pulls to the back of the school. He makes his exit from the bus, going directly to the lockers to stow his things.

As Slade bends down to unlace his corrective shoes and take off his sock, Arnold realizes he's about to be paid in coins.

He's about to make fun of Slade, but notices that Slade is embarrassed.

Slade decides to tell Arnold how it is. "Hey, I had to sneak this out and I knew they would never notice change missing. You know Baptists can't gamble and my dad would spank me for sure if he found out."

Arnold takes the money, but does not seem to be getting any real joy out of it. This also strikes Slade as odd, but as he hadn't understood why two people were flipping instead of one, he didn't understand Arnold's reaction at this moment. He was the winner; he didn't have to gloat, but Arnold had won, he had beaten the odds and won. He should at least feel happy or accomplished or something.

It's as if Arnold could see the wheels spinning in Slade's head. Even at fourteen, Arnold has a knack for reading people, and he can see that Slade has exactly zero clue what happened to him, and for whatever reason, at that moment, Arnold decides to come clean and share.

"Hey man, you know why you lost right? I mean, you figured it out?"

With a curious look, Slade says, "Ya, man, shit ass luck. The odds are even, but I had a bad run of luck and it sucks ass."

"No, man. Look, we hustled you, and you never had a chance to win." Arnold goes into the explanation of why two people were flipping coins, so it would seem natural for a third person to join. It was a setup from the beginning. They weren't gambling with each other and in fact, the quarters were not even exchanging hands, they made it look that way.

In the same way, they had a signal, and one or the other would make sure that for the most part, one would have tails and the other would have heads, meaning, of course, that Slade would rarely be the odd man out and would lose most of the time. It wasn't that difficult to see a coin in your palm before slapping it on the back of your other hand, then slightly flip it for the desired landing.

It all made sense, including why Arnold wasn't happy with "beating the odds." The odds had nothing to do with the game.

"Before you even ask, no, you can't have your cash back, call it a cheap lesson. And you can't tell a soul what we did. It's our secret; only a select few know what is up and how to handle it!"

Slade heads off to class and somehow isn't in poor spirits. He's also not happy or angry. *What is it?* He's not used to this feeling and is struggling with it.

Then it hits him. He's motivated and hungry for more action. Hustle is a new concept. This hustle is not gambling with odds and math to be calculated and won. In fact, not gambling at all; this is a manipulation of the game with distraction. A distraction that even intelligent people will miss that renders the odds meaningless.

Slade never struggled to know things in his highly sheltered life. Everything has been black and white. There are questions and answers, and you can read a little here, talk to a few people there, and that's that.

But this, this is new! This is a complete unknown. It's as if there's another kind of existence. Can good people cheat? This is a paradox. Arnold is a good person. Slade knows it. Slade knows Arnold is good, but he's also a cheater? Arnold's also a hustler?

Slade likes the paradox and the grit of it. The fact that it's also against his father's rules makes it that much more desirable.

Arnold and Slade would become real friends over the next few years of riding the bus. The antics on the bus of Arnold starting and Slade following would be a centerpiece of entertainment and indeed drive the respect of the neighborhood teenagers as they all entered high school.

Slade would not gamble at all from this moment until late in high school. Fear would keep him paralyzed and an observer only. But he and Arnold would become friends, allowing Arnold to show him more and more glimpses of this new and exciting world that Slade had just discovered.

Slade was curious.

CHAPTER THREE

OUT OF POCKET

Sitting on the back of the bleachers in the high school gymnasium during a pep rally, the high school boys engage as boys will with a banter of "one-upmanship."

Arnold showed Slade a blister on his hand. "This is what I get from working at the restaurant."

Slade quickly shows Arnold a slice on his hand and a large bruise on his forearm. "This is what you get when a big ass wooden planter box falls on you when some idiot is not paying attention unloading at our warehouse. At least you're getting paid real cash. I get like fifty dollars a month whenever the old man feels like tossing me a bone."

"Slow your roll, Fatman. My pay is a whopping twenty-five dollars a week. I'm telling you, it's child labor. There should be a law."

"Well, Arnold, there is. I'm not sure you would win since you've already taken the hardship driver's license. You technically agreed to support your family as they're in hardship."

"No way, Fatman, you can't sue your own family. There's no law like that."

"Sure there is, Arnold," Slade said in a tone he rarely took with his friend. Slade is about to go into a rant, and Arnold can tell it. Instead of listening, Arnold raises his hands and says, "Ok, you win, Fatman! Arguing with you is like arguing with a wall. I'm not doing doin' it.

"Here, you fly, I buy." Arnold handed Slade a five-dollar bill and said, "Snag us some popcorn and a couple of cokes."

"You want your usual Dr. Pepper?" asks Slade.

"You know it," says Arnold. It was common to call all soft drinks "cokes" in central Texas at the time, like calling all facial tissues Kleenex regardless of the brand.

Arnold got his hardship driver's license[24] at fifteen, Texas's earliest legal driving age limit. In Slade's mind, this, too, was cheating the system, as there was no real reason that he could see for Arnold to have one. A license also meant that Arnold would get a truck as a freshman in high school. Driving as a freshman was almost unheard of and a serious status symbol.

Slade was the first person Arnold drove to show his new truck to. Although Slade wasn't allowed to leave with Arnold, he did sit in the truck while parked in the street in front of Slade's house.

"Dude, this is a cool ride. I bet you can get some Vikettes in here for lunch." The school mascot was a Viking, so the female dance squad members were called Vikettes.

"Man, screw them stuck-up bitches. I'll snag a real chic." Neither of the boys had a clue what they would do with a girl at this point, but they were starting to imagine it often.

Slade poked at Arnold: "Well, you won't be doing shit if you don't get this broke-ass radio fixed. How is it you get this cool ride and no tunes? I was hopin' to sneak in some listening time while you were here."

"Man, I'm glad I don't have your parents. That shit's rough. No stereo in the house. You still get no TV and shit, or have they laxed [slang for relaxed] up some?"

"No, man, still stuck on an hour and a half, but it ain't that bad. TV is full of bad stuff anyway. I'm not missing anything," says Slade.

---

[24] In Texas, there is a type of license that is given to underaged persons who would otherwise not be eligible to drive. It's given when not having a license would result in unusual "hardship" for your family. Some other states like Florida, Indiana, Arkansas and Kentucky also have similar licenses, but each differ in requirements.

Arnold is uncomfortable and changes the subject. He feels sorry for his friend but knows he can't help him and does not want to push him. He's heard the stories about the beatings Slade took when he was younger, even though Slade calls them spankings. Having never been spanked, Arnold can't imagine what it's like but knows it can't be good.

"Hey, back off on the stereo, Fatman. I'll have a new one soon enough. My old man and I talked about it when I bought the truck, and I already have it ordered."

Arnold would almost always "go off campus" for lunch and invite Slade. He would refuse, fearful of losing his ability to hang out with Arnold if discovered by his father. Arnold understood that Slade's fear of his father was real.

Again feeling a little sorry for him, Arnold would tell Slade where he was going and would usually come back with the food they could share in the parking lot together.

As first and second years moved to junior year, this lunch thing would become a daily routine for the two and carry through the end of high school. They would sit in the back parking lot telling tales and making plans as teenagers often do.

"Hey, Fatman, don't be bogarting all the fries; we're sharing those. I swear you eat enough for three people.

When are you gonna get your license? You know you can get it at sixteen without hardship or anything."

"Ya, but my parents have to sign and consent, plus I have to take a driving class," Slade replies.

"Take that easy driving class; ya know that one old coach what's-his-name teaches. Everyone passes that shit."

"I can't, I would have to drop orchestra or trigonometry, and my parents are not hearing of it.

"Dude, I can't even spell tiggomoetry [Arnold mangles the word] or what the fuck ever. Why do you take that shit? It's not even required."

"Well, if I take it, I can place out in college and be a step ahead. The faster I finish college, the faster I get out of the house."

"Dude, you gotta get a car first, which means a license. How are you gonna get it if they won't sign?" Arnold states matter of factly.

"Well, I've found a school I can attend in the summer, and when I turn seventeen, they can't tell me no anymore because they don't have to approve if I pass the tests. They agreed to let me go to the class since it's right down the road from the warehouse. I'll work the afternoon shift and take the class, which starts right after that. I'm surprised they're letting me take it, but Mom told Pop I could help drive the rounds and pick up plants and stuff from the stores, and he said ok."

"That sucks. You got six more months without a ride. Hell, you'll be a senior before anyone here knows you got a ride. Damn, I'm glad I don't have your parents," he says, disgusted.

Arnold called that one right. Time crawled for Slade, and the next six months seemed like six years, but finally, the day arrived, and his license hit his mailbox.

"I think this is it," Slade's mom yells as she walks into the house, having picked up the mail. "I think it's your driver's license," she beams, more to herself than to Slade. My boy is becoming a man."

It's an otherwise typical early Friday afternoon between Slade's junior and senior high school years in the summer. Slade finished up his daily grind of household chores. At seventeen, he's almost six feet tall, and while still a large person, all of his childhood "pudginess" has vanished, and his voice has dropped a few octaves noticeably.

Yet even with these physical changes, Slade does not feel any different. He still constantly fears the repercussions of saying or doing anything against his father, like a man standing in the middle of the road about to cave in from an earthquake tremor. The fear is palpable, and Slade still can't imagine that he could overpower his father. In his mind, it would be game over. Slade hasn't been whipped for roughly three years, but it's clear by his deference (to the point of cowardice) towards the patriarch of the house that he's still the same little boy afraid he might be whipped at any moment when his father walks in the room.

"Maybe you'll be useful when you start paying your way around here instead of us driving you around everywhere," booms his father to the room at large.

"Can I borrow the keys and eat at Arnold's restaurant?" Slade disregards his father's snide putdown. Before his father has the last say, his mom speaks up in a rare moment. "Slade, of course you can. We all agreed as soon as your license came in the mail, you could use the car."

"Well, you better bring the suburban home with more gas than when you left. And not a scratch. Grab a pen and paper," his father counters, motioning to follow him to the garage door.

The two walk through the garage to the family suburban parked in the driveway. In the same way some people like gasoline, Slade is pleasantly attracted to the smell of fresh sawdust swirling in the air as his father pulls the heavy garage door open.

"We're not wasting money on one of those fancy garage door openers, 'cause that makes you lazy," his father repeats the mantra every time he opens the door.

Slade can't remember when the garage was used for a car. It's been filled with saws and working tables of all kinds, used for making wooden crates and knick-knack shelves for the family plant business.

As they walk out into the early evening air, it's still a warm and humid ninety degrees, quite normal for early July in central Texas. Slade is unclear why he's out here and what the pen and paper are for, but then his father points out scratches and dings.

"You need to note all of these, and there better not be any more of them when you get back, or you'll have to pay to have them fixed. And don't forget to replace the gas. I'm not paying for you to be out being a playboy."

Ever since the day when he had to sneak coins out of the house in his shoes, Slade hides his money out of the reach of his parents. He has over six hundred dollars hidden in his closet in a big box of marbles. In 1982, this was no small sum. Slade feels the strangest urge to tell his father how easy it will be to keep the tank full but realizes it will give his secret away.

"You can use my Suburban tonight, but you'll need to get your car, pay your own insurance and upkeep. I'll bet you stay home when you stop freeloading and start paying your way. You don't know how easy you have it, boy." His father takes two keys from his keychain and hands them to Slade. "Make sure you keep it locked. You know what kind of people hang out in the city. Nothing but bad news."

Slade takes the keys and walks back in to tell his mother goodbye; she smiles and says, "Please drive safe and call us if you need anything. You won't be in trouble. We love you."

Getting his driver's license also represents something powerful for Slade. It's the first thing that Slade owns that his parents didn't give him. And they can't take it away. It came from the state: the state seal is on it. Seeing this little piece of plastic makes ownership of it real. It's the catalyst for a bit of disagreement that Slade has had brewing to become a full-blown war.

Slade is growing disillusioned by the duplicity he's noticing in his parents. They say things like "prepare Slade for the real world," then restrict him with the expectation that he stay here and work the stupid family plant business so they can retire and live off of him.

He also can't wrap his head around why his mother is acting like this when she has been completely on board with the punitive and restrictive life Slade's led all his life.

Slade yearns to know more about the world he's only caught rare glimpses of. He's slowly been granted some freedoms, like study groups after school where he'll sneak some time watching TV and listening to top-forty pop music, or going out to eat with the school orchestra after a performance, riding with other parents who play the radio and listen to genres other than gospel music. It seems that with every experience outside his parents' control, he notices more and more that things don't fit perfectly into the "church family" atmosphere he's lived in all his life.

Slade now believes that the only way to learn and discover will be to rebel. The beliefs, however, are still far from action. He feels the need to know yet fears the consequences of such learning. He's conflicted. These feelings have manifested exponentially since he passed his driving test a few weeks back. The thought that he has something that his parents can't take away provides him with control. It drives and fuels him to make his own decisions like nothing ever before.

His adolescent hormones are peaking, and the pull between rebellion and fear is almost constant in Slade's head regarding his home life. At the moment, fear is WAY out front, yet losing ground at an increasing pace. This internal war will allow Slade to look with fresh eyes at the world around him. Slade hops into the truck and backs out into his rural neighborhood, recently incorporated into the city. His father was none too happy about that either. "Now we pay all these city taxes so the freeloaders can sit around drunk all day. And what do we get for it? Street lights that keep me awake at night and sidewalks for these little hellions around here to ride those skateboards on? Waste of my money." He remembers his father's rant.

Well, it wasn't long before someone shot out the streetlights his father complained about, and the street was once again primarily dark. Slade took care as he backed out and pulled to the four-way stop up the road from his house. The stop signs were partially covered by overhanging trees and shrubs, lacking maintenance in the neighborhood that Slade was starting to notice wasn't nearly as nice even as the ones across that two-lane road.

He had never been to Arnold's restaurant but knew where it was and how to get there.

Ever since that day on the basketball court where Arnold had hustled Slade, the two had bonded and had become almost inseparable at school and were often found together when Slade was allowed to leave his house. While the two seemed close from the outside, a relationship that starts with one person taking advantage of another is tricky; such was the case with Arnold and Slade. A "keeping of score" had been initiated that first day and would constantly be there to one extent or another.

But the two shared many commonalities and would build on these areas of positive support for each other. They would discuss what it was like to work for the family business and that they were treated like slave labor as neither one was even paid minimum wage. As they discovered more and more common ground and had more conversations about family life, Slade heard about the different family life Arnold experienced. This alone was enough to drive Slade to stay close to Arnold.

Slade was amazed to learn that Arnold had a pool table in his house. Pool wasn't played by good people in Slade's world unless you were playing on the tables at the church camp. Only low-life people who drank and went to bars did this. Adults all outgrew this bad behavior, so it made no sense in Slade's head.

Slade walked in the restaurant's front door, which was dimly lit and mostly packed. The smell of garlic and pasta sauce fill the air. Slade had not planned on eating, but he was getting hungry!

The hostess asked how many were in the party, to which Slade replied, "I'm here to see Arnold."

About that time, Arnold pops out of the kitchen area, greeting him, "Hey, Fatman! I'm back here!" Being nine months older and eighteen, Arnold had also grown physically over the last six months. He, like Slade, was pushing six feet tall, and the wiry boy was replaced with a thin, lean young man with a voice a couple of octaves lower and his face showing a full "five o'clock shadow."

As Slade walks into the bright kitchen, Arnold says, "Hey, don't use the front door; family comes in the back." Slade knows this is a serious compliment. Over the years he has come to understand that Arnold's Italian heritage means a lot to him and that to Arnold, family is sacred above all else. To be called family is a big deal. Arnold and Slade had become closer over the last few years, but this was the first time he called Slade "family." Slade is not exactly comfortable with this new designation, but he rolls with it as with many new things.

Arnold makes up a large plate of gnocchi that they share as they dive into a familiar dialog. "Well, Fatman, you did it. You got that license. It seems like forever ago when we talked about it. I figured your old man would swoop in a fuck it up for you at the last minute somehow."

"Ya, well, not this time. I have it and it's like I'm free! Man, I can't wait to get out of that fucking house. THAT is what seems like forever away. I'm tired of being a pussy all the time," Slade says with anger in his voice. This attitude is new. Arnold has never seen Slade openly angry at his parents.

Then, for the first time, Slade took an open action. "Hey man, don't bogart the snuff. Pass it over," he demanded.

"Damn, you're for real! You ain't takin' shit no more," and Arnold tosses him the can.

Slade takes a good-sized dip, as he has seen his friend do on many occasions. He quickly asks for a cup, and Arnold says, "Plenty of spitters around here, Fatman," as he tosses him a Styrofoam cup and a napkin to stuff inside. He feels his head dizzy but is determined and acts cool.

With that singular act, Slade feels tougher and more robust.

Breaking a rule has made him this way. This experience is what gritty feels like, Slade thinks to himself, and he can't help but smile a little.

At closing time, as the last set of dishes goes into the industrial dishwasher, Arnold casually says, "We're gonna play some cards. Grandma's playin'. It'll get interesting for sure. Full family tonight!"

Slade had heard the stories of Arnold's grandmother but had never met her. The same was true of the rest of Arnold's family. Arnold was the only person he had met. It seemed they would all be here, and Slade was intrigued as he thought back to one of the many tailgate lunches.

"Man, you got your family shit, but my grandma is a real piece of work. She fucking hates my mom for being Irish, ya, know, cause Grandma thinks Italians should hate all Irish people. Fucking old bat. She'll start cussing and ranting at my mom for no reason when she sees her. It's nutso. She should still live with my uncle out in Vegas. He's her favorite, but I guess he got tired of her bitch ass and sent her here. Now she's here sucking off us and being a bitch to my mom all the time. Pop won't say shit to her, so my mom takes it and ignores the old bat."

The way Arnold describes his family couldn't be accurate, and Slade writes it off as an embellishment to make his family seem like something out of a movie. Grandmas don't cuss and aren't mean; they're sweet older people, as uncles and aunts are nurturing, and cousins are people to be instantly trusted. This is the world view Slade had been given and that he fully believed.

This person Arnold described couldn't exist. He must be exaggerating as he did out on the tailgate during lunch. Slade's looking forward to seeing the real version of Arnold's grandma and not this imaginary bad person Arnold embellished into existence.

Arnold's mom and dad arrive and pop into the kitchen. His dad's a short but burly man, while his mother is a full head taller than his dad and lean. They somehow looked well-dressed and comfortable at the same time.

Arnold introduces Slade in a way that's also not what Slade is used to. Adult first name introductions. "Slade, these are my folks, Dean and Susan," and motioning back at Slade, "this is Slade."

It's immediately apparent where Arnold gets his booming personality. Dean sticks out his hand and says, "Damned glad to meet ya, Fatman!" (with a large emphasis on fat), letting out a big full, belly laugh.

"Oh, ignore him," Susan says as she steps closer to Slade. "We're glad to know you. Arnold tells us all about you, and we're glad you were able to get out and come down tonight. Did Arnold feed you? Do you need anything?"

In a tiny interaction, it was clear that Susan wasn't afraid of her husband and was somehow allowed to step up and take control of the conversation.

This is like nothing Slade had ever seen. A full-grown adult, cussing in front of a child (Slade still saw himself as a child.) And they were loud. And a woman stepping in and taking over a conversation? This is simply not allowed in Slade's world.

The shocking conversation from Susan continues as she asks, "Is the old bat coming tonight?" referring to Arnold's grandmother.

Arnold had talked about his grandmother and how she hated his mom, all based on her nationality. While Arnold's father's parents were born in Italy, his mother's family was originally from Ireland. Or at least that was how Arnold's grandmother saw it. They were like fourth or fifth-generation Americans, while Arnold's grandmother, having moved to America with her husband shortly after they were married, was a direct immigrant from Italy. Arnold's grandparents had settled in New Jersey, where she eventually had three boys, including Arnold's father.

Arnold's father and mother met in New Jersey, and, with the disapproval and disappointment of his mother, they married and promptly moved to Texas.

As the grandmother arrives, Slade notices she is driving a brand-new Lincoln Mark VI. While he doesn't know much about cars, he knows this one was expensive. Looking across the parking lot, he also notices it has a twin that he would later learn belonged to Susan.

Grandma is a short woman with a slight humpback, and when she walked in the room, everyone seemed to give her deference as if SHE were in charge. She looked over at me and snapped, "Who are you? Why are you here?"

Dean pipes in and says, "It's ok, ma, that's Arnold's friend. He's a good guy. They finished up some gnocchi." Then after a slight pause and head tilt toward the kitchen, he adds, "in the back."

There's a significance to Dean telling Grandma that Slade had eaten in the kitchen that Slade certainly didn't understand but would later find out. Only the family eats in the back, ever. Slade eating back, there was a sign of endearment that Arnold had shown Slade without Slade even knowing or understanding it.

Grandma's whole demeanor changes, and she walks over. "You must be a hell of a guy then. Where are your people from?"

Slade replies, "We're a full-on mix, even have some Cherokee in there somewhere. We don't have anything like y'all have."

This seems to be good enough for her. Grandma's demeanor changes once again. She's shaken Slade's idea of what a grandmother should be.

She looks at Susan and almost snarls, "Why are you here? I was hoping to have a good night, but with a goddamned Irish in the house, I'll have shit luck for sure. I should have stayed home."

No one flinches as if it was a normal comment. Slade is floored: Women don't speak this way, no one talks to the family like this, and everyone seems ok with it. Slade can't even process at this point.

Even Susan doesn't react, as if she expects it and is used to it. Slade is perplexed by these people. Susan would take charge and step between the head of the household to talk to him, yet a grandmother could be downright mean to her, and Susan acts as if she'd said hello.

Grandma went on. "I thought you were gonna get another car and stop copying me? You couldn't stand it, could you."

Susan pops right back. "You know fuck well that I ordered my car first, and you got lucky and pulled yours off the lot. Don't give me shit. Go buy a different car if you don't like it."

Well, at least this part makes some sense to Slade. The reaction part, but the fact that a mother would drop an f-bomb in front of her child was nothing Slade thought could ever happen. He's seen such things as he snuck in some TV shows here and there but assumed this was fake and that no real person would ever behave in such a manner.

Grandma starts to come back when Dean steps in. "Ok, that's enough shit, are we gonna play or not? Let's get some cards in the air."

Arnold quickly pulls a few tables back, double-checks the front door to ensure it's locked, and changes the white tablecloth for a heavy green one, felt or something. They each started pulling up chairs.

As stunned as Slade was by the language and the mean-spiritedness of it all, he was equally dumbfounded that they would all sit down together as if a major blow-up had not happened. Surely this couldn't be so normal that they moved on. This wasn't how people acted in public. People were outwardly kind and respectful in public places in Slade's world; this was different.

Slade can't allow himself to see that the beatings and the mental abuse his father gave him and his mom were anything other than the required acts. He'd been taught that this was how it had to be and that a loving God was a vengeful God that would punish his children out of love. And then it was also that a loving earthly father would punish his family out of love. Many beatings would come with the words, "I'm spanking you because I love you."

Amidst all this internal revelation, Slade's inner war was going at full force. Every time a new version of the world appeared, it fueled him to learn more outside of his parents' hold. In this moment, rebellion was beating down fear.

So when Dean said, "Hey, wanna play?" the rebel in Slade's head was screaming YES!!!!

As Slade looked at Arnold, he could see the ever-subtle "no, you don't want to play in this game" look. Slade didn't understand that Arnold was protecting him.

At this moment, Slade couldn't remember that Arnold had been hustling since that day over three years ago on the basketball court and that he hadn't learned anything about gambling.

All Slade could hear was that he was going to break his father's rules and use the money he had kept hidden to do it. Slade felt free. Slade said yes and took a seat with the family, and the cards were dealt.

It's often difficult to know what you don't know, but at this moment, Slade thought he knew something about poker: he was wrong and about to relearn the same lesson from the basketball court flipping quarters. Don't play a game where you don't understand the rules. This is the path to being hustled.

The game begins, and Slade immediately notices that they're not playing what he thinks of as poker, which is Five-card Draw. Five-card Draw is exactly like it sounds: everyone gets Five cards, and then you bet. Then everyone gets a "draw" of up to three cards to replace what's in your hand, then you bet again. Then everyone shows, and the best hand gets the money. This is the only card game Slade knows about. He's seen it in old movies, and they called it poker; being naive, Slade has no reason to think there are variants to the game.

They started playing something called Five-card Stud, then Seven-card Stud, then Hold-em, then another game that looked like others but was called Lowball, where the worst hand won. Slade's head is spinning.

He notices that people fold (quit a hand by throwing the cards to the middle.) This is also new. Slade thought you had to stay in until the end, no matter what.

So, to save the embarrassment of quitting the game, Slade starts folding, a lot. He also tried to start paying attention and learning, but the strange actions kept happening.

During one hand, someone said, "This is table stakes." Slade has zero clue what this means but notices that there are two piles of money in the middle of the table instead of one. Then everyone starts screaming at Grandma: "THIS IS TABLE STAKES, NOT OUT OF POCKET!" She had pulled money from her bank bag and put it on the table in the middle of the hand. This was a rule violation, but Slade didn't understand.

She screamed back: "OK, then! I'll fold!"

Slade finally decides to play through, as he thought he had a good hand. He did not; it cost him two hundred dollars, one-third of the money he had squirreled away. He was devastated. Arnold could see it. He stepped in to stop the pain.

"C'mon, Fatman, let's get out of here. The older people are about to get snippy. I've wanted to show you my new stereo. Let's check it out."

It was one hundred percent a lie. Slade had seen the stereo right after Arnold got it and drove his truck to Slade's house a week earlier. But Slade took the exit, fearful of losing more money.

As the two walked out, Arnold scolded Slade. "What the fuck, man?! Didn't you see me wave you out? You got no chance in that game. They have real money and will wait you out."

"But I've got six hundred dollars. I had a shot."

"No, you did not, Grandma easily had ten thousand in that bag, and she's probably on the light end with the rest of the table. My old man stakes me. Anything I win or lose is on him. I'm not even good enough to play in that game."

Arnold sees that Slade doesn't understand the games, so he focuses on the money aspect. Over the last four years, he learned that directly arguing with Slade wasn't a good move. All good hustlers know which angle to work at any time, even if they're working it to protect their friend.

The two do the "handshake, pull in a hug," including the firm back slap as they prepare to part, then walk to their cars. As Slade hops in and starts to drive home, his mind is racing.

On the one hand, he's sad almost to the point of depression over losing one-third of his money. This loss will be a cornerstone of learning for Slade, and though he'll not play serious poker anytime soon, it will drive him to know when to gamble and when not to.

Two rules that Arnold shared in the evening ring in his ears:

Know all the rules and understand that if you don't know how to break them, you don't know them.

Never bet money you can't afford to throw in the street.

But on the other hand, Slade's charged and energized with his new observations and validation that there is a whole new world out here. People are not all like the "church family". Slade is determined to find more of this world where grandmothers cuss, women stand up to men, and children can be heard and seen.

Even though he does not know what that means, Slade wants to see the gritty world.

Snapping back to reality, he realizes he likely has snuff granules in his teeth.

Reverting quickly to that little boy, he pulls into a convenience store to fill the suburban with gas as his father instructed. He also grabs a coke and violently rinses his mouth until no snuff granules are present as he grimaces into the rearview mirror of the suburban.

As Slade makes it the rest of the way home, he feels the freedom slipping further away, he still wants to be free, but the fear is once again WAY out in the lead.

CHAPTER FOUR

THE SIDE HOLE

Arnold and Slade are high school seniors but rarely see each other during the regular school day as they have no classes in common. But like a ritual, they have lunch together right up through the end of the year.

"Hey, Arnold, my ride or yours?" Slade asks as he drops his books in his locker.

"Let's take yours, I'm runnin' on fumes and I don't want to waste time fillin' up, we still gonna hit the Chinese buffet?" Arnold answers and asks all in one breath.

"For sure, man, I'm starved, and it's Friday; they have those peel-'em shrimps!"

As they hop into Slade's truck, Slade recalls when he first got it, of course, being smothered with direction from his parents. He specifically recalled his mother's warning. "Now, Slade, while I agree it's time to get your own car, are you sure you want to do it without talking to your father? You know he wants the best for you and to make sure you don't get swindled. There are a lot of bad people out there who will take advantage of the upstanding young man I've raised you to be."

"Yes, Mom, I got this," Slade said. "A friend at school's dad works a car lot and has a clean 1972 pickup all ready for me. I've saved enough cash over the years to buy it. Pop doesn't like me driving his Suburban, that should make him happy."

"Well, you should leave before he gets here. You know how he gets if he's not leading all the decisions all the time," his mom replied with more disdain than Slade had ever heard.

Despite the lurking fight over getting his truck, it had gone off without a hitch and was a non-event. His father's only reply when he drove it home was that he had to park it in the street so "that old junker does not leak in my driveway."

As the two pull out of the school parking lot, Slade immediately returns to the present. They could see the Vikettes carrying the High School Senior Graduation banner across the parking lot:

To success we hold the key
We're the class of '83

in bright purple and gold letters. The two looked at each other and immediately started laughing. Neither one wanted anything to do with all that "rah-rah shit." This lunch would be one of the last school lunches Arnold and Slade would spend together. Graduation was next week, and then it was summer break.

For Slade, this meant fifty-plus hour work weeks for the family business. As his mom had predicted when he got his license, Slade would make the rounds between the warehouse and stores with loads of plants daily. It was a dull routine only broken by the weekend's yard work and house chores.. Summers were not a break for Slade, but he was allowed to visit Arnold occasionally at his restaurant.

Slade climbs the back steps and enters through the screen door at the back of Arnold's restaurant. The door springs, slamming it shut with a bang behind him. Immediately Arnold says, "Hey Fatman, 'sup?" but not with his usual joviality. Arnold is a little off, and Slade notices it instantly.

"Sup, man," Slade said back. "Shoot me the snuff. You ok?

"Ya, those fucks failed me cause I missed a stupid test during the flood last year. They never said shit about me making it up, and I have to do the whole fucking year again."

Now Slade knew good and well that you don't have to repeat a whole year over one test and that many people missed tests during the flash floods that were common here in central Texas. Everyone got a chance to make them up. But he let this one slide so his friend could save face.

Arnold had failed twelfth grade.

The night went on as usual. "Fatman, how many times I gotta tell you? Lay off the fucking bacon. That shit's for the customers," Arnold scolded Slade.

"Ya, ya, I'm paying for it doing all these fuckin' dishes, so blow me," Slade replies. The two laugh and carry on as Slade snags yet another slice of bacon, still warm, out of the full-size oven.

Summer rolls on and soon ends as Slade prepares for his first day of college.

His work in high school indeed paid off, as he would start with twenty full college hours. By the end of his first semester, he would technically be a Sophomore and on his way to graduating in three years rather than four. This suited Slade fine, as he would move out the instant he graduated.

Slade was stuck at home for the time being. In yet another way of controlling him, his parents didn't pay him enough to afford to go to college and live on his own. The brainwashing was all-encompassing, and Slade believed that to honor and obey your parents was absolute, regardless of your age. The thought of rebelling was still not a reality for Slade. And while not a reality, it was becoming a dream. Things at home were getting harder, and Slade felt suffocated.

At this point, it wasn't just the mental stress of wanting to make his own decisions, but the physical side of things were difficult as well. Slade was never alone, and a closed bedroom door wasn't allowed. One of the many rules of the church was that masturbation was a mortal sin. Slade had all the normal urges of an adolescent teenage boy, but the fear was so overwhelming that he would not even dare attempt it in his father's house. The physical stress that had been building for years, even for a "late bloomer" adolescent like Slade, and he had no clue nor understanding of what to do with it.

Suddenly, Slade's mom comes bursting into the house in a state. Slade was surprised to see her as it was way earlier than usual for her to be home.

"Oh my goodness, your grandmother had a massive stroke. We need to get to her right away. Where is your father?" she cries. Slade's mom was in a state of franticness and tears as she spoke.

But then, in a blink, she transformed into full control mode, ordering the family around as Slade's father came in from the garage. "Just pack a quick bag. I need to be there if we're gonna lose her," she barked. "Let's get loaded and on the road–five minutes!"

They made it to the tiny hospital in Slade's mother's hometown of Brownwood, Texas, within two hours. His grandmother was in recovery and showing signs of improvement but was significantly speech impaired. The doctors (from what Slade could overhear down the hall) said his grandmother would eventually make a full recovery but that, at this point, she would need constant care either with family or in a facility. They expected to release her from the hospital within three to four weeks.

A few weeks later, at the dinner table, Slade's mother confided, "Well, I spoke with all of your useless uncles, and none of them will take care of Mama, of course, so she'll have to move in here with us."

"That makes sense to me," Slade's father interrupted. "We'll put her in Slade's room, and Slade can take the sofa couch until we can figure something else out," his father said as if Slade wasn't in the room.

Slade wasn't ever too sure what to expect from his father, but it certainly wasn't this. He had never seen his father agree to anything his mother had suggested. He seemed to have some "slight addition or change" to make sure everyone remembered that he was fully in charge. But not this time; he agreed. With this anomaly in mind, Slade surmised that they had previously discussed this without him and had decided to take his room without even as much of a second thought. This wasn't a conversation. It was an announcement.

Slade had been kicked out of his own room, and his mind is suddenly racing:

What about my stuff?

Where will I hide my cash?

What if my parents find my cash?

A million things run through his head, and he quickly blurts out, "Well, I can get some boxes and clean them out for her. I'll get that all done this weekend."

"You're such a good son," his mom replied, "and a good grandson. Mama will be thrilled. "It worked, Slade thought. They see me as being helpful and supportive when in fact, I'm protecting myself from them.

After almost eight months of sleeping on the couch and basically living out of boxes in the living room, Slade was suffocating at a whole new level as he finished out his freshman year of college. Living like this, his family literally knew every move he made, and he had exactly zero privacy. The lack of good sleep was also wearing on him. The pull-out couch wore on his bones as the thin mattress allowed the bars and the tiny springs to develop more noticeable lumps. Slade often wondered if it would be better to sleep on the floor or not even bother to pull out the bed. Again, fear kept him from doing anything but thinking about it. Years of spankings had taught Slade that there was no winning an argument with his father.

As Slade was folding up the bedding and getting ready to start the day, he was pondering what the summer might look like for him. Just then his father came in through the garage door bringing in with him that familiar whiff of sawdust.

"Well, it's done, we have the house," his father exclaimed.

Slade was perplexed. He said, "What house, what do you mean? "As usual, Slade was still treated as a child to be seen and not heard. He'd been kept in the dark that his parents were getting a bigger house with a large "mother-in-law" master bedroom suite. It became crystal clear to Slade that his grandmother was here to stay.

"It needs a bit of fixin' up, but we should all be in there in six months tops, before any kind of winter sets in," said his father in a perky manner. "As long as your lazy college boy self does some real work for a change. You better get your working pants on. This loafin' life of yours is over as of right now!" he admonished Slade.

The summer was one of the hottest on record, with more than eighty days of triple-digit temperatures. That time was literally hell for Slade. He started every morning at five and usually ended around eight at night. He was physically exhausted. Even with the usual four-hour break in the hottest part of the day, it still left an eleven-hour workday. He knew this was against any interpretation of any labor law, but he carefully and purposefully buried this truth deep inside himself.. There was no world - real or imagined - that Slade could challenge his father, even over what amounted to indentured servitude.

His mental state wasn't much better as this was a seven-day-a-week effort. He was left with almost no time to see Arnold. Arnold did stop by from time to time, but the conversations were short as Slade's father would come out and shout – "breaks over, boy, back to work, daylight's a burnin'." And as if out of sheer spite he would add, "Always good to see you, Arnold!" Other than his name, his father knew exactly nothing about Slade's friend. Then out of nowhere, came another unexpected turn.

"Well, boy, you probably noticed we finished out this room and bathroom first, and we can slap on some outlet covers and throw in some carpet this weekend. This'll be your room. You can move in here while we finish out the rest. The house will be safer with someone in it. The rest will be slow going as you have to get back to school (there was a snarl to that sentence) and won't be around to carry your load.

You won't be scared sleepin' in a house by yourself, will ya? (again with a snarl).

"No, I'll be good," was all Slade could muster. He was excited but afraid to show it for fear his father would change his mind if he detected that Slade liked it.

Since this house wasn't yet in Slade's father's possession he had real privacy which allowed the normal course of masturbation. It felt like an act of rebellion which only added to the frequency and intensity of the act.

Slade was settling into this quasi-new-found freedom. His parents couldn't tell if he was home or not (his father would not pay to have a phone installed "just for Slade"), allowing him to hang out on weeknights with Arnold.

"Hey Fatman, glad you're finally free! I told the old folks it was like visiting you in prison or something over there. Hard fucking labor and all. Dude, all of us around the neighborhood have known that your old man was a hard ass all these years, but he's next level."

"Ya, I wasn't sure how much more I could take. They're not up my ass twenty-four-seven, but you know it can't last forever. Still, I'm good; I feel like I can breathe. What do you think, are you gonna move out anytime or chill at your old folk's place?" Slade asks.

Arnold seems to pause as if thinking about it, then says, "I knocked it out of the park and have my diploma. I see no need for college. The restaurant is my career. So, ya, I need my own spot—ya know, for the ladies," he says with a big grin. "I'm thinkin' after the spring rush is over; things slow down at the restaurant around UT[25] midterms. An easy time to move, and my folks are good with it. I'll look for some houses to rent. I'm squirreling away some extra cash."

"Ya, shit, I won't be ready then, I gotta hang with them so I can afford school."

---

[25] Ut is how all locals refer to The University of Texas, at Austin

"It's all good brother, you can make it. You've gone this far, just hang tough," Arnold replies with a genuine tone of support for his friend.

As the parties are being planned for NYE '85, Slade realizes that he is an upperclassman on paper. He also notices that his grades are not great. And while a three seven-five in Electrical Engineering at the University of Texas is good, Slade knows he's slipping. He doesn't like college and, in many ways sees it as a "checkbox" activity without any real purpose. One more thing to complete to get out from under the oppressive thumb of his father. College was his parents' dream and that alone is becoming enough for Slade to dislike it.

In what seemed like the fastest three months of Slade's life and midway through the spring semester, the family moves into the new house. The last of the carpet is laid, and appliances are installed. "No more walking around in your skivvies, boy! We got women folk in the house now," his father rants. In a couple of months when summer break starts, you can get back to work on the business and give your poor mother a break."

Slade feels like a caged tiger; the suffocation is back like never before. The war of freedom and fear is raging in his head and this time freedom is screaming for attention- louder than ever before.

Slade goes to get a haircut the next day. "Slade, I love your hair, thick and full," she said. "You know, you can let this grow really long if you wanted to. Then get yourself an earring or two, and it will look gooood." Slade promptly takes that advice and walks across the street to the mall to have an earring pierced with one of those little guns.

Like the driver's license, a pierced ear was something that was HIS. He bought it with his own money."Hey, I'm home," Slade says as he bounds in the door and walks to his room.

His father is in his recliner. "Boy, look at me" his father roars. "What is that? Is that an earring?"

His mom shuffles in from the kitchen. In an unusual act of defiance, he stands to full height and puffs out his chest ever so slightly, and declares, "Yes, yes it is. Pretty cool, don't 'cha think?"

Slade's father turns beet red. "Take that shit out of your head this instant! I'll not have some faggot on the way to hell livin' in my house."

Slade is taken aback. He can't ever remember his father using a curse word, ever.

Slade starts to protest, but his father booms, "RIGHT NOW, OR GET OUT!"

Slade reaches up and pulls the earring from his ear and heads to his room. The night ends in silence.

The power that Slade felt earlier in the day is gone; fear had beaten him once again, and in his bed, he lay silent and angry—at himself. Was he tired of being a pussy like he had told his friend earlier, or was he all talk, no action? His ears are ringing: his blood pressure rises with anger as he falls asleep.

Slade had forgotten his parents were leaving the next day for two weeks to attend a convention. Slade's mom walks into his room early in the morning, right before they leave.

"Now Slade, remember that your aunt and uncle will be here by noon. They'll take care of Mama, and you need to take care of yourself. Make sure you clean up after yourself. Your aunt is no more your maid than I am," his mother said as if talking to a seven-year-old. You don't need to worry about letting them in, you can still make it to school on time. they know where the spare key is."

"Yes, ma'am," Slade replies, but his mind is far, far away. He's already planning to blow off classes and go see Arnold as soon as his parents are gone. And that is exactly what he does.

"Hey man, got a sec?" Slade says in an unusually serious voice as he walks in the kitchen door of his friend's restaurant.

"Dude, what's up? You look like your dog died or something."

"Man, I can't take it anymore. I gotta get out of that house. I gotta find a job and move out, and I got two weeks to do it."

"It's all doable, my brother! The timing is perfect!" Arnold replies. "I saw a place yesterday, something big. We can move in together. This will work!" Arnold is rambling with excitement. "Dude, you go find a job, any job, we can qualify and I got a stash. I can float you the upfront if you're a little short. Dude, this will be THE SHIT!!" Arnold is extremely excited and Slade is floored. He wasn't expecting an answer, let alone a solution.

Could he do this? Was it time?

With that, Slade reaches into his pocket and grabs the earring, and pushes it back into his ear. The rebellion has started.

Slade skips classes over the next two weeks and fills out about twenty job applications, finally landing one at a local parts store in a not-so-great part of town. The pay is more than minimum wage. Slade's done the math and can afford the rent with a little left over. His decision is made! He's moving out.

Arnold and Slade meet the agent at their new little house, sign the lease and get the keys. It's a pretty simple process in 1985.

Slade heads back to his parents' home and is loading up the last of his things as they pull into the driveway. At this point, everything Slade owns fits easily into the back of his pickup.

His parents stare oddly at his truck as they step out of the family Suburban. "What are you doing? That seems like a lot of stuff to get rid of, and if you throw out that bed, where are you gonna sleep boy?" his father queries.

"I'm moving out," Slade declares. "In fact, that was my last box. My key is on the kitchen table."

Slade is standing at full height looking down at his father with a clear look of defiance..

"What are you talking about? I don't approve. Let's get this unpacked. Boy, I don't have time for this nonsense and your mother is tired. You need to get to the warehouse first thing in the morning to deliver the new set of plants that came in."

Slade has the courage needed to respond with confidence, "That's another thing, I QUIT. I got another job and I start in a week," he says with satisfaction.

Angrily his father retorts in a passive-aggressive tone. "Well, you'll fall flat on your face, boy, you don't know how easy you have it. I guess you're gonna go live a life of sin. Don't think we don't know what is going on when you're in the bathroom taking all those long showers. You're going straight to hell, boy!" his father says condescendingly.

His mother's tears are flowing as she walks around the car toward Slade.

"Oh, Slade, please don't do this to me. I love you. We love you. Tommy, tell him you love him and that we don't want him to leave us," his mother pleads. "You're breaking my heart," she continues in soft tones.

Slade's demeanor softens considerably seeing his mother cry.

"Mom, I've made my decision, this is something I need to do. You've told me you've been preparing me for the outside world and now's my time to experience it. Everything'll work out, I still love you and it will be fine," Slade says, almost choking. With that, his mom's expression changed. She's angry, taking a passive-aggressive stance similar to his father's.

"Well, I guess I failed at raising you, right? You're gonna run off and abandon us and the business? You don't really love me." The guilt trickled out of her mouth like sour grapes.

She had mistaken Slade's soft tones and kindness towards her as weak. She couldn't have been further off the mark. Slade is VERY angry. All at once things are becoming clear to him. He's seen this duality all his life, but never overtly.

His mother is a puppeteer master. For all the talk of " father in charge" of the household, she embodies control and props his father up as the MAN. Passive aggression and faux caring are her M.O. She has wielded them well. In a world dominated by men, she learned how to dominate from behind. Slade remembers it was his pastor who warned about this kind of mother: a mother who does not give motherly love, but "smotherly" love is all about command and control.

Memories begin flooding in. His mother reminded his father of how embarrassed they were at church over some misbehavior on Slade's part resulting in a whipping. One time she whipped him in public and another as she stood beside his father when welts appeared on his legs, telling him she loved him and that " spanking equaled love. Or the times she used that damsel in distress expression "Oh, my goodness," while acting faint then two minutes later whipping everyone into shape to load up for the hospital to see her mother. Or hypocritically speaking fondly of her father as a drinker and a gambler while condemning any and all such behavior in others while at church.

This was back gaslighting at its finest Slade had learned through observation., as most children do. Right up to this moment, she weaponized her affections. In a second she went from being hurt over losing him, to blaming Slade for her failure as a parent.

It was all about her, and it *always* had been! She was a narcissist. At this realization, Slade matured in a matter of moments. He took on a stoic stance of indifference.

"I wish you both well, but as I've said, my decision is made." And with a blank stare, he turned, climbed into his truck and popped in a cassette of Beastie Boys. He wanted them to hear the "devil's music". He blasts the music, as he maliciously drives away at fifteen mph, the lyrics "You gotta fight for your right to party" fading.

Slade and Arnold are all moved in. As Slade is fading off to sleep that night, he thinks back over the whirlwind of the past two weeks and has a sudden realization. He missed the midterms. To graduate with a degree in Electrical Engineering from the University of Texas, upperclassmen or not, this is an almost certain "sco-pro" or scholastic probation event. He'll have to deal with that tomorrow.

Slade is up early to get down to UT and as he walks into the administration building, he's not sure what to expect or even how he'll deal with school. He had not planned for a work and school schedule. Slade had seen an exit from his "cage" of a home and nothing else mattered.

No other options existed except applying for student aid if Slade wanted to continue at UT. He would need his parents to cosign and there was exactly ZERO chance he would go down that path. In one fell swoop Slade leaves the UT campus, never to return as a student.

Eager to begin a new chapter in his life he arrives early to his new job at the parts store to be ready for his first day. Slade does not know much about cars, but this job is about being able to research parts and quickly locate them in the large books at each end of the counter. Parts stores were light years away from being computerized. Manual lookup is a skill to be mastered. He had a good teacher, Allan.

Allan was a bit older than Slade with a strong upper body build that made him appear shorter than his six-foot two-inch frame. Wavy and unruly blond hair and a full beard with a slight tinge of red contrast his piercing green eyes.

He speaks slowly but without any accent, Slade can discern.

Allan taught Slade the ropes of the parts business, and they bonded over Copenhagen snuff. As the first week of work ends, Allan asks Slade after work if he wanted to have a drink and play some pool. Slade's legally allowed to imbibe at nineteen.

"Well, ok, but how much is it? I don't have a lot of cash built up right. I just moved out and stuff, ya know, all the deposits kinda cleaned me out," Slade confesses.

"No sweat, man. I'll spot you a couple of beers and I got the hook-up on the pool. Johnny won't charge us."

"Well, hell ya, never say no to free beer," Slade says with a grin.

Slade hops in his truck and follows Allan down the street a little less than a mile from the parts store in one of the rougher parts of town. Even though Slade has driven through the area, and seen buildings in ill repair and cars in bad shape, he has no understanding of what rough means. To him, it's not much different than where he grew up.

He pulls into a parking place in front of a long, dingy, brown building with half-round windows that go from about a foot off the ground to the top of the slight overhang of the roof. The parking places stop at a foot-high sidewalk that runs the length of the building and are directly off the street such that if you back out, you're immediately in the street. Slade makes note of this and thinks he'll have to be careful backing out.

A large red and black sign on top of the building with chipped paint and light bulbs inside each letter blinks "The Side Hole" and underneath Billiards and Beer.

Slade pushes open the front door noticing the reflective window tint is peeling off. A sad little bell attached to the top of the door makes a slight "dinging" as the pair stroll in. The guy behind the bar looks up. "Hey, Allan! Want a table?"

"Sure, thanks, Johnny, and start a tab for me and my friend Slade here."

Johnny is well-built, almost like a bodybuilder. He's over six feet with curly dark brown hair sticking out from under a baseball cap with some logo Slade doesn't recognize. He's got big clear blue eyes and a broad smile with perfectly white teeth. This guy could be a magazine model.

Slade's never been in any place like this before. It's like a foreign land. He isn't sure why, but he likes this foreign land and is taking in every detail as not to forget it.

The place has a distinct smell as you walk in. Cigarettes for sure, but something else as well, an old house smell like his grandmother's in Brownwood. His mother called it "musty."

The blue carpet is short and worn. It might have been multi-colored or had a pattern to it at one point, but the stains had removed any clear view of such.

As Slade looks to the left, he sees row after row of pool tables. Every table has a long thin light about half the total length of the table, hanging above it, and centered promoting some kind of beer. All the way to the back, a wall is lined with pinball machines and a door in the right corner reads "Women".

He realizes why he had not seen the tint on the front windows. From the inside, they're all boarded up with painted pool balls on them. This seems odd, why replace glass with plywood?

The bar is on the right as they walk in and is chest high running about thirty feet. As Slade looks closer he notices it's a tall table with wood paneling with a top covered in blue laminate that probably matched the flooring at some point. It's a walk-up bar with no seating. He also deduces that there must be coolers under it as he hears a door sliding open and closed as the bartender gets the beer for him and Allan.

Further back away from the door, a jukebox can be seen in the corner, and near that another door that reads "Men."

There are some little square tables along the wall near the jukebox just big enough for four people to sit at plus a few more standing tables farther out from the wall.

What appears to be the remnants of an old wall stands between the first row of pool tables and the remainder. While steel six-inch square floor-to-ceiling structural pillars painted white can be seen all through the building, there are some carpeted concrete bench-high walls between most of them. Open areas allow people to walk to the back pool tables. These pillars also have little tables attached to every other one so that when you sit on one of the concrete benches, you have a table at the right height for a drink.

He also observes that the row of pool tables near the bar seems different. There are fewer of them, and they seem bigger and further apart. Not wanting to let on that he has never been to a pool hall before, he observes and does not ask.

Allan grabs a little black tray of pool balls from the chest-high counter and says, "Snag the beers, let's play nine-ball." Slade is totally clueless as to what nine-ball is.

He knows there are a total of sixteen pool balls. One is the cue ball and is solid white. The rest are numbered one through fifteen. One through seven are solid colors, the eight-ball is solid black and nine through fifteen are striped. He once played eight-ball at a church in the fellowship hall, but as far as he knew, eight-ball was the only kind of pool. One person shoots in all of the stripes or all of the solids, then the eight-ball last. If you sink the eight-ball early you lose. If not, then the first person to knock the eight-ball in after all of their own balls wins. A simple game Slade thinks. Nine ball sounds simpler.

Slade replies to Allan, "Well, to be honest, I've not played pool much. I played some at church when I was a kid, but we played Eight-ball."

Allan is laughing in a serious belly laugh, "Hey Johnny, this guy is a hustler for sure, he told me, get this, that he's only played at CHURCH!" Johnny the bartender leans around some new customers who walked in and joins Allan, laughing. Slade doesn't get it. What had he said that was funny? He walks over to grab a cue stick from one of the many holders around the pool hall. He rolls the stick across the pool table like he's seen someone do at the church to see if the cue was straight. Allan looks over and is about to start in with another round noticing the stick being rolled on the table, but stops as he notices the perplexed look on Slade's face.

"Oh, man, you were being for real, damn, I thought you were saying some shit and then were acting like you didn't know what's up rolling a stick like that on a table. Look, have you really not played much or what?"

"No man, the truth is I've never even been in a pool hall before. I mean, I love this place,, but it's like nothing I know about or have ever seen. And, what's wrong with checking to see if a cue is straight?"

"Well, look" Allan takes his cue and rests the skinny end on the rail and the fat end on the center of the table. "This is the best way to check. All of the off-the-wall cues are gonna be crooked. It doesn't matter that much, to be honest, it's something you tell newbies to do. If you're playing off the wall you'll be playing with a crooked pool cue."

Allan puts the balls into a diamond shape using one end of the triangle rack and says, "Look, like this. Get the one-ball up front here and the nine-ball in the center and nothing else matters. Keep them tight and lift the rack. You break."

Slade leans down and lines up to shoot the cue into the one-ball. He has his index finger and middle finger on each side of his pool cue and it's resting on the back rail like he had seen the men at the church do it.

Allan looks up and says, "Ok, stop. We got some work to do brother. How about you let me break, then we finish this rack and have a beer and chat a bit. I can show you some stuff and we can come back on a weekday or something when no one is here and you can practice up."

"I'm good with that, thanks man, always up for learning new games!"

Allan walks over and breaks with a loud crack and the balls go flying around the table, with the nine ball falling into the side pocket. Slade remarks, "Oh, you lose? The nine ball went in out of order (applying the same logic used in eight-ball)."

"Well, no, in nine-ball, I win. You win if you make it on the snap." Seeing that Slade didn't get the lingo, Allan adds, "Ya know, the break, the snap."

"Ahh, ya, I can see I've got some stuff to learn."

The two grab the balls and place them back in the little square rack and walk back to the little tables grabbing another beer on the way. Allan points to a few people and explains who is gambling and what the quarters on the table mean. It's a complete blur and Slade realizes that this place doesn't just look foreign, it IS foreign. He LOVES it. From the constant music from the jukebox to the dirty carpet, all of it. This is REAL life, these are real people. Everybody is cursing all the time and no one cares. Slade is drawn to this kind of world as it's unlike anything he could have ever imagined. He's not dreaming, this is real.

Slade gets home, forgetting that it's Arnold's night off. Arnold is watching something on TV when he walks in, "Hey Fatman, where you been? Smells like a bar – look at you!"

"Ya, I went to The Side Hole and..."

Arnold cuts him off. "WHAT! Dude, you went alone? That place is blood and eyeballs (making a reference to bare-knuckle fighting where someone literally loses an eye) on the weekends; you gotta be careful." Arnold is full-on protective. "Man, if you ever go back there, you need backup and someone you know to be there in a spot."

"No, man, it was all good. I went with this guy from work, Allan, he goes there all the time. He knows the bartender, he even hooked us up with free pool."

"Ok, well, be careful. Let me know when you're going next time, I'll swing by after work and we can kill a few beers and close it down. I think I remember that bartender, Johnny, or something? Right?"

"Ya." Slade is shocked to know Arnold went there. "So you went there, but I'm not supposed to? What the hell?"

"Well, I went with my cousin Lenzo a few times, ya know he picked up cash for a bookie for a while and I rode along when I was a kid. He told me not to ever go in there alone, so I didn't."

"Who the hell is Lenzo? A sports bookie? That is illegal shit, man. I had no idea you had real criminals in the family, shit well, pretty cool. Dude, I need to get some more of the real stories here, I can't believe all these years, you never told me shit."

"Look, never mention it, ok? I'm not supposed to talk about it, he's gone, like a new name and shit. Man, dude, I'm serious, I shouldn't have said anything, It's my ass and my family's too if anyone ever finds out I said shit."

"Ok, ya, sure, brother, I got it. Never again, never heard a word," agrees Slade. "But The Side Hole man, I loved that place. I'm gonna go there more, learn to play pool some, with Johnny hooking Allan up for free pool and cheap beer, it's a cool place to hang out!"

"All good, Fatman, just be careful."

Slade heads off to sleep, his head still reeling from the past few weeks. Time to get some rest and set the alarm. Tomorrow is his first Saturday at the parts store and it's supposed to be their busiest day of the week.

CHAPTER FIVE

DO THE HUSTLE

"**H**ey Slade, you still think you want to go back to The Side Hole? Plenty of other places we can grab a beer if pool isn't your deal, ya know," says Allan as he walks into the parts store. Allen has been thinking about Slade being out of place in the pool hall.

"Oh, for sure. I want to learn to play better, plus I liked that place, I mean really."

"Well, It's a good cheap place to play pool, but other than that, c'mon man, that place is a dump and it can get rough sometimes, you gotta watch yourself."

"Ya, my friend Arnold said he was surprised I went there and was glad I wasn't alone. He might come up sometime after he leaves his restaurant. He's a good pool player, he had a table in his house growing up (Slade had never seen Arnold play pool, but did believe his friend.)

"Ok, well look, let's start with some basics. Your friend didn't teach you shit, but I will. You're right-handed correct?

"Well, yes, but I do some things left-handed, does that matter?"

"No, but if you ever get good at pool, that'll come in handy. I want you to hold your hand like this the rest of the day, then when we get off work, I'll show you why and we'll put it into practice." Allan holds up his left hand and makes an "OK" sign putting his index finger and thumb together. "Start like this." Slade copies him. "Now keep your thumb and finger together and sliiiide your thumb up until it touches your middle finger, like this. You see that little hole under your pointer finger and your middle finger where your thumb comes together? THAT is where the pool cue goes.

"This feels funky," Slade says.

"Ya, do it anyway, all day, when you're not flippin' pages looking for a part for one of these fucking idiot customers or stocking. You hold that position. Then in the next few pool games, that's the ONLY way you get to hold the pool cue, comfortable or not."

And the lessons begin.

Slade is focused on holding his fingers the right way and barely notices when a customer is standing in front of him clearing his throat. He looks up, smiles, and asks how he can help. The customer replies rather gruffly "Yes, I need a top radiator hose for a 1968 Volkswagen Beetle".

Slade goes to the end of the counter and puts his nose in the radiator hose book flipping pages to the "V" section to look for the hose. "Go fast but never rush" he remembers the first advice from Allan ringing in his head. At the same moment he's perusing the book Allan walks up to stand beside him. Slade feels his glare, he looks up to see Allen has a big grin on his face. "Dude, he is fucking with you".

"What?!" Slade replies, "he doesn't want a radiator hose?

"No, man", Allan continues, "Beetles are air-cooled, they do not have radiators". It's a joke. Allan turns to the guy on the other side of the counter and both are laughing. "Man, that never gets old," the guy says. Then to Slade, he says, "I do need an upper radiator hose, but for a 1977 F150 Ford truck."

Slade quickly works on finding the hose in the books, then heads to the back to retrieve it. When he returns the customer already has the damaged one with him to compare to the new one.

"An exact match" the customer replies, as Slade lays it on the calendar. "Great," says Slade, "that will be fifteen dollars and eighty-two cents" walking to the register. Slade rings the customer up and takes the twenty dollar bill from the customer when he notices that Allan has the strangest of looks on his face while watching him give

69

change. Slade hands the customer his receipt and thanks him, then turns to Allan perplexed, "Hey, did I fuck up?"

"Sorry for not getting that those Beetles are air-cooled, I didn't know".

"I also can't believe that guy came in here and lied to me. That is a (Slade almost says SIN, but catches himself) well, an uncool thing to do, lying," he stammers. "No man, it's all good, says Allan who adds for good measure, adds, "That guy is a shade-tree[26] and in here all the time. He does that bit on all of the new parts guys."

As lunchtime arrives, the local "roach coach"[27] pulls into the parking lot and the mechanics from next door start to line up. Allan flips the sign to CLOSED and he and Slade head out as well. While standing in line Allan asks "How did you know how much that hose was going to be this morning? You told him the price INCLUDING tax before you even rang it up."

"Oh, easy," Slade replies. "I knew it was fourteen dollars and eighty-nine cents because the sticker is on it with the price, I figured the tax and added it right quick."

"In your head?! You added six and a quarter percent of fourteen eighty-nine just like that? What the fuck man, are you some sort of genius or something?" Slade begins to answer, but Allan cuts him off.

"Dude, how is someone so fucking smart so fucking ignorant? Man, I am not trying to be mean or nothing but I was thinking about stuff after we were at the pool hall Friday. You do not know what is going on. I mean, it's like you have been living under a rock. It was clear you haven't had much beer ever. And, again, not being mean, but you do not even cuss right, it's like you are trying out some of the words for

---

[26] Shade-Tree is a person who repairs cars one the side and not at an official repair shop. A mechanic who works under a "shade tree".

[27] A Roach Coach was common slang in the 80's for what we would call a food truck today

the first time. I did think you were putting on an act for a while but I can see you really do not know what is what."

Allen continues, "That is why I asked about going somewhere else. Somewhere more tame? I thought you might be, well, slow if you know what I mean. But, fuck me, I don't know what to think, you ain't slow that shit is for sure. You have most of the back room memorized already. I can tell by how you go back for parts, no pausing, you head right for them."

The two grab a couple of sandwiches and drinks and head back inside the parts store as the truck pulls up to re-supply them. The driver unloads and hands Allan the invoice, and heads right back out.

"Look, pay attention tonight" Allan continues; "remember what I was telling you about the people gambling and listen to the lingo. Learn the pool hall like you are learning the parts store. There is more to playing pool than shooting the balls in the holes. We will start you there, but with your noggin in the right place, you can pick up some decent side money if you want it" Allan says finishing up his sandwich. "Let's get this place stacked and straight and we will hit the Side Hole right after we leave. School is about to be in session."

When the two arrive at the Side hole after work, Allan starts by teaching Slade the basics using repetitive learning. Do it until it's so natural, you do it without thinking. He's building muscle memory. This first of many, many nights starts Slade as Allan's student and this student learns quickly.

In a short number of days, the lessons become more and more advanced.

"Ok, line up each ball about six inches apart this time, starting right here," Allan says while pointing at the little "foot spot" that all pool tables have. This is the spot where one lines up the lead ball when you rack the balls to play a standard game.

Just as Allan's telling Slade what to do, a tall, thin but well-endowed blond girl walks into the pool hall. Slade loses focus as she walks directly up to them.

"Hey Allan, you got my stuff?"

Allan motions her toward the back near the pinball machines. This girl is focused on talking to Allan so Slade goes back to practice.

The goal of this exercise is not only to pocket the pool ball but to control the speed of the cue ball such that it'll stop in an ideal location to make the next shot. The pool hall term for this is "getting shape". Playing pool well is much more like chess than checkers. You need to be able to make balls in pockets, but also to set up for the next series of shots.

Slade positions up the balls as Allan and his friend walk back towards him. She pats Slade on the butt, saying, "Nice ass," with a giggle, and walks out the door.

"Holy shit, she was HOT," Slade says, "you tappin' that or what?" Even after only a short time in the pool hall Slade is doing as Allan had said and is quick to pick up the lingo and the "way of things". Here, women were playthings and seemed to want to be. The more vulgar you spoke to and about them, the more attention you got.

"Ya, no, she's a customer, never mix business with pleasure, my man. But I can hook you up if you want. She works at the strip club up the road and she seemed to like you well enough for a few rounds at least." They both grinned big.

"Business?" Slade said. What am I missing here, he wondered.

"Hey man, look, it's no big deal, but some folks need product and I can get it for them. It's a side hustle for a little cash to throw around. I take care of it for friends and such, but I don't put that shit in my nose. I stick to my liquid poison, thanks!"

Allan is a drug dealer. Slade's mind is racing once again.

Allan is a nice guy. A soft-spoken teacher who charges Slade nothing. Slade contemplates, this isn't what drug dealers are like. He'd heard his racist preacher talk about them, the evil bringers who kill people for looking at them wrong, corrupters of little children. They were Mexicans or Black. White people didn't deal or do drugs.

This is yet another glass-shattering moment for Slade. All of the stories he heard in church and at home must be lies.

He's starting over in his new church: The Side Hole.

Those thoughts happened in a flash and then Slade got right back to practicing pool. A short three weeks and a few other basic lessons later, Slade's regularly shooting six balls flawlessly, even when interrupted.

"Ok, here's the deal," Allan says to Slade, who seems to be wearing down at practice. "You get this drill up to nine balls and clear the table without a miss ten times in a row, then we'll move to break shots and play a few games.

"Look man, stick with it, think about it. three weeks ago, I was hounding your ass in the parts store on how to hold your shooting hand, then we went to keeping your elbow stationary and your forty-five-degree stance to the cue ball. Look at you holding your rock for the next shot and getting in shape time and time again without even thinking. You don't even know this but you're already better than seventy-five percent of the people that come in here. Don't stop!"

A week later those learned routines were working well. Slade would stop at the pool hall on the way home, then when he had made nine in a row clean five consecutive times, he called it a night and headed home.

"Hey Fatman," Arnold says as Slade gets home as usual at about two-thirty am, "I don't know how you do it with no sleep, brother, I need my eight!"

"I've never needed that much. My shift at the parts store doesn't start until ten tomorrow," replies Slade. "When are you gonna come up and show me all those pool shark moves I've heard about all these years? I don't suck much these days."

"I'll come up this week for sure. I got a new dishwasher trained so I can bail from work and go straight there. No one in The Side Hole would know if I smelled like a kitchen," Arnold joked and took a dig at Slade's new hangout at the same time.

Sure enough, Arnold came popping into The Side Hole later that week. "Man, this place never changes, like when I was a kid."

"Arnold? Is that you?" Johnny the bartender asks

"Hey, Johnny, ya, It's been a bit, still got the good business going on?"

"For sure man, let me know if you need anything."

"Whoa there, Fatman, you playin' on the nine footers? That's for the big boys."

"Ya," Allan says, "work out on these and the rest are easier to adjust to. Oh, hey, Allan, this is my friend, Arnold. Arnold, meet Allan. he's been helpin' me." The two shake hands and seem comfortable with each other.

"Hey, I think I remember you. You can draw[28] your rock like crazy right?' Arnold asks

"Ya, man, that's me. You used to come in with that old bookie, Phil, and run beers for Johnny when you first got that big-ass pickup. You still got that thing?" asks Allan.

"Naa, I got a Camaro these days. If I need to haul shit, I call Fatman here," replies Arnold. You still taking care of the dancers?"

"Ya man, pays the bills," says Allan.

There's more to Arnold than Slade knew. This was interesting and unsettling all at the same time. Slade felt betrayed, but he did not understand why. That feeling was interrupted as A few college-looking kids walked into the joint, a little too clean and buttoned up for the place. Allan and Arnold lock eyes, then Arnold says, "Spot or rail?"

Allan replies, "Rail."

Slade is totally clueless as to what is happening, but Arnold says in a loud voice, "Closest to the rail, a nickel a shot pay at a quarter?" Slade knows that nickel is five dollars and a quarter is twenty-five

---

[28] To draw your cue ball or "rock" is to make contact with the object ball with reverse spin of the cue ball such that after contact the cue ball will reverse itself and roll back toward the shooter.

74

dollars. They'll play until someone has lost twenty-five dollars, but other than that he's still lost.

Allan replies, "C'mon WOP[29], I'll take your cash, AGAIN!"

Slade is confused, but he pays close attention. If race slamming were normal, Arnold wouldn't brush off being called a Wop. This goes against the grain of his proud Italian–American heritage.

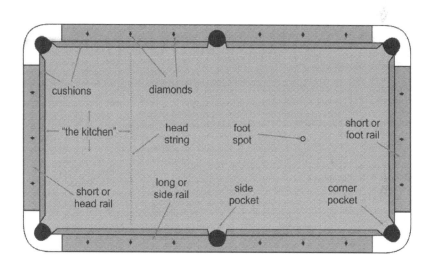

Allan and Arnold each pitch a quarter. The one closest to the near rail of the pool hall wins. They're keeping count of how far ahead one person is with a penny. It's placed just under the rail of the pool table. If Arnold wins it's moved one diamond (the little white spots on the top part of the wooden rail of a pool table) to the right and if Allan wins, the penny is moved one dot to the left.

---

[29] WOP is derogatory slang word (without papers) given to immigrants, especially at the turn of the last century, yet particularly reserved, for Itialian Americans.

Slade remembers learning how to line up angles using the little diamonds that are evenly located on all pool tables. Slade quickly counts and sees that if the penny crosses the side pocket on either side, it's pay-off time. Slowly but surely, the penny keeps progressing left and Allan gets paid over and over.

The college kids that walked in grabbed a pitcher of beer and sit at a nearby table watching intently.

Allan starts to tease Arnold who is visibly frustrated.

"You've always sucked at this, I'm almost embarrassed to keep taking your cash at this point. Just go drink a beer, or let Slade kick your ass playing pool or something, you got no shot here."

At this point, one of the college kids laughs.

Arnold whirls and snaps at him. "Hey, college boy, keep it to yourself unless you want to come over here and let Allan take some of your daddy's money, or is it your girlfriend's? She's kinda dumpy, so you must be moochin' off her or somethin'. "The girl turns to the laughing kid and says, "Really, nothin', you just gonna sit there?"

Then the kid hops up. In an arrogant tone that reeks of privilege, he blurts out, "This looks easy enough, but not with him," pointing at Allan. "I'll play you, you with the mouth," motioning to Arnold. "That's if you have any money left? And, for the record, it's not my daddy's or my girlfriend's money, I have my own money thank you very much. What are y'all playing for?"

"Five dollars a throw, and we pay up every twenty-five dollars," Arnold informs him, this time without using any slang.

The college kid then responds with full snark, "Oh, small time, I see. Well (he glances back over his shoulder to his friends as he wants them to pay attention to his response) I don't play small time like that. If you want to gamble with me, we make it twenty a throw and pay off at a hundred. But I get it if you can't afford it, that's a lot of money for a worker like you."

Arnold steps back and contemplates. He turns his back to the college kid and pulls out some cash counting it.

Then he whips back around, puts his cash away, and says, "Sure thing, I can do that. Let's go. We take turns. Closest to the rail wins."

They start to pitch. Arnold wins some and the college kid wins some, but after about twenty minutes, Arnold moves his penny across the side pocket and declares, "That's five. Pay up."

The kid whips out a hundred-dollar bill like it's a one-dollar bill and announces in an arrogant tone. "Okay, I know the game. Let's up it. Fifty a throw, pay at two-fifty unless that's too much for you." He turns to his friends and whispers, "I have him."

Arnold looks a little embarrassed, but after a quick talk with Allan, he proclaims, "You're on." This time, the game is much shorter and Arnold is moving the penny across the side pocket in his favor for the win in about ten minutes.

The college kid is frustrated and all but throws the money on the table, then turns and barks at the girl at his table, "Get me a beer, he can't get lucky all night."

Then spinning back towards Arnold he snaps, "Again?"

This time Arnold wins the first four in a row; each one of Arnold's tosses lands ever so slightly closer to the rail than the college kids does. The college kid lands a super close one that Arnold doesn't beat, but the next two are Arnolds and again, Arnold is telling the kid to pay up.

The college kid is getting madder and madder, drinking faster and faster, and his tosses are getting progressively worse.

Arnold collects another two hundred and fifty dollars from the college kid putting him two thousand six hundred dollars ahead. This IS a lot of money in 1985 with the median rent right about four hundred dollars a month. It's Arnold's turn to goad the kid. With a distinct jab to his voice, he says "Again?"

The college kid's friends are all out of their seats and are grabbing their friend. "Hey, man, let's ditch this dump and go find some real fun. Fuck these clowns anyway." Then the girl leans in close and says, "Hey, you fought hard for me, let's go, I'll get you your real prize later."

With that, they start to head for the door, and about the time they get to the bar, the kid wads up some bills and throws them at Johnny the bartender. "I got money to burn, don't mean shit to me," and with that, they're gone.

Arnold turns to Allan with a big grin, "Well that didn't suck. Here's a dime for you. We good?"

"For sure, easy," says Allan with a grin to match Arnold's. "There's a sucker born every minute."Arnold quips back the line often attributed to PT Barnum: "- and two to take him."

Slade is catching up all at once. This was a hustle. This is another version of what Arnold had done to Slade all those years ago at Burnet Jr High. But what was the trick? Back then, it was manipulating the quarters, but here, what if the guy had been able to get them even closer to the rail?

Seeing the confused look on Slade's face, Allan and Arnold walk over. Slade says, "He never had a shot. As if on cue, they both pitched a quarter on the nearest pool table and the quarters landed and "hopped back" slightly, settling on the table slightly under the rail edge. "We can do that all night," Arnold says.

Slade is amazed; he's never seen anything like it. He had no idea a quarter could be controlled like this.

"I gotta bail y'all," says Allan as he heads for the door. He stops and asks Johnny, "So how much did that punk throw over the counter?"

"Three dollars," replies Johnny. "I'll take insults like that all day long," he laughs.

"Cool," says Allan, who drops a twenty in the tip jar and walks out the door. Allan then glancing back at Slade says; "I think that was the last class before finals my man; next up, you get in the game".

Slade turns to Arnold with an inquisitive look and says, "So, what, do you guys practice things like this then make up games to get people to bet and take their money?"

"Yes, that's it exactly. NEVER take a prop bet if a player's offering to bet you they can do something, no matter how wild it sounds. You should assume they can do it and NOT bet with them.

"Here's an example. This guy who used to come in all the time, Smokey. He could roll a pool ball down the table, then put a cue ball in his mouth and spit it out and sink the rolling ball," says Arnold.

"What the fuck, that is bullshit, who comes up with that shit," Slade asks.

"Ok Fatman, have you ever heard of pitching quarters closest to the rail before today?"

"Well, no, I guess not," Slade says.

"And there you are. It's ALL a hustle."

Slade is looking at Arnold with a frustrated and puzzled look. "So, that was all a hustle from the start. You and Allan were not ever gambling at all? Like at school way back?"

"For sure. Why gamble when you can steal?" Arnold says with a laugh.

Slade is irritated. "What the fuck, seriously, how could you have kept this from me all these years? So, you do this all the time, and clearly, you know Allan better than you let on. Why don't I know this? How are we friends if I don't know any of it?"

"Whoa there, Fatman, slow your roll. Think this through man. Look, I know what it was like for you with your old man and everything. There is no way I'm gonna be the reason you took another beating. What if you liked it or were good at it, then your old man found out. Dude, no chance I risk that shit."

Slade flinched with that and corrected his friend, "Whipping, not beating."

"NO, look, we're coming clean here. It is what it is, and it sucks, but your father beat your ass. We all heard stories, and people saw the marks on your legs in gym class, and of course, no one said anything. No one wants anything to do with that. Lots of kids have stories, but yours seemed awfully bad."

"I mean, we all take licks[30] at school."

It all comes rushing in on Slade. Overcoming him almost to the point of tears. He knows the biggest lies are the ones he's told himself all these years.

"Look, Fatman. That's over, you're out. You're free. They do not control you anymore. You want to know about the hustle, man, let's go to school. Someone as smart as you who can keep all those numbers and shit in your head, you'll be a natural. I know Allan has been showing you some stuff, he told me. I will come clean too; I have been keeping tabs to make sure you are good. As I say, I am not comin' between you and family, but at this point, you seem like you are leaving them behind for real."

Slade is recovering, still feeling a little betrayed by his friend, he channels this as his face immediately starts shifting to an arrogant stance. "Damn straight, being the smartest person in the room has its perks!" He says as he slips into his newly adopted persona.

Because he's free to BE smart without fear of his father using it against him and he feels the power of this freedom as the last hold of his father is removed.

And Arnold continues. "Look, that was a simple move. Rich kids all tend to be the same, shame them a little and let them make all the moves. Act like you're the one under pressure. I mean, that whole bit with me counting the money.

"Ya," Slade says, "I was wondering if you were gonna be able to cover it if you lost."

---

[30] Corporal punishment was still the norm in public school systems through the late 1980's in Texas, including the large metropolitan areas and in the state capital of Austin.

"I've been doing this a while. I have my bankroll in order," Arnold says, pulling out a literal roll of money with a rubber band around it. As he takes the band off, Slade sees that it's all hundreds. "Five-thousand-dollar rolls, I have at least three of these on me at all times, plus a little mini stack of five dollars or so with little bills, flash cash. Ya know, in case I want to play some fool, some alligator."

"Alligator?" Slade says.

"Man, we do need to get you in school," says Arnold. "Basically, alligator is a test to see who has the most money on them. winner takes all.

"WHAT?" Slade says. "Why would anyone risk that, lose all your money in one shot, I mean. People got to know you have money if they know about a game called alligator right?"

"Man, I'm telling you Fatman, people are stupid and prideful. They walk in here after cashing their six-hundred-dollar paycheck and think they have all the money in the world. Their eyes would pop out of their heads like yours did if they saw five dimes in cash, much less fifteen. Never flash your real money, only what you need to show to win. They show six hundred, I show eight hundred, then next week, they come in with a smooth dime and I'm ready with fifteen hundred. Then, after a while, you'll not see them and the next suckers come in. This place and a few others are revolving doors for idiots."

"So, if you do all this hustle and have the cash, why are you still working at your parents' restaurant?"

Arnold seems puzzled by the question. "This is money, that is family," Arnold replies. "That'll be my restaurant one day. I can't leave the family in a lurch. My sister can work the front as a greeter and stuff, help with making the desserts, but she'll never run the place."

"I've never seen your sister; how old is she?"

"Dude, she's thirteen and all but useless. The folks don't make her do shit. I've been in the fuckin' kitchen since I was ten. She's coasting along. Anyway, I'll never bail on the family."

Slade's trying to take this in as it's the exact opposite of what he's feeling about his own family. He wants nothing to do with them or their plant business. He's been betrayed and lied to his entire life. He has zero loyalty.

Slade is seeing that while Arnold might have his path in life all set and connected with his family, Slade is certainly still forging his own where there are not even guideposts. One step at a time.

Over the next few months, Slade continues to get better and better at pool and is itching to run a real hustle on his own; not the little games here and there he has been playing to "get his feet wet" as Allan has said. He is taking it all in watching for the egos one night, eagerly searching for the right time and the right person.

About that time, Slade hears a familiar group of motorcycles pull up. A guy Slade had come to know as King Henry walks in with his usual crew of people. Henry is a large well-built black man, a known drug dealer from the east side of town. Easily six-six and two hundred and fifty pounds, he makes an impression when he walks in a room. He comes into The Side Hole from time to time and considers himself a good pool player.

A few weeks ago, I would not have even had a shot, Slade thinks, but now, I should be golden.

Most of Henry's crew also play a little pool, but everyone knows Henry is the best of them. He loves to gamble and he's a hustler in his own right.

Slade has adopted the arrogance that came with the realization that he IS the smartest person in the room most of the time. Arnold had said it, and Slade had taken it to heart: "Someone as smart as you who can keep all those numbers and shit in your head, you'll be a natural."

I am the smartest person in the room. Slade reminds himself once again.

Henry sees Slade and says with a goading tone, dragging out his words, "Welllll, look at the meat on that bone[31]. You gonna gamble some or just watch little man?" As he says this, he looks over to Allan and Arnold in the back corner of the bar, in some ways talking to them as much as to Slade.

"Hey, King Henry," Slade said, using the man's full nickname to show respect, "I can't handle you, you know that would be like stealing, but I'll take a shot at one of your crew. I trust you—give me someone in the middle. Match me up fair and I'll gamble some."

"Well, you're comin' up in the world, little man. Let's do something," Henry replies, a little surprised.

"Look, I'm not rolled[32] like y'all and I don't have no stakehorse[33], so let's be friendly, first to three for fifty cents?"

"Done," says Henry. "You play Curly here, should be even from what I seen you shootin'."

Slade settles in and plays, thinking to himself, go slow, you have all night. Don't win big or make anything fancy, no big breaks. After six rounds, Slade's been paid five times and Curly has been paid only once, so Slade is up two hundred dollars. Henry has been watching and decides it is time to step in.

"Man, you're in stroke[34] tonight little man. I think you and me should have a go.

"Look Henry, I'm all about the gamble, but I can't take you, I'm just giving it away."

"Well, you asked to get in, man, I got to get my shot to get the cash back. Let's go some rounds, you know I'll adjust if It's out of line."

Slade agrees, and they keep the bet the same, Slade gets the first break and snaps the nine-ball right out of the gate. The next two

---

[31] This is slang for seeing someone as an easy target to get money from; It's a jab, an insult
[32] Short for bankrolled meaning not having as much money
[33] A stakehorse is someone who is backing another person who is gambling for a percentage of the bet
[34] In stoke mans playing pool at the top of your game

games are equally short as the break lines up easy combination shots that any player could make and win, and Slade does.

Henry says, "Well, no weight for you, you're seriously in dead pop tonight."

"No, man, come on, you know that was luck there man, let's see what happens when that goes away."

The next round isn't so fast and Henry wins three before Slade does and the two are even.

On and on the games go with Slade winning one set, then getting right there on the last shot of the next, and the eight or the nine doesn't quite fall in. Slade looks nervous and a little tired, but at the same time makes a little comment when Henry misses and loud enough for his crew to hear. But the comments are sympathetic. "Oh shit, you musta pissed off the pool gods this week, that was heading dead in."

After a few more rounds of this back-and-forth, Henry's had enough. "Man, I gotta get out and take care of some business little man. you're a shooter. Get your stack together and I'll be back and show you what It's like playin' a player. I'm off my game some tonight. I must have irritated the pool gods, 'cause you ain't that good, but you're still bettin' on my money so I'll be back to get it."

With that Henry motions to his crew and they head toward the door.

Just as they are about out, Slade sets the hook for the next game. "Hey Henry," he shouts across the pool hall, "I have a question for you."

"Shoot, little man," Henry replies.

"How long does your money have to be in my pocket before it's mine?"

Henry gives a slight grin while nodding and replies, "Ok little man, I gotcha, you a playa. I'll be back and we see how much of one for the reals.

Slade knows he's set Henry up perfectly. He won two hundred dollars from Henry's crew but was careful to break even with Henry in a brilliant show. That was the goal here.

Slade has graduated school to the next level by NOT WINNING. Sometimes *you have to lose to win*, and that is exactly what Slade's done to set up a big win later.

As Slade hears the motorcycles fade into the distance, he turns to Allan and Arnold who have been watching from a corner table, and throws up a fist in victory and says, "Ya, look at the meat on that bone!" repeating what Henry had said to him.

As he walks over to the table, Arnold says, "Damn, Fatman, you got this shit down. You own his ass. He'll be back next week and you'll smoke him and he'll have to pay up or lose face to his crew. Remember, you can sheer a sheep many times, you can only gut him once, so win but don't clean him out."

Slade looks around as if to see who Arnold might be talking to, then back to his friend. "Oh, you were talking to me—as if!" Slade says with his usual arrogance. "Dude, I do own him and his crew. I can eat off that for a month or two before he gets tired of paying me."

Slade coins a line of his own: "What do they say at the Barber Shop? NEXT!!!'"

As the night goes on, Slade picks up a few games and leaves with ten dollars more than he came in with. He loves it and is longing for more.

Slade is rearranging his schedule at the parts store as he's making more money hustling pool than working at the store full time, but this schedule was quickly getting in the way.

A couple of weeks after his interactions with Henry and nine months after he started at the store and subsequently dropped out of UT, he quits the parts store to hustle full-time.

His manager starts to tell him what a mistake it is to quit and that he knows how much time Slade's been spending at "that pool hall".

"Slade, I'm telling you, I know what I'm talking about here. I've been where you are, this is a mistake son. Please think this over and do not throw away what you have here. Let's take a moment and pray on it."

Slade could have let almost anything go; except that. It brought back way too much of the hurt from the life in the cult of his upbringing. So he turns and with full arrogance and assuredness replies, "Those of you who think you know everything really annoy the shit out of us that do." Slade of course has adopted the Isaac Asimov quote into the pool hall vernacular from the original —" *People who think they know everything are a great annoyance to those of us who do*"

Slade is a player.

CHAPTER SIX

POOL HALL LIFE

"Well, today was my last day," Slade says to Johnny as he walks into The Side Hole. "I'm officially a bum without a job!"

"What the hell, seriously, what are you gonna do for cash?" Johnny asks quizzically, laughing. "I could see it a mile away. It was a matter of time. You got way too good way too fast not to." He says right after, "I saw you setting King Henry up too. That was pure hustle right there. I think you'll be fine."

"Thanks, Johnny," says Slade. "...and speaking of Henry, he should be comin' in tonight. This could be the night I go ahead and collect on that setup. Just have to see what kind of mood he's in. I think I'll hit a few balls a bit to make sure I'm in stroke. Can I get a rack and a Diet Coke?"

"Sure thing," says Johnny. Slade slides a twenty in the tip jar and takes the balls to the table. He runs the drills that Allan had taught him not that long ago.

He reflects back for a moment when he got his first real taste of freedom, the day he got his driver's license. Man, had that only been 2 years ago? The world was still small for Slade then, and he was the meek follower of his parents, obeying every rule to the letter. In stark contrast, he had transformed into a young man bucking any authority and, in fact, any establishment of any kind. He had no job, and no accountability to anyone but himself.

And for the first time ever, Slade wasn't afraid.

After a few hours, Slade takes a break. Johnny is in the back of the pool hall brushing tables to remove all those tiny little balls of felt that build up after a night's play and getting ready for the evening crowd to come in. Hey Johnny, Slade hollers, "I'm gonna drop the balls here," as he sets them on the bar, "and run up the road for a bite. I'm thinking Taco Hell—you want anything?"

"Nah, I'm good. See you in a bit," Johnny hollers back.

As Slade is driving to get some food, he drives by the parts store he had quit earlier that same day and notices Allan outside taking a smoke break and talking to another hot chick from the strip club. This girl catches Slade's eye. A tall thin redhead with enough curves to be striking. So he pulls into the parking lot and rolls down the window.

"Hey, Allan and Amanda—right?"

The girl replies first. "Well, sweetie, that's my stage name, but I'll have you screamin' my real name later. It's Ramona," she says with a wink and a pop of her hips.

Slade takes the cue and replies. "I'll swing by the club; what time is your shift up?"

"Two, as usual, sweetie. see you later." Ramona turns and hops into a cab.

"You gonna nail that, huh," says Allan.

"Why the hell not? She's HOT!" Slade replies. "It might be a two-fer night: nailing Ramona AND cashing in on the setup I did on Henry. He's supposed to show at The Side Hole tonight. I'll clean Henry out of his cash, then go a few rounds with Ramona to cap the night!"

"Man, be careful with Ramona. She'll be trying to get her hooks into ya. Word is she's looking for something on the regular."

Allan nods back toward the parts store and asks as much as states, "They told me you weren't comin' back to work. Henry will for sure be a good starting roll to work from. I'll swing by to catch some of the action and get some down on the rail. 'Cause for now, no one knows how good you are. Nobody's gonna think you have a shot at winning. We've done well keeping you under the radar."

"Cool, I'll see you later. Gonna snag some food. I'm freaking starved," replies Slade. "And thanks for the heads up on Ramona. Hell, it might be less hassle to have a steady piece of ass these days anyway with the shit goin 'round," Slade continues with a large grin.

Slade pops into the fast-food Mexican restaurant for a few burritos and a drink. He takes them back to his car and relaxes. His thoughts drift. *What a life, no one hounding me, telling me what to do, how to talk or not to talk. No chores, no schedule, absolute freedom!*

Slade drives back to The Side Hole and notices a few motorcycles out front, but not the entire crew of King Henry. His eyes adjust to the light as he walks in, and he notices a couple of Henry's crew playing on the main nine-foot table in the front, a few more of them hanging out drinking beer.

"Hey y'all, skippin' out without King Henry tonight?" Slade asks.

"Nah, man, he had some business. He'll be 'round in a bit," one of the crew says.

"Cool. You want to get in a few games cheap before he gets here? I could use the warm-up. Henry was out of stroke when we played last time, but I can't count on that shit again," Slade says with his usual arrogant tone in contrast to the submissive language he used the first time he met Henry. Yet another part of the hustle was coming to Slade as a fish to water.

"Nah, man, I better not," his crew member says. "If I clean you out before Henry gets here, he gonna be pissed, but you right about one thing: you better get good an in stroke. Henry, don't miss much." He removes the balls from the table and takes them back to the bar.

About that time, the sad little bell on the front door dings, and Henry comes in, big as life.

Henry, in his overbearing and booming voice, enters the bar, motions to all, and with his usual drawn out "Weelllllll – look at the meat on that bone," this time directed at Slade. "You ready to play some little man?"

"Sure thing, but I'm not warmed up. Can I get in a practice game or something? Slade asks, knowing good and well that this is very much against gambling etiquette, but does it anyway, still trying to hold on to the "newbie" concept that Henry blindly sees in Slade.

"Look, man, not how this works," says Henry in a demeaning tone. "You come to the hall, you come ready! Practice on your own dime. Grab a rack. I will be PRO-FESSSSSSOR Henry today!"

With a feigned defeated look, Slade goes to the bar and says loudly, "Gimme a rack, Johnny," then, more quietly, "Blue circle[35] me."

Slade also notices that Allan sauntered in and is at one of the stand-up tables in earshot of the main nine-foot table with a beer.

"Ok, what are we doing, Henry? Make it fair, man, you gotta spot me somethin'. We both know I got lucky last time and barely broke my ass even."

"Screw that little man, even is even where I'm at – you get down four or five, then you talk to me on getting a spot," Henry replies in a sharp and definitive tone. "And I ain't got all night to break your ass either, so we gonna play this time – we're racing, not playing ahead[36]. You come to play or dick around boy?" Henry asks in a full aggressive, arrogant stance.

Slade sees it and acts appropriately intimidated. "Sure, ok King Henry, we can race. What are you thinkin'?"

---

[35] a cue ball with a blue circle is slightly heavier and of better quality than the "standard" blue dot que at the time; the higher quality ensures a ball that is more balanced and predictable as it rolls

[36] racing means that the first person to win X games, while playing ahead means the first person to win X number MORE games than the other person. In the latter scenario It's possible to have played twenty-five games and the score would be twelve to thirteen and no winner would have been determined

"Race to three for five. Can you afford that little man? I don't want you to be sleeping on the street or anything," Henry says, laughing to his crew, who all join in as if on queue.

"Ok, I'll do that. You don't have to be a dick, Henry. Let's play," Slade says, acting as if Henry has hurt his feelings. "Here's my five; we post up[37] each round so you know I'm good; how's that?" Slade continues with the feigned hurt still in his tone. This is yet another "newbie mistake" by Slade, and he knows it. You would never ask someone like Henry, who has the reputation for having plenty of cash, to post up before the game. This has the two-fold impact of Henry being put on the spot to post the cash and driving home in Henry's mind that Slade is still a newbie.

About that time, Allan appears close to the table where the two players are about to post up the cash. "Hey, Slade, man, that ain't cool; you don't post up with players–" he starts, but then Henry cuts Allan off.

"It's all good, Allan, my man. Little man don't know no better, we'll post up. How about you hold the dough for us. While you at it, make sure the rail don't outrun the action[38], don't want anyone thinking there's funny business when I take the boy out.

"All good," says Allan, "can't see this one getting much rail anyway. "Who's stupid enough to bet against you?"

Slade can overhear this and lowers his head and eyes, looking as if he's already lost. Allan thinks to himself, *damn,* Slade IS good, He's playing right into his part.

"Ok, call it for the break," Slade says, as he tosses a quarter in the air.

"Tails never fails," says Henry, and as they look, sure enough, the quarter lands tails up. Henry has won the first break.

---

[37] meaning put up the cash in advance of the game
[38] meaning that the amount of money wagered on the side or not directly with the two players who are competing is not more than the actual bet between Henry and Slade

Slade takes out two pennies and slides them under the rail at the foot of the table behind the rack as he racks the balls for the first game. He then repeats so everyone can hear it: "Race to three for five, let's do it!"

Henry breaks and fails to sink a ball, so Slade is up.

Slade leans over the table and there's a visible transformation. His face isn't a face of worry, it's one of confidence and concentration. He glances up at Henry and shows him his confidence before he lowers his head once again for his first shot, which is perfect and smooth.

The one-ball glides into the corner pocket, and the cue ball sets up perfectly for an easy shot of the two-ball into the side pocket. Slade goes on like this, not missing a shot until he gets to the six-ball.

The six-ball stops and "rattles" but does not fall into the corner pocket, which appears to be a big mistake as the ball is left sitting in front of the pocket.

But then it's clear, this too, was a perfect shot as the queue ball comes to rest behind the eight and nine balls which are sitting close together in the center of the table. They're blocking the cue from the six-ball. Henry will have to try a difficult kick shot[39] .

Slade decides it is the time to shed the newbie facade and attempt to rattle Henry, right here in the beginning.

He turns to Henry and uses the line he made up when Henry left the pool hall the week before. "Hey Henry (dropping the "King" this time as well). You know what they say at the barber shop right? .....NEEEEXXXXXTTT......!" he says, letting it hang in the air before backing away to let Henry shoot.

Henry is furious. All at once he realizes that Slade is better than he's let on. He can't simply walk away, he has to stay and play or risk losing face with his crew. Henry leans down for the kick shot, and the

---

[39] where you bounce the cue ball off a rail and try to "kick" the object ball into the pocket

six-ball slides into the corner pocket..... But the cue ball follows it in. A scratch shot[40]. Slade has "ball in hand"[41].

It's short work and Slade wins the first game. But much more importantly, Slade has rattled Henry. Henry starts missing shots he should be making while Slade is all but flawless.

Three sets of races to three in and Slade's won all three. Slade turns to Henry.

"Is this fast enough for you? Are you ready to quit? I get it if you are, It's a little embarrassing for you," Slade asserts in a quiet tone so that only Henry can hear his insult. Slade wants to rattle Henry, not shame him into a bar fight.

Henry glares at Slade and goes to rack the balls, sliding the pennies back in place behind the rack to start the next set.

Two more quick sets and Slade decides to push it even more. This will end it or make for a big win. Slade is satisfied with the twenty-five hundred dollars he's up. *THIS* is the time he ponders.

"Hey Henry, we did say we could talk about a spot after four or five sets ahead. I'm up five so if you want the eight, you got it." Then Slade paused and added, "But you gotta up it to a dime a set."

"Boy, you think you can hustle a playa?" asks Henry.

"Well..." Slade lets it hang, knowing he need not answer anything more.

"Ok, little man, let's see what you made of, then, for reals. I'll take that eight, but for two dimes a set, or you can stay in the little league," Henry says, trying to throw Slade on his heels.

"Done." Slade drops two thousand on the table in front of Allan. Slade also shows his roll of cash so Henry can see it, signaling that he's not going anywhere and that the two thousand is not intimidating.

---

[40] an error where a player fails to make contact with the object ball which must then contact a rail or when the cue ball leaves the field of play by falling off the table or into a pocket

[41] a specific and in this case official BCA pool rule; after a scratch shot, the incoming player may place the cue ball anywhere on the table for the next shot

They flip for the first break as they start the new set. Henry tries regaining some of his vibrato and spouts off his usual, "tails never fails". As the quarter lands heads up, Slade responds, "...until it does."

Just before Slade starts to break, he looks up.

"NEXT!"

That's all he says.

Slade snaps the nine in on the break then proceeds to break and run[42] the next two games to cap the race to three set.

Slade quickly snaps up the four thousand from the table, then lays two thousand back in its place and says, "...again?" while motioning to Henry.

Four sets later, with Henry only winning a total of three games across all of the sets, Henry has had enough. By this time, Slade knows It's time to back off and not add any more insult to injury. Henry's lost twelve thousand five hundred dollars and while he can afford it, no one likes to lose.

As Slade puts the four thousand of the last set in his pocket, he walks up to Henry with his fist out for a fist bump. His mind is racing back to his first meeting with Henry.

East side parts store

It was after the new year 1986 and Slade's manager had told him he would need to go to the east side store to fill in for some of the counter people who were out sick for a few days.

The east side was the side of town where years of redlining and persecution had caused black people to live in impoverishment. These were the facts Slade had remembered from some of his brief time at UT, but this was also in harsh contrast to what he had been taught in his church, that black people chose to live here and were lazy and

---

[42] when a player does not miss a single shot and wins the game

broke, sucking off of the welfare system causing all of the white peoples taxes to go up.

Slade had heard about the "black side of town" all his life and especially from the church elders who spoke of the hatred black people had for white people and that if they were in groups to be careful and get away from them as they would likely "kill you as soon as look at you."

With all of the revelations of the wrongness of what he had learned growing up, Slade decides to approach going "over there" with as much of an open mind as possible. He is realizing that what he had learned at UT was likely the real truth. But even then, indoctrination at this level makes unlearning his bias uncomfortable and difficult.

But once Slade was there on the east side, waiting on customers and interacting with the other counter guys he saw it. The people who came into the store were a normal mix of folks. No bloodthirsty mobs of people looking to do Slade harm, no glaring stares, just folks. Folks with broken cars, looking for parts to fix them just like the people from his other store.

He noticed that this side of town wasn't as "taken care of" as some parts of town, but not all that different from the parts store where his job was with a lack of sidewalks and many street lights that didn't work. But the east side did seem somehow poorer.

Slade stayed late, having a few beers with the other counter employees, who were all black. In central Texas, it wasn't uncommon for January to be in the mid-seventies. This was precisely the weather: clear, sunny, and seventy-five.

A group of guys on motorcycles pull up and one of the counter guys leans into Slade, "Hey, this is King Henry. He's cool, but he's also the biggest drug dealer on this side of town; show respect.

Henry, being in charge and wanting to set that out plainly, walks right up to Slade.

"Boy, what you doin' here? It's almost dark, dontcha know it ain't safe for a white boy over here after dark?"

Slade is caught flat-footed, but this isn't the place to be scared, whatever is gonna happen, he decides.

Slade replies carefully. "King Henry, I'm not lookin' for trouble; I'm just havin' a beer with these guys, we work together. But if I'm not welcome, I'll bail."

Henry steps up close to Slade, and even though Slade isn't small, Henry is a full half a foot taller and bigger overall. Then he says with a wide grin, "It's all good, I'm fucking with you," he pauses, "Brother White. If these boys asked you for a beer, then you must be good people somehow. I'll take one of those beers." He then stuck his fist out for a fist bump and Slade did the same. It was a sign of respect and every bit as meaningful as a handshake.

****

As Slade's thoughts race back to the present, he realizes that Henry has reached out his fist and is bumping Slade back; he nods up at Slade. And as he had done in the parking lot of the east side parts store when they had first met, he says to Slade, "We good," and pauses, "Brother White."

Henry lets out a big laugh and motions to his crew. "Let's bail boys, nights a wastin' and we got some bills to pay!" And with that, Henry is gone.

When Slade turns to go talk to Allan he notices that Arnold has arrived. With all of his focus on Henry, he'd missed Arnold's entrance. It's as if he's seeing the rest of the pool hall all at once. Slade realizes a large portion of the pool hall is eyeing him.

Arnold walks over. "DAMN Fatman — LOOK AT THE MEAT ON THAT BONE!" he says, enunciating each word as if it were a sentence all its own. A few of the people watching start walking over and giving high fives and fist bumps to Slade, treating him like a celebrity.

Slade grabs a beer and describes the game shot by shot. People are hanging on his every word. Allan and Arnold chime in every so often with, "See, I told you how you needed to practice this or that". But at this moment, this is the Slade Show.

This is Slade's Side Hole.

Slade leaves in time to go pick up Ramona. Walking through the parking lot up to the strip club, he sees a group of cabs parked outside. He slides a driver a hundred-dollar bill and says, "I need you to be at my place in two hours. I'll give you another one of these," waving another greenback..

He walks in as the lights are turned on, signaling closing time, and quickly spots the striking redhead. She gives him a big smile.

"I'm all tipped out, let's bail," she says. Slade lightly pops her on the butt as they walk out the door.

They waste no time once inside Slade's place. "I need a shower," says Ramona. Slade is waiting as she finishes, holding a towel for her. As she reaches for it, he immediately drops it to the floor and pulls her wet body in close. The two intertwine and eventually make it to the bed where, as he had been earlier instructed, he screams *RAMONA* as he finishes!

The two lay in bed while Slade talks about the night and his game with Henry. As if on cue Slade sees the headlights of the cab pulling into the driveway. He rolls over and grabs Ramona's clothes, motioning to the door. "I got you a ride and it's all paid for. " He stands and pulls on his jeans.

Ramona looks at him with slight disappointment, which Slade ignores completely., "It's all covered, tip too, so you don't need to give him any cash."

She quickly puts on her clothes and, a little deflated, heads out the front door. She turns to get a good night's kiss. Slade steps back and says, "Man, that was a lot of fun. Come up to The Side Hole sometime and we can do it again." She plops down into the cab. Slade closes the door and goes inside to fall immediately into a deep sleep.

Over the course of the next few months, Slade plays on his new status and sets up rail bets knowing he is the favorite. He'd lose and collect the cash, lots of it!.

Then, when someone came in who thought they could win, Slade would obliterate and humiliate them enough to get their cash.

Ramona comes by more often. One night when she decides to push it a bit, asking Slade, "Hey, so, can we be like regular fuck buddies, nothing serious, on the regular or something?"

As with everything, Slade had played her as well, and answered, "Sure, why not? He won't have to put real effort into his new play toy. The cash is flowing in and Slade was getting good at spreading it around for show and for influence. Cash was every bit as much of a tool as the new twenty-five hundred dollar pool cue Slade had custom-made.

Slade thought he had it all under control.

One of the people Slade had met "throwing cash around" was an ex-biker named Salazar turned bouncer at a local country music nightclub. Slade liked having Salazar around in case things got out of hand or if someone acts like they weren't going to pay up. Salazar on the other hand, liked the girls Slade introduced him to and the free beer! On one seemingly typical evening at The Side Hole, Salazar and Slade were playing pool (not gambling at all) and drinking beer. All of a sudden the front door slams and in walks a girl in a frantic state, out of breath screaming, "He's after me!" Before the door closes, a guy comes running after her in a rage. The girl runs right past Slade and Salazar and the guy heads toward the pair to get to her. Salazar being the macho hero type,, steps right in front of him and says, "Slow down there, we ain't putin' up with that shit in here." The next moments seem to unfold in slow motion as if the world went silent. The guy pulls a snub-nosed pistol from somewhere and presses it firmly on Salazar's forehead. He stares directly at Salazar, "Say what *cabron*?"

Slade's blood is rushing through his veins and he hears it pounding in his ears, but it was excitement, not fear. A strange sensation indeed. Slade still has his pool cue in his hand, as does Salazar. At that moment, Slade is afraid Salazar might take the macho bit too far and try to do something. No matter how fast you are, you can't outrun a bullet of a gun pressed against your forehead. Slade eases his pool cue to Salazar's foot and applies pressure as if to say *don't even think of it.* Then, as quick as the gun appeared, the gunman put it away and came back in the room and Slade observed things moving at normal speeds. The girl heads towards the door, and the oddest thing happens. The guy pushes her to the ground and then runs out. The girl gets up and immediately runs after him?!

Slade turns to Salazar and Salazar says, "Ummm, my fucking foot." Slade still has the cue pressed against Salazar's foot and quickly removes it. Slade says, "Well, that was some fucked up shit right here," and drains his beer. "Let's get the hell out of here. We can hit the strip joint and snag a couple of bitches and work out some kinks, I'm buyin', you in?"

"Hell ya," says Salazar, and the two head out the door.

The next day Slade is rolling out of bed as usual late morning, but today he's on a mission. He decides he also needs a gun and heads to the local gun shop to get not one, but two. One for the car and the other to carry.

He walks out of the shop with two new guns, holsters, extra clips, and plenty of ammo. He paid for it in cash, so as to leave no paper trail. Such is life in Texas in the eighties.[43] Buying a gun is like buying a bicycle at a toy store. Slade climbs into his truck and looks for a place to keep his "stash gun. He reflects on his new normal. He briefly thinks back to two years earlier when the only people he thought

---

[43] It's not much harder to get a gun in 2023 in Texas as you can go to a gun show and get one same day, but, at a "reputable dealer" you would have to fill out paperwork and wait a week or so

might have a gun were the most evil and vile people on the earth, as his church leaders professed.

He quickly recalibrates his thoughts: most people have a gun, and most people have it with them. Slade has two; with laser sights.

Slade is a hustler.

CHAPTER SEVEN

THE GARAGE GAME

T he Side Hole is where Slade starts and ends most days. He's more than a regular, it's *"Slade's pool hall"*.

"Hey Johnny, can I get a set of balls, I'm gonna tune up a bit, I gotta stay in stroke ya know. I gots bills to pay!" Slade laughs as he says it.

"Sure thing, man, let me clean up a bit and we can shoot a few games before the square-Johns[44] start rolling in," replies Johnny.

But as Slade rolls the balls out on the table, a group of college kids come waking in. Slade knew they might show up this week since it was the start of Spring Break, but not this early in the day.

"Hey, do y'all have tournaments here, or a pool league?" one of the college kids asks, walking closer to Slade.

"Hey, I don't work here, but I've seen tournaments here on weekends. I'm not sure about that pool league thing," Slade lies, as smooth as silk. He knows full well there's a pool league full of those snobby players who are "too good to gamble", blah, blah, blah. They're always talking about "making nationals" or "regionals" or something. Slade has a tinge of animosity toward the pool leagues that have started to pop up. Corporate sponsors are trying to clean up the game and there's a family-friendly pool hall that he heard about. The fucking corporate establishment ruins everything, Slade thinks to himself.

---

[44] regular working folks who don't understand or necessarily know a hustle is going on

"Hmm, well, ok, who does work here?" the kid asks.

"He does," Slade replies, motioning to Johnny. The kid walks over and starts talking to Johnny as Slade heads back to set up the table. Instead of the normal line of balls for practice that Allan had taught Slade, he racks a standard full rack as if playing eight-ball[45]. He then sets the cue ball and breaks. The balls don't spread very far apart and no balls fall in the pockets. Slade cusses rather loudly SHIT! Then he moves to make his first shot. The college kid walks over. "Hey, you're Slade, right?"

"Yep," Slade replies "Who's askin'?"

"I play in a pool league in Dallas and a few of the members who play here told me this was your place, and that you gamble some. So nice try fuckin'up the break, and acting like you didn't know about the pool league. We know who you are. Wanna play some?" the kid asks Slade after insulting him, with as much snarl as he can muster and a head motion toward the table.

"For sure, what do you have in mind?" Slade replies as he's thinking to himself this is NICE. These chumps come to me. They think winning a few games in the clean pool league *in Dallas* means they can hang with a real pool player like me.

"Let's do nine-ball, full BCA Rules[46] and we lag[47] for the break," says the kid.

Slade agrees. They lag. Slade *accidentally* pockets his cue ball on the return from the top rail, automatically giving the college kid a first break.

"So what's the action, you on a budget or a trust fund?" Slade asks with a chip on his shoulder in an attempt to rattle the kid.

---

[45] all fifteen balls situated with the one-ball up front, alternating stripes and solids with the eight-ball in the middle

[46] the official pool rules by Billiards Congress of America

[47] With the balls in hand behind the head string, one player to the left and one to the right of the head spot, the balls are shot simultaneously to the foot cushion allowing them to bounce and roll back to the head end of the table. The player whose ball is the closest to the innermost edge of the head cushion wins the lag.

"Let's go fifty dollars a rack," says the kid.

Slade quickly replies, "So, let's do races to three for one-fifty?"

The kid replies, "Sounds good."

I've got him, Slade thinks. Slade moved the bet from fifty a game to as much as one-fifty and this kid didn't even notice. He's not a rounder,[48] assesses Slade.

The play starts and after about an hour, the kid is motioning to his friends who have grabbed a nearby table that he has had enough and is ready to leave. He turns to Slade.

"You're better than they said you were, good game man, I appreciate you not being a jerk about beating me. You should consider a pool league. I know people like you think it's all too clean but I'm not as naive as you think. You could put together a real team and make nationals no problem."

Slade looks at the kid and replies, "Look, no offense here, but what the fuck do I need with a trophy and a first-place prize that won't cover first-class airfare and a room in Vegas? This isn't playtime, this is business for me."

And with that, the kid is out.

"Man, you're getting good at reading people, you knew NOT to rile him up or insult him, you just played and he paid off," observes Johnny.

"How much did you take him for? I saw y'all uppin' the bet, but I couldn't quite hear,"

"Right at fifteen hundred. I stuck a dollar in your jar, so you might want to clean that out. Get me a beer would ya. I think I'm gonna call it and chill. It wasn't such a bad day so I might as well kick back early tonight." Slade admires his winnings.

As Slade opens his second beer, some ladies walk in from the local strip club. "Hey there, hottie," calls a tall skinny blond. Slade seems to

---

[48] a person who makes money gambling and hustling; making the rounds

remember her name Becky as she smacks Slade on the butt, "How's it hanging?"

Without missing a beat, Slade replies, "Long and to the left babe, like always!"

Slade has learned how women are supposed to be treated in this world and with that in mind, he leans in across the bar closer to Johnny and says in almost a whisper, "Ya know why women are like linoleum?"

"Why," asks Johnny.

"Cause if you lay 'em right the first time, you can walk on 'em for life." He turns and walks to the table where the ladies are sitting and pulls up a chair to join them.

The girls giggle a bit as he takes his seat.

"We know who you are," says the blond. "Ramona tells us all about you."

"Does she now," Slade replies. "Well, the parts about me being hell in bed are true, as for the rest, y'all know it's all a show, ladies," Slade orders a round for the table and waits for Ramona to show up, then the two make their way to his place.

This night he does not send her out the door when they're done twisting in the sheets. He rolls over and falls fast asleep. When he wakes the next day he serves her a cup of coffee in a to-go cup. He calls for his now regular cab driver and lets her know her usual ride is waiting. Then with a quick motion, he heads for the shower after giving her a quick peck on her forehead.

A few nights later Slade's stopped practicing and is about to put the balls away when in walks Little Donnie; the best of the top pool players in town. Everybody who's anybody in the rounder world knows LD (his common nickname).

"Well, well, well, what are you doing slumming down here man? Shouldn't you be hustlin' the rich boys back at Eric's; the land of top-shelf drinks and made-to-order burgers?" Slade asks with arrogance.

"Man, makin' the rounds like everyone else, you know this was my place LONG before it was yours!" Donnie quips back.

Most people know LD's story; he had been playing pool and hustling since he could see over the edge of the table at The Side Hole.

"Sure man, but not anymore. This IS my house now, and don't forget it!" Slade added for good measure. Slade looks over at Johnny and says, "Set LD up on the far end table, no charge." Slade also gives a barely noticeable nod to Johnny, the signal that the action is about to go down.

Johnny takes a set of balls to the back of the pool hall and sets them on the table. Then he pauses and has a short conversation with LD that no one can hear. Johnny then walks back behind the bar. Slade orders a beer while observing things for a bit. Just as Johnny delivers Slade's beer, Arnold walks in.

"Hey Johnny, make it two," Slade adds. "Arnold looks thirsty."

"Hey man, sorry, I've not been around much," Arnold starts to say, but Slade leans in closely, "Hey, LD back table, stay awake!"

"Ahh, on it! Action!" Arnold says. "I'm gonna wander and keep an eye." Arnold takes his beer from Johnny and walks to a nearby table, steadily eyeballing LD. A few of the regulars start to come in, and the same set of college kids from Dallas from a few nights earlier show up.

"Hey," the kid says, walking up to Slade, "I see you're not top dog in here tonight, and he" motioning to LD "isn't too *good* to play league."

"What the fuck," Slade says in a loud voice. "LD, you a league player? You have one of those cute little finger gloves[49] too?" making fun of them.

---

[49] a pool playing glove that fits only across the thumb, middle and index fingers

"I'm not some small-time hustler like you. I'll win nationals this year in team nine-ball and individual one pocket[50] LD snips back, then continues, "You can't hang and you know it!"

"Hey, this is not the land of Simonis felt[51] and perfect rails. You're in my house, so slow your roll some. We all know you're good, but you throw out a little weight and I'll happily show you more than *small-time* gamble!" snaps Slade.

Slade ever so slightly targets his glance at Arnold, who is moving toward the college kids. More people start to pay attention to the back-and-forth banter between Slade and LD.

"Ok, man, you got it. Let me shut you up," says LD. "You got the six and the eight, I keep the snap[52]." This is a considerable spot, meaning that if a player sinks the six, the eight or the nine, they win. But regardless of who wins, the person given the spot gets the next break. People familiar with gambling know it's no small thing to give this much weight.

"Hell no. I need the snap or I'll just sit in my seat and watch you run racks and pay you to do it. How about; fuck that, I'll take the six and the snap." Slade snaps.

"Man, I'm not one of the chumps you hustle in here, I know you can get to the six often enough if you have the snap every time. Last offer, you got the six and eight winner breaks," barks LD.

"Done; race to three for five barks Slade, as he plops the rack on the table.

Arnold turns to the group of college kids. "Y'all want some on the rail or are you spectators? Slade said you had some gamble."

"You really think Slade can beat LD?" questions the college kid. "I watched LD run fifteen in a row[53] last week. I mean Slade is good, but not that good, even with the spot."

---

[50] a difficult pool game where one must make all balls in only one pocket on the table
[51] high-end pool table felt that gives a more consistent and predictable roll
[52] the break or opening shot
[53] to break and not miss for fifteen racks of nine ball in a row

"Dude, Slade is gonna rattle him for sure! I've seen it plenty," declares Arnold.

Johnny the bartender walks up behind Arnold and says. "I'll take two dollars a set on LD if you're taking rail action."

"I am, and I'll take up to two dimes a set. Bring it," Arnold states arrogantly.

Lewis, wearing his typical blue jean overalls slowly walks up acting as if he hasn't a clue who Slade or Arnold is, and in a slow drawl says, "I'll take five dollars of that action on LD."

"Done" snaps Arnold louder and with even more arrogance.

Across the pool hall, they hear Slade shout, "Mother fucking lucky bastard!" as the two-ball and the nine-ball line up for an easy combo shot after LD breaks the first rack. "You can't keep that luck shit up all night so enjoy it while it lasts," he continues.

"Well, it seems your boy is the one getting rattled," the college kid leans in and says to Arnold. Then he adds, "I'll take the rest of the action, what is left thirteen hundred a set? Let's make it a smooth fifteen hundred for easy math."

"Done!" says Arnold, and they turn to see LD make the nine on the break and notice that LD and Slade are playing as hard of a verbal game as pool.

"That's the hill[54] LD says as Slade, starts to rack the balls.

Nothing falls on the break this time and Slade easily runs to the six-ball for the win. Slade then adds "NEXT", which has become his go-to line. He snaps the nine-ball himself and laughs, then says even louder; "hill-hill bitch, hope you get to shoot again".

Slade breaks but does not make a ball. LD needs to make a hard shot on the one-ball, but the table seems like it will be an easy run after that. LD makes the difficult one-ball shot and then proceeds to run out. With that, he turns Slade's phrase on him. "NEXT".

---

[54] When playing a race, the "hill" means" one more game for the win

At a glance, Slade seems flustered. But then, as LD fails to make a ball on the break, suddenly Slade becomes completely composed; as if a light switch was flipped and the room that was dim becomes bright. Silently, smoothly and with full composure Slade runs the table to the six, then breaks and runs two more times winning the set. Slade and LD are even. The gameplay continues in silence and the noisy pool hall has fallen mostly silent right along with the two players. It seems that the show has ended and the two warriors are on the green felt field of battle and have lost all concerns with the observers in the audience. This has become a war between two of the best.

Slade plays an almost flawless pool game thereafter, rarely missing and when he does, he leaves LD in a hard position to make the next shot. LD has started to miss shots he shouldn't ever miss; he's the one who's rattled. It seems that it's the silence that's done him in.

Arnold turns to Johnny, "Again?" Johnny replies, "No, LD is shaken, I'm out, eight hundred is enough for me." Lewis says in his slow drawl as he spits in a cup he's holding, "LD is a player, He'll come around, I'm in."

"You're down six thousand, no shame in losing and quitting," Arnold says to the college kid.

"Up it to two thousand?" the kid asks.

"Done," says Arnold.

And as if on queue Slade breaks and starts another set. He immediately roars "- OOOONNN THE SNAP!" and breaks especially hard and loud and sure enough, the nine sails into the pocket as if on command.

Falling back to his quiet attack, Slade pours on the speed, shooting fast and smooth in dead silence. LD is missing all the time. LD loses more sets in less than thirty minutes.

The college kid hands Arnold two thousand more and says, "I'm done, you were right. I've never seen LD get rattled, but your boy did it. He's not supposed to win ever, you know." He slams the last of his beer down and, motioning to the door, he and his friends walk out.

Slade smiled broadly, knowing that this whole thing had been a ruse.

LD didn't "happen" to walk in, and neither did Arnold. Slade had called Arnold earlier that day and made sure he would come in. At this point, the role of Arnold being the teacher and Slade being the learner had all but faded away. Arnold was Slade's primary frontman for the rail bets. The long-time friendship between Slade and Arnold made Slade trust Arnold despite their sometimes disagreements on the best way to "do the hustle". Slade also knew that Arnold had this side of the equation down to art which showed up here when Arnold pulled the regular named Lewis in to add to the fake betters along with Johnny the bartender. The whole goal was to get the college kids to make rail bets, and they never had a chance to win; none.

Slade, Johnny, and Lewis walk over to where Arnold is starting to count out the money.

Arnold looks up and says, "Well done y'all. Let's get this chopped up," as he lays the twelve thousand from the college kid on the table. "Here's yours back, Johnny." Then to Lewis, he says, "And yours as well," handing him the rest of the pretend bets.

"Thank you, sir," says Lewis with a grin.

Arnold then says, "So, standard chop ten percent each for rails, fifteen percent for me for running point, and split the balance fifty-fifty. That's thirty-nine hundred each for the players," Arnold announces as he counts out cash for all involved.

LD turns to Slade, "Good call man, I wasn't sure you were on the up and up with me, but that was the nuts[55]." LD often used poker slang as much as pool hall slang to remind everyone that he ran a poker game in addition to other hustles.

---

[55] a poker term meaning the best possible hand

"Hey man, I wouldn't hustle you like that," replies Slade. "If nothing else, I respect the rounders' rules[56]."

"Oh, I know that, I wasn't sure the kids were all that you said they were. I've seen them poking around Eric's but we never got them to bite. You did it right."

"Ya, not even work," Slade said; his broad grin had quickly become replaced with a distinct look of boredom. "I should wander over to your pool hall more often." Slade continues as LD is heading out of The Side Hole. "I won't be hustling up any of your action, but good to show my face around so people will know I'm in. Plus, I wasn't kidding about the burgers, Eric's does make a tasty burger! For sure, man, come around, you have moves and you did me a solid here today. I will introduce you around and we will see what we can stir up. I'm out," LD replies as the door closes behind him.

"Hey man, let's find some other kind of action," Slade says to Arnold as he takes his cut. "This shit's too easy. I could have been drunk as a skunk and won that shit, not even a challenge." His face remained stone cold, bored.

"Hey, I know about this garage game; I've played it a few times. It's not hard like playing at the restaurant with grandma and shit, these guys are mostly drinking and having fun, but they throw around a lot of cash," pined in Arnold. Fuck-it, I'm in says Slade, I will learn on the way, let's bolt, Slade says and the two walk out and hop in Slade's truck.

"Why is it called a garage game?" Slade asks seriously. "Oh, It's poker, but they play in their garage; They're mechanics, ya know, brake jobs and shit," Arnold replies. "It's a dime buy-in, they play with chips and some cash, but It's table stakes[57]. Arnold and Slade head

---

[56] rounders don't hustle rounders when square-Johns are involved

[57] whatever you start a hand with is what you're playing with for that hand. If the bet of another player exceeds the amount you have, then you're considered "ALL IN" and while other players can continue to bet, you'll not win any part of that second pot which is also called a "side-pot

towards the outskirts of town, and as they turn off the highway, they come upon a sign that reads BRAKES.

As they walk in, they notice one of those padded folding tables with a sheet spread across it and a mismatch of folding chairs around it near the back of the garage bay.

"Hey Arnold," one of the guys says, "glad you could make it, as he's pulling out a case with chips in it. Arnold motions to his friend. "This is Slade. This guy is family!"

"Good news then, all friends of Arnold are welcome here. Grab a chair and a beer from the cooler. We play dealer's choice[58]. It's also table stakes, and the buy-in is a dime."

"Here ya go," Slade hands the guy his thousand and pops open his beer.

As the cards start being dealt, Slade notices that he's not familiar with the games, but taking heed of the lessons learned from the last poker game, he folds instead of betting when he does not understand the game.

"Hey man, do you play or just fold?" says one of the guys at the table to Slade, then continues he quips, "We like to play here"!

Slade is kind of new to poker," says Arnold before Slade can answer.

"Ya, I'm trying to see if I understand the rules and shit before I hand over the chips," Slade finally says.

"Ah, I see. Hey, man, we'll help. I'll run the rules out for ya as we go," the guy says to Slade."

As the night continues, Slade is still playing tight[59] and observing more than anything.

"Man, you're sitting there waiting for the nuts! Where is the fun in that shit?" one of the players says to Slade. "I told you before, we like to play here. This ain't some pro-ass poker game, Play the cards!"

---

[58] the deal of the game rotates around the table and when It's a player's turn to deal, he also gets to call the rules of the game
[59] not betting often and folding unless the odds are high in favor of winning

With that comment, Slade understands what he's noticed. People are playing every hand all the way to the end and never folding, except when he plays a hand, then they seem to fold much more often. They've been watching me too, Slade thinks to himself; They're afraid that if I'm playing, I must have a good hand, and of course, they're correct.

Slade is every bit as bored as he was when he walked in. He came in looking for a thinking game, but this is the exact same mechanical hustle as the pool hall; no strategy, all tactics.

"Thanks for the game, y'all. I gotta get some rest and set up the restaurant and shit," says Arnold to the guy running the game.

"Man, that wasn't what I expected," Slade says in an almost indifferent tone to Arnold as they walk back to his truck.

"Ya man, they won't invite you back if you don't gamble some. You gotta get in there and play," says Arnold.

"Dude, have you done the math on those games? No one has an advantage until the very end. It's practically all luck the way they set up the rules. I mean, I'm no poker player, but I can do the simple math here. The only thing to do is play as slow and tight as you can so you're never behind, then no matter what, you leave a winner. That's what you told me to learn about poker. "Quit when you're winning," That is what you said, right? Or what?!"

"No, man, you're missing it; you gotta gamble in this game. You have gotta lose to win. Then when you're winning, you make an excuse to get out like I did and bail. I knew you weren't down, so it worked out. I'll make sure you're up before we bail the next time we play there," assures Arnold. "Just watch for the signal. I'll do a two-finger tap on the table and tell a joke about a fish.

"Don't overthink this man. Hustle with the flow."

Slade pulls into the parking lot of The Side Hole. As Arnold climbs out of the truck, he turns to Slade and says, "It was a good night, Fatman. Don't look so down. This is the good part; we're winners!!!"

Slade arrives home and sits in his truck for a moment in reflection. He has three thousand dollars more in his pocket than when he started the night. That's ten times the average monthly rent for most folks and yet, he wasn't at all excited about *just* the money. He wanted more—much, much more. Slade wanted a game to win, a strategic thinking game. Something like chess vs. checkers. Arnold does not understand this part and it's creating a quiet but growing rift between the two friends. Slade continues to think; This is about winning, but how we win is as important as IF we win.

Slade was a bored hustler.

CHAPTER EIGHT

REAL POKER

H ey Johnny, how's things?" Slade says to the bartender as he walks into The Side Hole.

"Good! Things settle in when football season starts. It's like it has a calming effect or something, people are not as snippy and my tips are usually better in the fall too," Johnny replies with a grin.

Slade is the type of regular that he serves himself. He walks behind the bar and grabs a set of balls and a Diet Coke then heads to the big table up front to start his practice routine.

He's deep in thought as muscle memory takes over. He starts to shoot balls in pockets like a machine. It has been six months since he played in "the garage" poker game for the first time. He recalls the complete letdown when he discovered that it was another "check the box" hustle. Sure, there was the occasional "you need to read how far to push or not push a person, but at the end of the day, it was mechanical, like the practice Slade was doing at the pool table. Easy money made it attractive to keep going back. Though he never seemed to win as much as Arnold (Arnold still tells Slade he folds too much and needs to loosen up), he never lost.

Slade is shaken out of his deep thoughts by the dinging sound of the sad bell hanging over the front door as Lewis saunters in. They have become more than acquaintances since Lewis helped with the side bets earlier that year. Slade began trusting Lewis to do more and even act as the front man running the rail when Arnold was directly involved with the action or not seen as neutral enough. Slade liked having Lewis around, as Arnold was not to be relied upon to do what Slade needed to be done. Although Arnold and Slade were almost inseparable, a result of a long-time friendship, they did not agree on how to hustle.. Arnold chased the excitement of the hustle while Slade relied on it to earn a living.

"Hey there, Fatman," Lewis says as he walks over to the pool table. The irony wasn't lost on Slade, as Lewis was rather plump. "How many of those duck shirts do you have?" "I've seen you in a duck or goose shirt almost every time I've seen you lately. I think I'll call you the duck man," Lewis says, laughing, then pauses, "Wait, no, Bird-Man! Bird-Man," he repeats as Arnold walks in the door.

"What's that, Lewis? Who's Bird-Man?"

"Fatman here! He keeps wearing all these "fuck a duck" shirts and shit, so I'm gonna call him Bird-Man."

"Hilarious, asshole," Slade finally says back. "I'm sure that nickname will help me get laid."

Johnny, the bartender, can't help but overhear and chime in, "Man, I like it. Bird-Man rolls off the tongue, don't it?"

Arnold repeats slowly, trying to imitate Lewis's drawl. "Bird-Man, rack them balls, and let's play some." The whole group laughs. Fatman's nickname has been replaced with Bird-Man.

Slade and Arnold practice, and LD walks in. "Damn, twice in a year," Slade says to LD. "What are you doing here, man? It's still early. You can't be on the move yet. Is the action that slow over there at Eric's?"

"Nah, I'm meeting Phil the bookie up here. He said he was meeting some other players here to settle up, so I reckon I'd save him a trip to Eric's. I'm starting my game back up this week, too, so I want to make sure and ask him in person. He's a good draw," LD continues with a grin.

"Damn, that reminds me," Lewis says, "I owe him two dollars. I can settle up while he's here."

"Man, you guys know better than that shit," Slade says. "I'll never understand why smart rounders like y'all bet one cent on fucking sports. That shit's a loser unless you're the bookie. You know that, right? I mean, would you flip quarters with eleven to ten odds? Hell no, you wouldn't."

Slade looks up and realizes everyone's looking behind him, and most have funny little grins on their faces. He turns to see Phil standing right behind him,

a large man, easily six feet six inches tall. Slade guesses he's in his mid-to-late-fifties. Dark black hair without a speck of gray, but the lines on his face reveal his age or at least some wear and tear. His dark brown eyes still sparkle like those of a younger man, and he speaks with the confidence of a rounder who's stood the test of time. The word in rounder circles is that Phil's loaded. If you bet with Phil, the story goes on. You'll get paid in full and on time.

"Are you tryin' to ruin my business and send me to the poor house?" Phil says comically to Slade. "Don't be telling people the odds, I might lose all my customers."

"Hey Phil, I...um, you snuck up behind me. I didn't see you come in. I'm not sure we ever met formally," Slade continues. "I've seen you in here, of course, but you kind of usually keep to yourself. I'm Slade." He sticks out his hand.

Arnold says, "damn, you gonna ask for a fucking autograph too? Hey, Phil, call him Bird-Man!"

"I see Lewis is up to his naming stunts again," Phil says, pointing at Slade's shirt, immediately making the connection with the name. "Nice to meet you, Slade. If you ever want some sports action, you call me up. I've heard about you. The newest Side Hole rounder, and not doin' too bad for yourself the way I hear it. I'll set you up on a five-dime limit to start."

"Damn, Bird-man!" Lewis says. "Phil keeps tabs on shit. We all know it, but he likes you. He doesn't hand out limits like that. He maxes me at twenty-five hundred a week."

Phil has turned his attention to LD. "Hey, let's walk over here and talk some," as the two move out of earshot.

Phil focuses on the business at hand. "Damn, man, that was tough for you this week, LD. A lot of people didn't like the call at the end of the Cowboys game. Without that penalty, they almost certainly cover the spread," Phil says, as a way to have some small talk.

Phil treats his customers like people; this is all part of the service. It's personal with Phil, not transactional.

"Ya, fuck I know it," says LD. "Here's what I'm down. Twenty-seven fifty; you can count it."

"You know better than that, LD. I trust you," Phil says as he folds the stack of bills and stuffs them into the pocket of his long-leg track pants. With the bookie business handled, LD shifts the conversation to his poker game.

"You comin' to the game tonight, right? Tex will be there, and some of your other customers too."

"I won't let you down, LD. I know I'm a draw. Everybody loves it when "*Wild Phil*" hits go-off mode!"[60] Phil replies in the third person making fun of himself.

Now it's Lewis's turn to pay, so he pulls Phil aside. "Hey, let's square up," Lewis says as he slides Phil two hundred and twenty dollars. Phil takes the cash from Lewis.

"Thanks for your good business," Phil says. Again, it's about customer service, especially when collecting. Easy for people to like you when they win and you show up to give them cash; the trick is to make them like you when you lose.

Phil announces to the group, "Well, I've got some more rounds to make. I'll see you tonight, LD." He then turns to Slade. "Hey, it was nice to meet you, little buddy; you got my number. I also run a craps game from time to time. I'll hit you up when it's on next. You can spread a little of that wealth of yours around."

"Thanks, Phil, Might take you up on it," Slade replies. He is in admiration of Phil and the business he's built. He feels warm to have

---

[60] when a rounder lets emotions take over and starts making bad bets trying to get even after a loss

one of the wealthiest rounders in central Texas know his name and invite him into his private games. Slade turns to see Arnold looking at him with a funny look.

Arnold was remembering a time when Slade looked at him the same way he looked at Phil: with wonder and inquisitiveness. The way a student looks at a professor when they're ready to learn. Arnold had known that Slade would grow past what Arnold could teach him, but today he sees it firsthand. His friend found a new teacher in Phil.

"Sup," Slade says to Arnold. "Something about Phil I need to know? You got a look; tell me."

"No, hey, Fatman, all good. I was thinking about tonight. If Phil's going to LD's game and hits go-off mode, that'll be some real cash in the air. We could get some." Arnold turns to LD, "Hey, you got a couple of seats for me and Fatman...uh, I mean Bird-Man," he adds, laughing.

"For sure," LD replies, "dime buy-in and five-dollar rebuys. We start at eight, I supply drinks and food, but no eating at the table. Table stakes, of course. Five/ten blinds, no limit Hold 'em, and we pass the deal." LD's fully describing the game.

"Cool, we'll be there," replies Arnold as LD heads out the door.

As soon as LD's out of earshot, Lewis pipes up; "Arnold, you know they got some real players over there, not a chump game. They're for real and have real cash. Checkbook, Danny the Drain, Tex O'Sullivan, Lorenzo; these are real players, ya know."

"C'mon Lewis, of course I know," Arnold replies, almost annoyed. "I've been playing cards since I pulled my wallet out of my diaper. I'm good."

Lewis replied sheepishly, "Ok, don't get on me, I was making sure you know. It's not just Phil playin', as I say, a real poker game."

Somewhere in the back of Slade's mind, "real poker game" was registering, but it was way back there. On the surface, where decisions are made, Slade appears arrogant, and bored with the mechanical nature of it all, and ready for anything but the grind.

"Well, if we're gonna play, I'm going to the house and shower. Doesn't seem like a game you want to show up late to," Slade announces. He walks out and hops in his truck without waiting for an answer. He's annoyed for some reason, but he can't quite put his finger on it. Way back in his mind, way, way back, this annoyance is driven by uncertainty. The uncertainty that should be setting off alarms to be careful instead seems to be pushing him to be even more aggressive than usual.

Arnold leaves The Side Hole with enough time to get to LD's game as the eight o'clock hour approaches. Slade and Arnold happen to pull up to LD's place for the game and walk up the drive together. Arnold turns to Slade and says, "Ok, this one, you do play tight and pick your spots when you know you have the nuts. This ain't no time to be fuckin' around, assume the nuts will always be there."

Slade is getting annoyed that Arnold is still trying to "teach" him. The fact is that Arnold does know much more than Slade about poker, but Slade feels he is the full-time rounder and there is absolutely nothing left to learn from Arnold. Slade became bored with his teaching method and, in his arrogance, ignored Arnold even while ignorant about some things.

Along with most of his bankroll, which has grown to about forty thousand dollars, Slade carries his boredom and arrogance to the game. While Slade was at home, he decided that he would show these "big-time" players that he was one of them. He would bring his "big stack" with him and flash it around a bit. Slade wants the people in this room to see it, to see that he's a success and that he has the cash to show for it.

The table is set, and the perfect fare of boredom, ignorance, and arrogance are on the menu. Slade walks in, unrolls a couple of stacks of cash, quickly counts off two thousand, and says, "I'll take two dimes."

From behind him, sitting at the table, a player comments to Slade, "Sure, take two. They're small." The player is making fun of the fact

119

that Slade is acting like two thousand is a large chunk of money and, at the same time, indicating that he thinks it's nothing. Slade turns to see which player is talking to him about the time LD starts to make introductions.

"So," starts LD, "this funny guy here in the sports coat is Checkbook or Jimmy." Then pointing as he goes around the table, "This is Tex, Danny, Sam Lorenzo, and I think you know Phil. Guys, this is Slade; he plays a good game of pool, so don't be getting hustled," LD says with a laugh. "I think most of y'all know Arnold."

"Oh, THIS is the Slade character we heard about? That was a slick move y'all did on those college kids. LD here tried to get them to bite at Eric's for a while, then you took them out over at that dump, The Side Hole, right?"

"Ya man," Slade kind of laughs and bristles simultaneously. "That's me, the king of the dump, The Side Hole." This fuels the arrogance and chip on his shoulder even more. Slade makes a note to try and beat this Danny guy and the smart-mouth Checkbook. He'll show them what a real player can do.

Slade takes his seat and is ready to play. As he starts to look around the room, something seems off. He can't quite put his finger on it, but something. A voice in his head reminds him that he is one of the best rounders in town, and these people don't seem to be giving him the respect he deserves. They know about his actions and how he beat some kids that even LD couldn't hustle, yet they treat him almost like a square john. And some of them ARE square johns. He's fighting hard to push this feeling away, but it's there, nagging at him in the background.

For the moment, he silences the voices as LD sits at the poker table and says, "Let's go; high card for first deal," and he starts to deal one card to each player. Slade gets the first Ace, and LD stops dealing. "Looks like Slade, or as I learned, Bird-Man, gets the first deal.

"Let's post up blinds[61] LD says to start the first game. As a reminder, it's no-limit five & ten blinds. We rotate the deal, but in this house, it's all Hold 'em all the time; no funny games."

Slade isn't sure what LD meant by "no limit," but he had the rest of it down, so he knew he was ready. Slade takes the deck and starts to deal.

He sets the deck beside him and looks at his two cards when LD says, "Hey, protect the deck."

As Slade is making a funny face, Arnold quickly adds, "Drop a chip on top of the deck so no one accidentally lands a card on it or something." Slade complies and instantly realizes this hustle is different. There's a structure here. A set of rules and a set of etiquette which is expected to be followed. This is beyond "pool hall lingo" which to some passes as the etiquette of sorts; this is a real structure that, if unknown or unfollowed, can have real consequences. And not just different from the pool hall. This is also unlike the chaos of the card games Slade remembers from church fundraisers or the restaurant, and certainly not from the garage game Slade's been playing. This is different, indeed. Slade quickly puts that away and decides he can learn as he earns; he is, in fact, the smartest person in the room; he lets the little voice in his head remind him.

"Oh, shit, sorry." Slade reacts quickly, not letting on. He had no clue he was supposed to do that. "Long damned day, fellas."

Checkbook, the third person to Slade's left, the first person after the big blind and also known as "under the gun," says, "Call," as he drops two five-dollar chips in front of him. After seeing his two cards, Slade immediately throws his hand in the middle to fold.

---

[61] this is the ante or required bet in poker. They're called blinds since you "make a wager" without seeing the cards; or; bet "blind". The first player to the left of the deal is the "small" blind and the second player to the left of the deal is the "big" blind. The amounts are called out in that order as the game initiates. After the initial deal of the cards, the third player can either call the big blind amount, raise the big blind amount by no less than the big blind, or fold

LD again quips, "Dude, wake the fuck up and pay attention. Don't fold without pressure; what the fuck kind of rookie are you?"

Phil the Bookie pipes up before Slade can speak. "Hey, LD, slow it up, man. Damn, first hand, the kid said he was tired. Don't come out being a dick. Save it until you're down ten dimes."

Turning to Slade, Phil continues. "All good little buddy. We have all had days."

Slade again apologizes, "Man fellas, sorry about that," as he takes a long drink of his Diet Coke. "Let's get some caffeine in these veins and wake the fuck up. I'm on it."

Slade notices that no one is looking at him, not even Arnold. Somehow, he knows this is not a good sign. How many meaningless little rules are there, Slade thinks to himself. *Just bad luck that I had to deal first, or I would have picked up all of this nonsense.* His little voice of arrogance is getting a bit louder in his head.

The hand continues without further incident, and Phil wins the first pot of the night. The deal passes, and the game continues. Two cards, flop, fourth street, and the river.

Slade finally gets a hand he likes, a pair of kings as his hole cards, so he says, "raise," When It's his turn and throws two green chips in the middle.

LD snaps again, and no one is coming in to rescue this time. "Hey man, this ain't no backroom bullshit game. Don't splash the fucking pot, or you're out, got it?"

"Ya, man, I got it."

"Your hand is dead, throw in your cards," says LD.

Slade complies and throws his hand in.

He understands, as he thinks it through, what splashing the pot means. It means putting your chips in the middle before all of the bets are made, and the dealer pulls the chips in. What he does not know is why this is a rule. He accepts it and moves on. He's pissed though, emotionally embarrassed. He knows the table thinks he doesn't know how to gamble because of a couple of LD's silly rules.

On the next hand, Slade doesn't even look at his two hole cards. *I'll show them how a player plays. I'm going to fuck them up.* When It's his turn, he ever so slightly slides his entire stack forward and, staring directly at LD, declares, "All in[62]."

Everyone folds, and Slade takes the blinds. He risked eighteen hundred and won fifteen grocery dollars, and yet he feels like he won a lot. He has his confidence back, and It's showing.

"Do you ever play pool, Checkbook?" Slade asks.

Checkbook looks at LD and slyly replies, "A little."

Slade knows this routine and says, "Ya, ok, got it, that good, huh? What about the rest of y'all? Do you all play?"

"Not me," says Danny. "I'm just a plumber," and the whole table laughs.

"He's the director of the local pipefitters union too; he leaves that out sometimes," Tex adds.

"Phil then says, "None of us play any, well, not like the four of you anyway," motioning to Slade, Arnold, LD, and Checkbook.

About that time, Slade decides It's time to show them again that he's a real player. Out of nowhere on fourth street, he pushes his chips forward ever so slightly and declares all in. There's about four hundred in the pot at this point, so he's ready to make a little win. Everyone around the table is folding, but the action stops at LD as he stares back at Slade.

Then LD does the same thing, pushing his chips in, and saying, "ALL IN." Slade isn't sure why LD didn't just call but decided not to ask. The rest of the table folds and Slade and LD turn their cards face up.

Slade reveals two pair, and LD reveals a set of aces. Slade hears LD say, "I got the nuts," before turning over his hand. As Slade looks over

---

[62] this means that you're betting all of the chips in front of you

the hand, he does a quick mental check of all possible combinations that could come out, and not one card in the deck can save his hand.

"Damn, I never put you there," and folds before the river card is turned.

"Time for a rebuy, I guess," Slade says, smiling.

Checkbook once again spouts off, "Better buy two. They're small."

Irritated, Slade says, "Five dimes, let's play," and hands LD five thousand dollars

Play continues, and in less than a round of the table, Slade is again buying chips. Within another two hours, Slade's bought in for right at thirty thousand dollars and only has about five thousand left in front of him.

Arnold stands up and says, "Hey, I'm taking a break. I gotta take a piss, and run to the store for some snuff. Fatman, you wanna go with?" Slade looks up and sees that Arnold is giving him the head nod to step out.

Slade hops up and walks to the door with Arnold. "Hey, snag me some snuff, too, while you're at the store, would ya?"

"Sure, but hey, man, you need to lick your wounds here and back out. You're already in too deep. Don't blow your full stack, brother."

Man, I've seen you do it all the time. You've pulled out of plenty. Just keep pressing; I get it. I'm good!" Slade replies, still annoyed that his friend, the part-time hustler, is trying to keep schooling him.

"No, man, this is not that game. I told you. Lewis told you. These are players; they can't be bullied. They have you, and you need to get out."

"Bullshit, I'll show you. I'm a fucking player, don't worry about me," Slade quips.

"Ok," says Arnold, "Back in a few. I'll snag you some snuff."

Slade is standing as Arnold walks back in. He hears Slade say, "ALL. IN."

Arnold peers around Slade. With a quick count, he can see that Slade's pushed about twelve thousand in.

Slade turns to Arnold and says, "I got the nuts. I hope he calls," as LD says, "All in."

Slade quickly turns his cards face up, revealing that he has Aces full, full house. What Slade missed in his excitement of having an exquisite hand is that it's not the best hand. There are two kings in the community cards, meaning four kings are a possible hand. LD then turns his hand over and says, "The actual nuts," revealing a pair of kings as his hole cards.

"Well, that was fun," Slade says with a laugh and adds, "but I think that's it for me tonight. How often do you do this, LD?"

"Once a month. I'll swing by The Side Hole and remind you."

Checkbook adds, "Hell, I'll send the fucking limo to your house; you go off like a rocket. Phil ain't got shit on you!"

Slade looks at Arnold as he walks to the door. "Hey, fucko, you got my snuff?"

"Sure, brother," Arnold replies and hands him the can of Copenhagen.

Slade is completely lost as he walks to his truck. Well, rent's paid, he thought. Slade lost forty thousand dollars, basically his entire bankroll. His short stack of five hundred is in the truck, but that doesn't cover shit. He'd have to look to see what else he might have squirreled away, but deep down, he knew it was next to nothing. For a gambler, not having cash was like not having any tools.

How does one even start without tools? Slade can suddenly hear himself ask out loud. Damn, I'm losing my mind, too, he thinks. All he hears are his father's angry words from the day he moved out: "You'll fall flat on your face, boy." Slade fears his father has been exemplary, and it's all he can do to drive home. He sits in his truck, swirling in the same thoughts over and over until some headlights snap him back to reality.

Earlier that night, he asked Ramona to swing by after her shift. He had forgotten about it until the cab pulled up to drop her off. Slade raps hard on the window before she can even open the door. The cabbie rolls it down; Slade throws one of his last hundred-dollar bills at him and says, "Take her ass home. I am in no fucking mood for her shit tonight." Then without even acknowledging Ramona, he turned and walked toward the house.

Slade is defeated fiscally and mentally; his will to hustle is gone.

CHAPTER NINE

LOSS

S lade keys the front door and walks into the house he shares with his friend Arnold. Absent-mindedly, Slade throws his keys on the coffee table and wanders to his room without turning on a light or even locking the front door behind him. He closes his bedroom door, pulls off his clothes and tosses them in a heap, and falls into bed with a thud.

Slade is devastated.

What the fuck am I gonna do? What have I been thinking? I'm not going to my parent's home. I'll live in my truck, first, he thinks desultory. Damn, I'm fucked. I don't have the cash to fight my way out. Contradicting himself, he thinks, who cares? At least the rent is paid for this month. He continues to spiral in a circle of depressing thoughts.

Slade tosses and turns and slips into a restless sleep. He barely hears Arnold as he opens his bedroom door. "Hey, Fatman, you ok, man? It ain't like you to sleep the day away. I know that shit was rough last night, but hey, get up, man."

Slade opens his eyes and sees bright daylight streaming through the tightly closed mini-blinds hanging over the small window in his bedroom.

"Ya, whatever, I'm fine. I need sleep. Man, I fucked up. I; I'meaned out, I'm not sure what I'm gonna do."

"Hey brother," Arnold replies, "it's all good, I got you. I'm heading to work but will see you at The Side Hole when I get off" Arnold walks out, closing the bedroom door behind him.

Slade rolls out of bed and rummages through his closet, finding the last of his emergency stash. He counts it. *Fuck.* He panics as there's only three hundred and eighty-five dollars. He's in full self-blame mode.

I took it all with me, and now it's gone, and I'm fucked! He screams out loud. He pulls on shorts and reaches for the wireless phone extending the antenna, then hits the speed dial for the pizza chain restaurant and orders a large thin-crust meat lovers pie. The person on the other end is unhappy with the f-bomb Slade blabbers, and Slade, sensitive to the grumpf on the other end of the line, apologizes. "Ya, sorry, It's been a long day; I'll pay cash." He hangs up and tosses the phone towards his nightstand, forgetting to push the antenna down. He doesn't care that it bends as it bounces off the stand and hits the floor. Forty-five minutes later, the doorbell rings and Slade hands the driver a twenty and says, "Keep it," not even considering the one hundred percent tip as he grabs the pie. Fuck it, he thinks, I'm broke anyway; who gives a shit! He eats some pizza, then wanders back to the bedroom to adjust the mini blinds to make the room pitch black. Once again, he falls to the bed.

Arnold's voice awakens Slade again, only its hours later at two-thirty AM. "Hey man, we missed you at The Side Hole," Arnold says. "I brought some gnocchi and salad home and threw it in the fridge. If you want a snack or something, feel free. There's plenty of beer and a few Jolts[63,] let me know if you need anything else," Arnold kindly offers his friend.

"I'm hitting the rack. We should make the rounds and hustle up some action in the next couple of days. You'll snap right back, brother. Wait and see."

Slade stares at Arnold blankly without a reply, then rolls back over and slips into a restless sleep. Fuck, he needs to snap out of it. That room has a funk to it, Arnold thinks to himself. Over the next few days,

---

[63] eighties cola promoted as having all the sugar and twice the caffeine as "regular" colas

it's the same. Slade stumbles out of bed, barely enough to shove something into his mouth. When he finally hits the shower, he notices his room stinks!

Arnold is worried as he pulls into The Side Hole on his way home from work. He thinks there is no reason not to hustle up some action or grab a cold beer because Slade is hiding at home. , Walking in he spots a familiar face, Phil, the bookie.

"Hey, Phil," Arnold says. "How's it hanging?"

"Oh, you know, long and strong," Phil replies, and the two laugh. "Where's our little buddy Slade?"

"Man, he's sick or something. He hasn't left the house since LD's poker game."

"WHAT?!" exclaims Phil. "That's no good. That was a week ago. Is it the flu or what? Is he puking his guts up?" Phil continues to inquire.

"No, man, nothing like that; he sorta eats and then sleeps almost the whole day. I have been bringing shit from the restaurant and stuff. He's kinda hanging low for a bit."

"No man, this ain't no good," says Phil. "I've seen this shit. We need to snap him out of it. I'm gonna page him. He needs to get his ass up here." Phil points to the phone, and Johnny, the bartender, sets it up on the bar. Phil dials and pops in his code to page Slade.

Phil says, sliding the phone to Arnold, you too, "Use whatever code you use for action and send it." Arnold complies and slides the phone back to Johnny, the bartender. But Slade won't get the page because, in his bedroom, the pager is silent. It's either out of power or out of service. Phil looks at Arnold. "Damn, it has been an hour, this shit is no good. We need to get him up and moving. I have seen this shit go bad before, and I won't let it happen again to one of our own," Phil shows a surprising amount of care for someone he does not know.

"You check on him tonight and see what is up. If you can't get him up and out of the house, page me tomorrow", "Leave the door open, and I'll swing by after you're gone. Oh, and make sure he doesn't have his pistol in his room. I don't want to get shot!"

"I'm on it. Thanks, Phil. I'm kind of worried about the asshole," Arnold admits, a little embarrassed that he hasn't taken any real action to help out his friend.

Arnold goes home and notices the smell in Slade's room. Even though it has improved, the piled-up dishes in the sink and empty beer bottles strewn about the kitchen table and floor leave a stench. Slade has had more beer than food lately it appears. He wanders into Slade's room in what has become a nightly routine over the last week. Arnold was a slob, but not Slade who likes his shit to be in order. Hell, most of the time, too much order, Arnold thinks.

"Hey, Fatman, did you get my page? Or Phil's? What the hell, you dodging me?", he says in his outside voice.

Slade rolls over and looks at his friend. His mouth is dry from drinking beer and replies in a whisper. "Ya, no page, man, I'm not dodgin'," was all he managed to say.

"Fuck Fatman, did you pay the pager bill that came in a couple of days ago?" Arnold states more than asks. He's more irritated than he wants to show. Softening a little, he adds, "I'll find the bill and take care of it." As Arnold looks across the dark room, he can tell Slade's rolled back over and isn't listening. Arnold pulls the drawer to Slade's nightstand, removes Slade's pistol then creeps out of the room; Slade does not stir or notice.

Walking into the living room he looks around for mail and finally finds a small pile under a pizza box with two pieces of cruddy old pizza. Flipping through the mail, he locates the pager bill, then tosses the rest back on the coffee table. He picks up other trash and beer cans strewn about and makes his way to the garage to throw it all into the big trash bin. He then wanders back to his room dropping the pager bill on his dresser drawer top along with Slade's pistol, his own wallet, and cash.

Man, I hope Phil can snap him out of it, Arnold thinks out loud as he plops down in the bed for some needed sleep.

The next day, Arnold, as requested, pages Phil with his usual "leaving" code – 688, the numbers that "spell" OUT on the phone.

As he receives the page Phil is standing in his walk-in closet at his house. He has a swing-out facade with shoes pulled open, revealing a space behind that is stacked floor-to-ceiling with wooden shoeboxes. Or at least at first glance, what they appear to be. Phil pulls the top back on one of them and *voila*! Inside are neat stacks of hundred-dollar bills.

Phil removes a handful, rolls them, then secures the roll with a rubber band. As he pushes the box back into place, It's apparent there are three distinct stacks of "shoe" boxes. The bottommost box of each stack has a number on it; 10; 20; 100, representing the denomination of each bill in each stack of boxes. Of course, there is no stack for fifty-dollar bills. As all-rounders know, the fifties are bad luck.

As Phil closes up his closet and snaps the exterior lock, he hollers goodbye to his housekeeper and heads out the front door.

He walks to his truck, still dripping with water droplets from a fresh wash. His maintenance man had finished the daily job at the top of the extended circle driveway in front of his house. Phil looks back up at his large home with manicured landscaping and pristine features and still longs for more.

He had wanted a family, but his wife was unable to have children. They discussed adoption, but he was afraid to reveal too much to anyone who might look closely at him or his sources of income. He didn't want to set himself up to be scrutinized. He had this beautiful ten thousand sq foot house filled with the finest of furniture put in place by some of the top interior decorators in town. His yard was landscaped with meticulous care right down to the angel fountain that was the centerpiece of the circle drive. But, it was a house, not a home of children and family, and what Phil wanted most was to have a family, a son; someone he could nurture and teach.

Phil thinks of this during his journey today. He's going to help a young man who reminds him so much of himself at that age. He will not repeat the mistakes of his own past and let people who are struggling "just figure it out".

From the first moment he heard of Slade hustling some college kids out of their daddy's money, he decided that he wanted Slade to become more than an apprentice. He would groom Slade to become his heir apparent; the son he never had.

Phil was determined to pass on his knowledge to Slade. Phil recognizes that Slade is more intelligent than most and isn't interested in *just* doing the hustle. Slade himself might not even fully see it yet, but to Phil, it's clear. Slade is into scheming and thinking up the strategy of the hustle. Building a business to last is his hope for Slade, not hopping from job to job. Phil is determined to help Slade. Today will start with a young man at his low point. Phil understands that this is where all good things start.

Without a doubt, Phil knows that you have to lose to win; the two define each other and are forever tied and required to be together as he pulls out of the driveway, Phil waves at his landscaper/maintenance man. Driving past the tee box of the fourth hole of the golf course—the centerpiece of his neighborhood—he waits at the gate until it swings open and pulls out onto the main road leading back into town.

He'll arrive at Slade and Arnold's place in about twenty minutes. Phil walks up to the door, rings the doorbell, and shouts, "Hey, Slade, buddy; you up, man. I need a favor. " When he's met with silence, Phil strolls into the house. He opens all the window coverings and mini-blinds in the living room to let the late morning sun in. He notices the living room has been "straightened up" some but needs a thorough cleaning as crumbs and beer can tabs are lying about. The kitchen is in a similar condition as the living room. Phil grabs a Jolt cola from the fridge and slowly walks toward Slade's room. He gingerly opens the door and again announces himself a little louder.

"Hey, little buddy, you up?"

Slade slowly stirs looking across the dim bedroom. Phil hurriedly walks past Slade's bed to the small window to raise the mini blinds. The room is lit up like a disco ball at a nightclub from the sun's blinding prismatic rays "Hey, little buddy, I need a favor Phil" repeats.

Slade sits slightly up in bed and replies in barely more than a whisper; "Hey Phil. Hey, man, I'm pretty much busted, so I can't help with action, plus, man, I feel like shit.

"Yeah, Hey, I know buddy, and if I wasn't in a bit of a jam, here I would let you be, but it's collection time and I need a driver. The guy I usually use had to go back to Mexico for a few weeks, so I'm short and I gotta make the runs. It won't work out well if I go solo'.

Slade couldn't have known if Phil was lying, in his current state, he wasn't sure if he had seen Phil with a driver or not. The fact was that Phil had no driver and never did, but Phil had thought it would be cool. As Slade climbs out of bed he barely manages, "Ok, Phil, of course, man whatever you need, let me hit the shower and throw on some clothes."

Phil inquires, "Hey, you got a sports coat in there somewhere? Do that and jeans, and pull your hair back in a ponytail (Slade's hair is well past shoulder length) without a hat." Collections are all a show and you need to look the part. Like, I'm the nice guy, but my driver here is all business if I need him to be. You get it, man, you know the game says Phil as upbeat as possible.

While in the bathroom, Slade purposely leaves the door cracked so he can hear Phil. For a moment, Slade feels more awake than he has in over a week, looking forward to getting out of the house.

"Sure Phil, I gotta coat; oh, and I've got those python boots too; hell might as well go all-in," Slade says without thinking. But as soon as he utters that familiar poker phrase, He's back at LD's power table in his head. It's like a gut punch and all of a sudden he's right back to a trance-like state. Kind of like PTSD after returning from a war zone. Slade's mind returns to the scene as a survivor in a battleground where he had no clue of the enemy's strategy.

As the shampoo starts to sting his eyes he's brought back to the present moment He quickly looks up to the showerhead and rinses them out and slowly finishes his shower He pulls on his jeans and t-shirt fully lacking emotion or even purpose. Phil hops up off of the couch looking at Slade walking barefoot although he enters the room fully dressed. "Hey, what about those boots?" Slade had completely forgotten them and immediately turned back towards his bedroom without a word. He pulled the boots from the back of the closet, again dressing in an almost mechanical way.

You should grab a pistol too, Phil then says. I never expect trouble, but you know the game" Phil repeats.

Sure Slade says flatly, as he goes to grab the Glock and the shoulder holster out of the truck. As the two load up in Phil's truck, Phil reminds Slade to head out of town on the main highway. "We start out at the edge of town and work our way back home," says Phil. "Mind yourself out in the sticks, those cedar choppers[64] like to pop their gums and see if they can get a rise out of young bucks like you. Blank stares make them uncomfortable. That's how to win."

Phil notices Slade is driving but barely listening, caught up in his own head. "HEY," Phil says sharply and has Slade's attention. "Look, little buddy, there's no shame in going broke. NONE, as is one ounce. It's the life of all rounders; we have all been broke at some point and sometimes more than once. It can get the best of us."

"The shame is in staying broke. You HAVE to get back out there. You find a nickel and make it a dime. Then make that a quarter, then after a bit, you have a few grocery dollars. you'll have to scratch and claw your way back. It's how you learn never to fall that far again"

And with that, Phil gave Slade his first lesson.

While on the road between the many stops, Phil kept the lessons flowing.

---

[64] derogatory slang for people who lived out in the area thick with cedar trees and were rumored to run meth

"Look, you need to make sure you know the games you're playing. Those guys at LDs game are no fucking joke. They're some of the best poker players in town. You never had a chance. Hell, I don't have a chance, but I know it and go to have fun. I need to be seen as a "go-off-Phil" from time to time or I might lose a customer. All players, from full square-john to full rounder, want to believe that they have a chance to get some of your money somehow. So, you have to let them have some."

Then came the clincher to shake Slade out of his depressed stupor. "If you're gonna be in this life for real, you have to have a plan, a strategy. You have to lose to win. Say it back to me."

Slade looks at Phil quizzically; "What?!"

"I mean it. Say it back to me, Phil repeats; you have to lose to win."

"You have to lose to win," Slade says.

Say it again.

You have to lose to win. Slade repeats for the third time and finally, it clicks. It's so simple, so hard, and counterintuitive at the same time. This is marketing; this is the show. you're not losing. You're making a show of losing.

"You're making yourself a draw?" Slade asks for confirmation, an attraction. You're bringing the action to you. Damn, I see it. For this brief moment, Slade left his funk, his brain was working, and he was in his sweet spot. Phil also knows that this phrase has many other meanings and that, at some point, he will teach his new protege, one thing at a time. Helping Slade learn some tools to pull himself out of this depression to get back to work is the focus of this conversation.

"That's it, that is it exactly!" Phil says with a grin and the sense of pride one sees on the face of a father looking at his child.

"Turn in here." Phil points to the left.

"This is our last stop today, then back to your house. We both go in, but then I'll step out while you collect on this one. I need to make a call right quick."

Slade immediately recognizes where they are; the brake shop where the garage game is played. Slade is a wholly different person than he had been a few short hours ago when Phil burst into his bedroom and all but pulled him out of bed. Slade's mind was alive, it was "looking for angles" and "plotting a way to win" even in this simple act of collecting money for his new mentor; Phil the bookie. In this moment, Slade snapped back because any cerebral challenge is the thing that excites Slade.

As they walk in, a guy comes out from under a car and sees Phil., "I've got you covered right back here," the car guy says. He then does a double-take and starts to say hey, aren't you? But Slade cuts him off before he can finish his sentence. "Ya, I come to play here with Arnold sometimes"

"He's my driver for a while," Phil adds. "Hey, I need to make a call in the office."

"Just square with Slade and we'll be out of your hair."

"Thanks, brother." Phil walks into the office, grabs the phone, and quickly keys in a number. It's the number for Jimmy aka "Checkbook".

"Swanson Realty," Jimmy answers the phone.

"Hey, Checkbook, this is Phil. I need to call in a favor man, and this one will square us fully on the *big one.*"

"Sure Phil, whatever you need," replies Checkbook.

"Look, on the DL, Slade isn't doing great and I need to keep an eye on him for a bit, but I've some business out of town the next few days, so I need you to shadow him, make sure he's in the game and not checked out. Also, be ready, I want him set with a place, so talk to the usual folks, ok? You watch him, you see the cash hit his hand, you move and don't wait on me"

"Done, I'll get to The Side Hole tonight and go from there," Checkbook says.

"Solid, I'll make sure he gets there, so don't let me down," Phil says in a stern tone. "This is important to me. I'll page when I'm back in town" then hangs up the phone.

Phil quickly dials another number, this time It's the main number to The Side Hole and Johnny picks up. "Side Hole, this is Johnny" Phil hears.

Hey Johnny, I'm calling in a *little favor*. "Ok, Johnny replies, happy to give one back; what do you need?"

"I'm sending Slade up to The Side Hole tonight. He'll think you owe four-forty, so give it to him and I'll square you next time I'm in. Are we good?" Phil asks. Easy and done, says Johnny, and the phone goes dead as Slade walks into the office.

"Ok, let's head home, man, this has been a good day."

Phil hands Slade three hundred dollars as the two head back to the truck. "Oh, no way, man, no charity, I ain't like that. I'll find that nickel and rub it until I have grocery dollars and go from there. I heard you today. I'll crawl back on my own," Slade says, almost in a normal voice and with his usual swagger. It's clear that hanging out with Phil has helped Slade's overall emotional state.

"Nothin' like that, these are your wages, you worked for me, and I'm paying you. I've got a reputation, too," When you work for Phil, you earn well. Plus, I have one more job for you."

"I'm gonna be out of town for the next couple of days and I need you to make one more collection for me. Johnny, the Side Hole bartender, owes four-forty, pick it up tonight, and when I'm back, I'll collect"

"Look, Phil, I'm happy to do it, but I'm not stupid, you know. You don't have a fucking driver gone back to Mexico, or I would have seen him before. I appreciate you pulling me out of the house, I probably needed a kick in the ass, but I'm still not taking charity here," Slade is adamant.

Look, ok, I know you're not stupid, and that driver bit was a ruse, but, it was also helpful, wasn't it?" he pokes Slade.

"I'm slowing down a bit, and from time to time, I might need someone to make some collection runs. some of the customers have seen your face and you know word gets around. I've got more options with you in the mix. We can even talk about a slice[65] at some point; you have been listening right, this is a business, not a charity. I'm investing in you," Phil says honestly.

"About how much did we pick up today? Phil asks.

"Seventeen thousand three fifty total after pick up and drop off, add the Johnny four forty and you have seventeen thousand seven ninety," Slade calculated in his head on the spot.

"Damn, you're like a fucking accountant," Phil says, looking at his little notebook, you're on to the dollar. See, I know a good investment!!! Take that micro stack of cash and make something, go get back in the game. The only shame is staying broke," Phil repeats.

Slade pops the truck into Park as they stop in his driveway, and he turns to look at Phil and feels somehow close to him as if he has known him a long time. "Hey, thanks for today, you did me a solid. I was in a whole other place when you got here today."

"You got it, little buddy, I'll be back in town in a few days, and I'll page you up. Let's do collections again next week, get you in front of a few more faces." "Slade arrives back at his house and opens the door to his dirty place; he is immediately embarrassed. He makes his way to his bedroom and swaps his boots for sneakers, then hangs the sports coat in the closet. He notices the phone lying on the floor and picks it up to straighten the bent antennae. It snaps off in his hand.

For some reason, Slade starts to get emotional. "Over a fucking antenna?" he says out loud. What the fuck? I'm talking to myself again. I must be losing it. I need more rest, he thinks and looks at his unmade bed. Then he remembers, he has to get the cash from Johnny tonight. He can't let Phil down too.

---

[65] Slice is slang for a percentage of the action; a "slice" of the pie.

Taking a deep breath, he walks to the kitchen and splashes his face with water, and grabs another Jolt. "There's no shame in being broke, only in staying broke". Slade repeats one of the lessons of the day out loud and hops in his truck to head to The Side Hole. Walking into The Side Hole, Slade beelines directly to Johnny at the bar. Johnny already has a set of balls ready for him and palms him some cash.

"Phil said you would be picking up this week." Slade nods and takes the balls and cash.

As he's putting the balls on the table, he sees Checkbook shooting some balls a couple of tables over. Normally Slade would wander over and exchange quips with him, as he usually is fairly sharp-tongued himself, but he's not feeling it tonight. Instead, he nods and tries to fall into the regular and mechanical "pool hall hustler" mode. It brings him no joy. But right now, it's all about making some money to get back in the game. Slade consoles himself.

Just as he's racking the balls to "shoot around," in walks a friend of Johnny's, Champ. That's what Slade remembers his name to be. A tall blond bodybuilder with thick wavy blond hair and steel blue eyes. In every way, this guy should be on a magazine cover somewhere. Slade also recalls that the guy's not too sharp, as if the stereotype wasn't already laid out in front of everyone.

Slade wasn't in top form, although he tried to be observant. All of a sudden realized that he had not seen Lewis standing around the table where Checkbook was playing; hell, he had a pool cue in his hand and was playing with Checkbook. Slade rallied up his willpower and thought, get it together man, you got bills to fucking pay; how do you miss that shit. He nods at Lewis as their eyes meet, and then Slade DOES notice that Lewis is staring at Champ. He must know something that Slade is missing. Then Johnny and Champ are arguing about something.

"Look, don't! You don't have a shot; he's WAY better than when you saw him before, you're the one who needs the weight, not the other way around, save your cash," Johnny says to Champ.

"Fuck you, man, you're jealous, you also said I would not get the gig, but I did, and they gave me an advance on the first shoot. I'm gonna double it," replies Champ as he walks toward Checkbook and Lewis.

"Hey man, will you warm me up, Checkbook? I'm gonna play some tonight" Champ asks.

"Sure, rack 'em up, we can play a few. Hell, I'll spot you some if you wanna play" says Checkbook encouragingly

"Na, I've my eyes set on one person. Then in a loud voice loud enough for Slade to overhear Champs goes on. "Word on the street is that he's rattled after losing his ass at LD's card game and can't make a ball. I might as well take advantage of that and finish his weak ass off; I never thought he was as good as y'all say anyway" boasts Champ to the entire pool hall

Lewis then jumps in the conversation. "Well Champ, I'll take some of that action, you get warmed up and come over, and I'll run the action for Bird-Man (trying out the new nickname). You got it; tell him he has the eight, race to three for five. Champ replies."

Slade hears this and his heart sinks a little, he only has three hundred dollars, and if he has learned anything, he knows he can't bet what he does not have no matter how good the odds are. For a moment, he considers using the money he's holding for Phil that he got from Johnny but immediately decides that's a shitty idea.

Lewis walks over to Slade motioning at Champ and says, "He's loaded tonight, we need to go slow, but we can get it all. He's a fucking idiot and his ego grows every time he looks at himself in the mirror behind the bar or one of those little girls giggles at him, he adds motioning at a table of college girls next to the jukebox."

I'll run the bets, he wants to race to three for five, how much of that are you gonna let me run? Lewis inquires softly.

"Look, man, I was gonna grab a beer and bail tonight, I didn't even bring much cash, and I know you know about LDs; I'm running thin, Slade says. So, It's your lucky night, you're gonna get the big end. You run it however you want, I'll start off at a dollar a race and pump every time I'm ahead. You press that bet every chance you get to whatever your bankroll can take. Every nod means I'll double my in; cool?"

"Hell ya Bird–Man, shit man, I was gonna float ya for it, you sure you wanna give up that much, he's probably carrying seventy-five hundred? Lewis clarifies.

I'm sure, man, I'm big happy if I walk with twenty-five hundred and you with five dimes, keep it going and let's do this, I'm warm whenever replies Slade

Slade moved into full-on mechanical mode and is practicing for real. Champ walks up to Slade while looking at Johnny as if to say, "*watch this, you jealous asshole*"; he says, "You got the eight, winner breaks, flip for the first break. We race to three for five dollars."

Done. My man Lewis will run all the cash, post up and let's go.

Slade glances at Johnny as he knows the two are long-time friends. Johnny looks back at Slade and mouths, I warned him; go.

Slade wins the flip and drops the eight-ball on the break to win the first game, followed quickly by a break and a combo on the nine-ball to win the next. The third game lasts a little longer, but after Slade breaks and does not make any balls at all, Champ misses the four-ball and Slade quickly and silently runs out to the eight-ball and wins the first race three to zero.

They continue to play as Slade goes dead silent. He has yet to miss a shot of any importance and Champ is missing all over the place. Champ is outmatched and to anyone watching who understands high-end pool, It's obvious that he has no chance at winning without a spot, much less the eight-ball that he's currently spotting Slade.

Lewis is working the rail and upping the bet, this time he proposed to go to race to three for six hundred and do away with the spot. It has exactly the effect that Lewis wants and Champ is super insulted as in his mind he's still the superior player (his ego won't let him think otherwise). How about seven-fifty instead says Champ and the game continues.

A couple more races won, and Slade pipes in. Hey Champ, let's get this over with. I'll spot you the eight and we can make the races a dime? Champ seems to be thinking it over and Slade adds, or you can lick your wounds and go cry in your beer over there, pointing at the table where the girls are still sitting and saying loud enough for them to hear. They all start giggling again, but this time laughing AT Champ.

Of course, that worked, and in five short races, with Slade winning four out of the five; it's over and Champ is busted. All totaled, Lewis and Slade, had won nine thousand dollars. The two walk over to where Checkbook is playing and watching with great intent to see how they are gonna chop up the money. Slade says, "Three dimes to me, you take care of Johnny, we good? Hell ya Bird-Man, you da man," Lewis replies in a slow drawl, one only Lewis could use and pull off.

Slade put the cash in his pocket, but it wasn't a happy moment. He had managed to claw back into the game a little and in only one night, but it was the wrong game. It was the same mechanical boring hustle that had led him to look for a strategic game at LDs in the first place.

He could remember being excited about something earlier that day, but for the life of him, he didn't know what it was.

He looked up at Checkbook and said, let's go to the strip club and blow some of this hard-earned cash; fuck it, who cares anyway.

Checkbook is remembering the second part of Phil's request and is preparing to put it in motion. His response shocked Slade, "Ya, not tonight, I have a better plan. You keep all of that cash and I'm going to get you a hook up. Ya know I'm a realtor, right? You come to the office next week and we will get you squared away, so don't be shoving that cash in no g-strings yet."

"Ya, Johnny said something like that and I heard Phil talking about you finding him his house and shit; what of it? No way I got the cash for a house man."

"That's where you're wrong my friend. You won enough for a duplex. You can live in half and collect rent for the other. It will be damn near rent-free livin'!" Slade was intrigued. "Interesting; well, what the fuck, I'll come to see you," he replied to Checkbook.

Checkbook then adds, "Give me your pager, If I find a hot spot, I will page you and have you meet me there."

Slade nods and, with a fist bump, walks out and climbs into his truck. This shit might work out Slade is thinking. His lease is up for renewal in a month with Arnold, so perfect time to bail. But how to tell Arnold?

Slade walks in the front door and hears Arnold pulling into the driveway as the door closes. "Well, glad you're out and about Fatman, I was wondering there for a bit," says Arnold. He pauses and has a serious face. Then adds, "Look, we need to talk about some shit, and man, know that no matter what, I got your back, the cash won't be a thing, I mean it. But, I'm gonna get a different place closer to the restaurant when this lease is up, this drive is killing me. Shit close to downtown isn't cheap, so if you can't swing your half at first, I'll cover you until you're back.

" I know that shit at LDs set you back some." Arnold blurts it all out like he was afraid to stop. I've not found a new place or anything like that yet, but I wanted to tell you before I even started looking for real. Arnold took a deep breath as if a weight had been lifted.

Slade looked at his friend with a big grin, his first smile in a while. "Hey, brother, It's all good, and man, I appreciate you having my back. I know you found this place out here, so I could afford it with you, I'm not that dense. And as we seem to have good timing, I've some news for you too."

He rambled on to Arnold, "I pulled my ass out of bed in time to clean Champ tonight. Lewis had the rail and was short, but I still pulled in three thousand. Checkbook was there and saw it, then let me know he could hook me up with a duplex or something, not sure really, but he said the three dimes were enough. So, my friend, we'll soon be livin' on our own, and it's all good!!!"

Arnold was genuinely happy with this news for his friend, but also thought to himself, shit, I wonder why Checkbook never hooked me up with that shit, knowing that his own ego would never allow him to "copy" Slade in anything at this point.

"I'm hitting the rack," says Arnold; "see ya at The Side Hole tomorrow; I should leave the restaurant early."

While lying in bed, for the first time in a week, he doesn't feel hopeless as his eyes close. Instead, it's the opposite: hope for a new day, no more than that. It's hope for a new home, a new life!

As he drifts to sleep, he hears Phil repeating, "You gotta lose to win."

CHAPTER TEN

A MAN OF CONFIDENCE

Slade's eyes open as sunlight enters his bedroom. When he got home last night, he forgot to close the blinds. It is a new week, and soon he will be shopping for a house, well, a duplex, something he will own and not rent. This is a new outlook and hope; It's nice not to have the heaviness on his shoulders. Slade WANTS to be happy.

Just as he's climbing out of bed, his pager buzzes. It's Checkbook. He walks to the nightstand, grabs the phone, and dials him. "Swanson Realty, this is Jimmy," Jimmy answers in his official voice.

"Hey man, this is Slade; what's up, my man? Are we gonna see that duplex or whatever?"

"For sure, it's not going to be on the market for long, so I want you to see it today and get an offer if you want. It's not far from The Side Hole but in a better neighborhood."

Jimmy gives Slade the directions and address, then asks him to meet him there in an hour.

Slade has a solid memory, so he doesn't bother writing down the address as he can visualize where it's located. He thanks Jimmy for hooking him up, as it would be cool to save some dough while he rebuilds his stack.

He hops in the shower, still thinking about what owning something as substantial as a duplex could mean. If he could pull this off, he would be a real estate owner before his twenty-second birthday, a mere four months away. He grins with pride and comparative arrogance as this potential purchase would happen WAY sooner than when his parents first bought anything.

For a brief moment, Slade flashes back to his father angrily, telling him, "You'll fall flat on your face, boy." That memory doubly motivates him. Not just to have a place and save some cash while subletting a portion of the property but to prove once and for all that he would not be "falling flat on his face," as his father repeated.

A saying Phil had said was etched in his mind and became a mantra: *there's no shame in going broke, only in staying broke.* Feeling cleaner and refreshed than usual, Slade walks outside to feel the crisp air brush against his face, a typical central Texas winter day of about forty-five degrees, and climbs into his truck. He starts it and lets it warm a bit. It shows its age, but it is not the time to spend cash on a new car. He taps the dash talking to his vehicle; you can make it; warm up.

Pulling up to the duplex, he sees Jimmy stepping out of his Lexus. The realtor business must pay pretty well, he thinks. Slade hears another truck pull up at the same time as he steps out of his truck and turns to see Phil. "Hey Phil, what's up? Was I supposed to meet up with you this morning?"

"No, little buddy, I heard you might be getting a place, so I thought I would come to check it out with you, then I thought we might make a day of it and "go round"[66] a bit."

The duplex is side-by-side, with the "A" side on the left and the "B" side on the right. The garage doors face the street with one on each side, "What is this door to?" Slade asks Jimmy. "Oh, that's the side garage door. The garage is attached to the house, but you must walk outside to get there."

It makes sense to Slade. He remembers a house his family rented when he was a kid also had a garage like that. Slade compared everything here to the homes he lived in as a child. As they walked in the main entrance which is located on the side of the duplex, Jimmy stopped to enter some numbers on a keypad. "It's fully wired for

---

[66] Hustle some people out of their cash

security. You can monitor it yourself or have a company do it; it will even call the fire department or police if you set it up to do it", Jimmy says.

"FANCY," says Phil as he walks in. "I have something like this; you might think about if you want "johnny-law" having your house call them, though. Mine just pages me", Phil continues.

Slade likes this. This place was better than anywhere he'd grown up in and had something in common with Phil's house, rumored to be pretty impressive up in the hills west of town. The living room is more significant than what Slade had expected. The entrance is made of ceramic tile squares, which meets a hardwood floor for part of the room. Next to the living room is a dining area and kitchen with new appliances, including a microwave mounted under one of the cabinets. The kitchen area is separated from the living room by a bar that runs the entire length of the kitchen.

"Wow, this could make a good serving area if you had folks over or something," observes Phil, running his hand down the length of the bar. Phil then turns to Jimmy, "How many bedrooms?" he asks. "Two, one is the master and has a toilet, double sinks, and a shower, and the other one here has a toilet and shower across the hall, Jimmy replies as he points down the hall.

Slade notices that the bedrooms are newly carpeted, and both bathroom areas use the same ceramic tile seen at the entrance. He's impressed with the size of the master bedroom; it has a higher ceiling than what he's been used to and a brand new ceiling fan, one that doesn't make a sound.

"Well, what do you think?" asks Jimmy.

"Man, I dig it. Good location and a cool place, but what will this cost me, like cash out-of-pocket and the payments and such?"

"Well, I ran some numbers here for you, it will be close to this, as he shows Slade a calculator with the amount, but there are usually some minor changes once you get the bank involved. But like I say, it will be close."

"If you can get me thirteen hundred in cash, we can make an offer for thirty-nine thousand. I'm all but certain that it will be accepted. From there with closing costs, taxes and insurance added in, your monthly bill will be right at four hundred and twelve dollars and some change per month."

"The other side is currently rented out to what is known as Section Eight tenants. It's a government program where the tenant pays part of the rent, and the government pays the rest. The government guarantees its part, but you're on your own to collect the remainder. Mind you; you can't evict them unless the government misses their rent portion. And they never do!" Jimmy informs. "In this case, the government portion is four hundred and eight dollars per month out of the five hundred and fifteen dollar lease."

"Well, hell, even if I don't get shit from them, I'm golden and living here for five grocery dollars a month. Dude, I'm IN," Slade says as he looks at Phil for approval.

Phil adds, "I don't see how you could go wrong."

"Can we look on the other side? I want to see what I might have to fix up or something if they move out on me, ya know, just want to make sure I don't have surprises," Slade says.

"They're not home and are aware we're gonna check it out."

As Slade walks in, he notices that the place is "almost" a mirror copy of the other side with a couple of crucial differences. The entrance had linoleum flooring, and the rest was faux wood. The appliances also looked a little old, and the ceiling fans were the kind he was familiar with: kind of noisy, long chains hanging down that moved in a circle as the fan went round and round. The carpet in the bedrooms was worn and would need to be replaced before a new tenant could be moved in. But most noticeable was no alarm system and plain locks.

Jimmy watched silently as Slade takes notice of all these details. "The old owner lived on the A side and had made a few upgrades.

That's why I picked this one for you to see. It's a good deal!" Jimmy said. Phil gave Checkbook a little nod and the slightest wink, and the deal was sealed, although Slade didn't know it.

"Cool, I've seen what I need," replied Slade. "Tell me about what's next. I don't know anything about getting a loan or anything like that."

"I've got it all covered for you. Our friend, Randy at the bank, knows what's up and what you need to get this done. Let's grab some lunch, and we can review the paperwork you'll need."

Slade is a bit nervous. What does Jimmy mean by paperwork? *I've got cash and a driver's license; what else is there?* Quickly Slade thinks of bringing Phil along for the paperwork part, too. "Hey Phil, you can come with us, then can go round some, hit the bowling alley. I've got my locker at Dart Bowl; we can round up a game."

"Sounds good, little buddy," Phil replies. "Let's hit Dart Bowl. They have some of the best enchiladas in town anyway."

"Oh hell ya, that sounds awesome. I'll see y'all there," Slade says as he hops in his truck.

As he's pulling away, he notices Phil shaking hands with Checkbook beside his car. Slade knows this move. Phil has passed Checkbook some cash for something.

Phil sticks his hand out to shake hands with Checkbook and passes him five hundred-dollar bills. "Thanks, Checkbook, this is what we needed for my little buddy, a little push to get him back on his feet. No one ever needs to know that those little upgrades came from me; we keep that between us, yes?" Phil asks but isn't asking.

"For sure, Phil, mum's the word," Jimmy replies. And I've got Randy all lined up to make sure this happens at the bank; we might need a little help making him look like a square john with a real job. No one ever checks that shit too carefully. As long as the money is there, it goes through.

Phil and Checkbook pull into the parking lot of the bowling alley as famous for its enchiladas as it is for being the oldest bowling alley in town. Slade's already arrived.

"What took y'all; you hit every light or drove like old ladies?" Slade jokes at Jimmy and Phil. Phil smiles widely at this, not because it's hilarious, but because he's genuinely glad to see Slade returning to himself with a bit of confidence and that sharp wit he's known for.

As the three place their orders at the counter and take their seats at the tables in the cafeteria of the bowling alley, they get down to business. Checkbook has a folder that he's opening up. Slade starts.

"Look, I'm a pretty smart guy, Jimmy, but I'm fully ignorant here, so please, you'll not insult me. Tell me everything I need to know straight up."

Phil is beaming with pride. He feels confident in Slade's words and attitude, and it's even more on point as Slade shows humility in admitting his ignorance. Phil has learned from experience authentic humility can ONLY exist when accompanied by confidence. Otherwise, it's fear and deflection. Jimmy replies, "All good, my man, I have it here in short, clean steps," as he flips a notepad around with a list of items for Slade to see:

- Cashier's check for $1,300.00 made out to ABC Mortgage
- Receipt showing where that money came from
- Bank statements for last three months
- Rental agreement where you live
- Two utility bills from that location
- Social Security Number
- Copy of Driver's License front and back
- w-2 showing that your gross income is $1,600.00 a month.

Slade reads the list and is taken aback. He thinks I don't have a w-2 as the three orders of enchiladas arrived. The steam rising and bringing up the sharp smell of onions and cheese lifts the anxiety that Slade is feeling at that moment. Phil leans close to Slade to reassure him, "Don't worry, little buddy, I know a guy who owns a print shop. We got this!"

Turning to Jimmy, he thanks Checkbook and agrees to meet at the bank with them the following day with the forms.

"Ok, great," says Jimmy, "I need you to sign here, and we can get moving. This is a contract that says you'll pay the thirty-nine thousand if you can get the loan to go through, bring the down payment to the closing, and that I am your agent. Since this is a quick close mortgage and we're buying this from FreddieMac[67], we don't have to post up earnest money or anything like that" He then slid Slade the contract.

Slade scanned it. Since he trusted Jimmy after reading the part that referenced "the contract was not binding" if the loan wasn't approved, he signs. Jimmy put it in his briefcase, slid Slade a folder with the list of items needed, and added, "The address to the bank is in there; ask for Randy when you arrive. If you don't see me, you can hang out in his office until I get there."

Phil and Slade say in unison, "Will do."

The three dig into the enchiladas that have cooled enough to eat. "Man, these never disappoint," says Jimmy. "What kinda trouble you two gonna get into? "Slade motioned out towards the lanes with his head. "You see those three over there in the matching gray shirts?" Jimmy acknowledges."They have too many dollars and not enough sense, and I think I'll help them get smarter," Slade states with a large grin.

Jimmy finishes the last of his enchiladas and leaves as he has work. Slade eyes the three and schemes to see what he can make happen. Time to pick up some walking around cash, Slade thinks, falling back into the mechanical hustle mindset. Everything is an opportunity; always look for the angle.

Slade exits the cafe and walks up to the bowling pit where the three have finished a game.

---

[67] Mortgage clearing house

"Hey, fellas, y'all in a league or something with the matchy-matchy shirts?" Slade says to the three bowlers with some snark and a chuckle.

"Yes, we are!" the largest of the three men snaps back. "What of it?"

"Hey, I was just funnin'. I'm in a league, too. What are y'all doing up here in the middle of the day? Is there a tournament or something?"

"Nah, we need to work on our games when the lanes have fresh oil and are still slick[68]."

"Oh, well, ok, basics, I get it. I was gonna see if y'all wanted to pot-bowl or something, but if you're still on the basics, then it might not be fair. Y'all have fun", Slade replies, walking away.

"Oh, no, we're not beginners. We're working on specific things. I carry a one-eighty-five average, and Jim here carries a one-ninety-two. We're up for a little pot-bowl action."

"Well, ya, sorry, those are respectable averages. What do you want to do? Winner take all or leave an out for second place to break even?"

"Let's go winner take all, and start cheap, say one hundred per man, then ramp up."

Slade fumbles through his pocket like he's not sure if he has a hundred dollars but then pulls out four twenties, a ten, and two fives and then announces he's in.

"Let me go over to my locker and get my stuff," Slade says as he walks away, winking at Phil. When he returns, Slade opens with a split that he misses converting, putting him in a hole to start the game. Jim says, "See, we told you: this fresh oil acts odd. That's why we're here practicing." Jim rolls a perfect strike.

The game continues but Slade does not recover. He ends up scoring a one-sixty-eight, while Jim wins with a one-ninety-five. Jim pulls his winnings from the stack on the table while Slade is again fumbling in

---

[68] Bowling balls react differently depending on how much conditioner oil is on a bowling lane; typically the more oil there is, the less a ball will curve down a lane.

his pockets. The big guy says, "Ready, or are you out of money?" laughing.

"Hey, just a minute, let me see if my friend has some cash on him. He's up here, I'll be right back."

"Hey," Jim says, "you need to get more than a hundred. When we pot bowl, we bowl four games on a ramp, meaning we double it each time. If you can't do the math, that's fifteen hundred you'll need to have. We're not small time here!"

"Ya, ok, give me a minute." Slade is excited as he walks up to Phil, sitting a bit away from the bowlers. "Man, this is way better than I thought," he tells Phil. "They upped the bet on me and locked in at double each round. I'll win the next three, but we might want to be ready to roll when I do. They will figure out quickly that I am hustling them, and these guys make my spidey sense tingle. Not for certain, but generally, rednecks can't be trusted to lose and walk away." Slade then pretends to take some cash from Phil and heads back to the three bowlers waiting to start the next game.

"Ok, I'm good," says Slade. "Here is my two hundred." Slade lays two hundred-dollar bills on the center table in the bowling pit where the rest have already placed their cash; the pot is at eight hundred.

Slade isn't messing around this round and never leaves an open frame[69]. He wins rolling a two-nineteen.

"Well, you pulled that last strike out of your ass to win that one, you better hope you keep that luck shit up. Brooklyn strikes[70] are few and far between in this house."

"Let's post, y'all," Slade says as he counts out four hundred dollars from the eight hundred dollars he's won.

The next game was much the same, but this time, Slade caps off the tenth frame with three perfect strikes finishing with a two thirty-five,

---

[69] In bowling closed frames are a strike or a spare and an open frame isn't.

[70] For a right-handed bowler hitting the head pin and the pin behind and to the right of It's called "the pocket" while hitting the head pin and the pin behind and to the left of It's called "Brooklyn". Brooklyn strikes are considered luck and not skill if all ten pens fall.

an excellent score. Without missing a beat, he scoops the sixteen hundred dollars from the table, quickly counting back out eight hundred dollars, which he slaps deliberately on the table as if it is an announcement.

"Hold it. These two don't have a chance, but I'll happily finish this. Let's me, and you go heads up, say two thousand bucks each for this last game?" Jim says.

"Sounds good to me," says Slade. He's been doing the math and knows he's up seventeen hundred dollars, so he's not worried about the bet.

On the other hand, he is a tad nervous about getting out of here quickly, so he says, "Hey, I'll be right back, gonna hit the head."

As Slade makes his way to the restroom, he grabs all the extra things from his locker and hands them to Phil with the keys. "Hey, throw all this stuff in the truck. If we must leave in a hurry, I'll grab my ball and shoes and head out. I'm about to pay the guy for the lanes, so there's no hassle. I have a bad feeling, and it's getting worse."

"Ok, little buddy, we'll trust your gut. I'll head to the truck and have it pulled up close, in case," replies Phil.

Slade goes to the restroom, stalls a bit, then returns to the bowling pit and drops his two thousand on the table. "Let's do this," he says. In the first frame,

Slade throws what looks like a perfect strike, but the ten-pin[71] does not fall. What is worse is that Slade misses the second time and has an open frame, a significant setback. Unrattled he seems calmer and more focused, a man of complete confidence as he approaches the lane for his next frame.

"Sometimes the pins fall, sometimes they don't; all I can do is throw a perfect ball," Slade says with an air of arrogance as he walks the lane to release the ball. It's a strike.

---

[71] Looking at the pins from the front, the ten pin is the pen on the far right on the back row.

Jim is playing a flawless game and has yet to leave an open frame, but he has noticed that Slade has rolled seven strikes back to back since the first open frame. He's become irritated and a bit rattled because he's losing. On Jim's next frame, he rolls a split, and Slade screams, "OUCH! Man, you did not deserve that one." He continues to mock him slightly. Jim manages to recover and does pick up the split to finish the ninth frame.

"Well, It's all in my hands," Slade says. "Three more strikes and that's a two-seventy-nine, and you can't catch me." And with that, Slade quickly turns and rolls three more strikes. He puts the four thousand dollars in his pocket and picks up his ball and shoes to head out of the pit. "Hey, hold up there. Man, you hustled us; we're gonna need that cash back. You're a little punk acting like you didn't know the game and might not have the cash. We don't put up with that shit here."

Slade had a step on them, and this wasn't the time to fight. Without taking a second to reply, he breaks into a dead sprint and heads to the door. The three bowlers are caught off-guard and try to give chase, but Jim gets tripped up out of the pit sending all three men to the ground angrily.

Slade hits the door at full speed and spots Phil's truck right out front, the front door slightly ajar. He hops in. Phil punches it, and the two speed out of the parking lot.

"Good call there, little buddy, spotting trouble is a big part of our life. Good to see you on your game again! How'd you make out in there, did you get a little walking around dough?"

"Well, ya, that's the good news. I'm telling you, these bowling rednecks gamble. It's nuts. I picked them off for thirty-seven hundred dollars. I dropped the guy who worked the alley two dollars, so the net was thirty-five hundred."

"Well, you can call it a day, little buddy. Let's go see a guy about some paper; we can swing back by the alley and get your truck later," Phil says as he's pulling into a gas station.

"I'll get it, and do you want me to drive?" Phil likes to be driven, it was an offer of respect, not one of trying to be in control.

"That would be great, little buddy. I'll swap over."

After filling up, Slade climbs back in the truck, asking where to.

"Just head on up this way (he points down the street) and hang a right at the fourth light. Then down a ways, you'll see a little print shop on the left. Just pull in there."

Slade does as instructed, and they pull into ATX Printing.

"Hey, hand me your driver's license. We can get all the papers we need here."

Slade is curious. Phil walks in and tells the girl behind the counter, "Tell Tony Phil is here, and I need a special one-off job ASAP." A distinct smell of fresh ink and something sharp emanates through the door as it swings open.

"Damn, how do you get used to that fucking smell," Phil says.

"Shit, that's awful!" Slade says.

Just then, a short, balding man in an ink-stained apron bursts through the doors.

"PHIL!!!! How the hell are you, my friend?" The man continues in slightly broken English that Slade discerns is of Italian origin, but isn't sure.

"How can I help you? Whatever you need, Tony will do for you. This, you know, friend Phil." Tony wipes his hands on his apron.

"Here is a license. I need the package we discussed, and we'll wait for it." replies Phil.

"Yes, yes, I have it almost ready. I just added the exact names. Gimme ten minutes." Tony turns to the girl. "Did you get them drinks, coffee, soda, or the good stuff? You take care of them. Do it now!" he barks at her.

"No-no, we're good," says Phil, "we'll wait outside; the ink gets to my little buddy," he says with a slight chuckle. Phil and Slade head outside, and in less than ten minutes, Tony appears with a folder.

"All things are here and done, my friend. The license is there too."

Phil slides Tony some cash which Slade is guessing is about a thousand dollars. Tony takes it and says, "Phiiilll, you're way too generous with Tony. I will help you, come anytime; always stop to help my friend Phil."

Phil nods and says, "Thanks, Tony, you're a good egg. Let me know if you want any action this weekend, and I'll get the lines in on Friday night."

Slade and Phil hop back in the truck, and Phil tells Slade, here is your w-2 and receipt for selling car parts for thirteen hundred. There's a polaroid in there of the parts, as well. Randy says it isn't required, but stuff like that makes them close the file and move on. Slade opens the folder and sees his license, a w-2 filled out, and a little yellow receipt that says sold for cash.

"All you need is the regular stuff and the cashier's check. We can pick that up at the bank when we meet Checkbook tomorrow; we'll get there early."

"Oh, wow, man, thanks, Phil; what do I owe for the w-2? You know how it is, we agree, no charity. I need to rub my nickels into a dime, not yours."

"Oh ya, I was getting to it; the w-2 was a dime."

Slade counts out the cash and hands it to Phil. "We're square, and thank you for pulling in a favor for me. I appreciate it."

"Let's get back to your truck. You can make your rounds and such, be seen at The Side Hole, and, get back in the groove. You know that's good for business," says Phil.

"Ya, I do, and don't worry, I'm not falling back into the funk, man; I'm on it. Arnold is meeting me up there later to see if I can pick up a game or two, but mostly be around," Slade replies, sounding like his old self again.

"Now you're talkin' right," says Phil.

As they pull into the parking lot beside Slade's truck, Phil says, "You should look at getting a new ride soon. I know a guy who can get you a good deal. That truck is looking a bit, well, rough. And I thought I saw some smoke when you started it up at the duplex earlier. You know how our business is: It's a show, little buddy. It's a show."

"Ok, let me get this duplex done, then I'll talk to your guy. I better stay full on the hustle and not get lax." Slade laughs as he steps out of the truck with his bowling ball and shoes. He looks to make sure the three rednecks have left, then heads toward the lockers.

I might want to dodge this place for a bit, he thinks. He then pulls a big bag out of the back of the locker, loads all his stuff into it, and carries it all to the truck.

As Slade hops in his truck, he knows Phil is right: This thing IS on its last legs.

He drives to The Side Hole to meet Arnold, who said he'd be off work early.

Time to get some cash for a new ride, Slade is thinking.

"Hey, Fatman," Arnold says as Slade walks in the door.

"It's Bird-Man!" says Lewis in a louder and friendlier voice than usual. He seems genuinely glad to see Slade.

"Hey y'all, what's shakin'? Any kind of action around today?"

"Ya, I need you to rail for me; they started this new foosball tournament, and some guys think they're players comin' in. Supposed to be a crew of three, and the real action starts when the third arrives. I'll handle the two until then; just work the rail. They hooked some idiot like this at Eric's last night. The two slow-played, hit the gas when the third got in and bet all the big cash on the rail. I've seen their best game, and it ain't shit. You could take 'em," Arnold adds to prop up Slade's ego. "They might pop in any time, so go lean on the bar or something; don't be over here by the table," Arnold quickly and quietly explains.

Slade walks up to the bar and looks over to Johnny. "Well, hell, give me a beer. It looks like I got the easy street tonight. Wanna order up one of those big supreme pizzas from that new place up the street? I'll kick back and be a pizza-eating idiot," he chuckles.

"Sure thing, I'll order it," Johnny says, picking up the phone from behind the bar. "You know it takes them at least an hour to deliver it."

Slade slides Johnny a hundred. "I'll cover it, and shoot me that beer, please."

About that time, the door swings open, and in walk two wiry-looking guys walk"Where're y'all's foosball tables?"

Johnny motions across the pool hall and says, "They take tokens. How many do you need?"

"Can I get five dollars' worth?" one of them replies and hands Johnny a five-dollar bill. Johnny slides him twenty tokens, and the two walk toward the foosball tables where Arnold and Lewis are playing.

Slade can't make out exactly what's being said, but it's clear that Arnold is working an angle and is about to hook the two.

Foosball is one game that Arnold is still better at than Slade, so it's good for Arnold's ego to be "the man in action." Slade is fully aware that the dynamic has shifted, and he's the alpha rounder, not Arnold. The part wearing on Slade is that Arnold keeps pushing for excitement and acting like boring, more profitable angles are the wrong thing to do.

Arnold's voice is louder, and he can be heard saying, "What about the bartender? Or some random person like that guy leaning on the bar with the silly duck t-shirt (pointing at Slade.) They can hold the cash each game?"

With that, Slade starts to look at Arnold and, walking in that direction points to his chest. "Are y'all talking about me? What do y'all want? I'm having a beer and some pizza if it ever arrives. I didn't do anything."

"No, no, no, It's nothing like that, my friend. We need someone to hold the cash for us. Come on over; we're gambling here," Arnold says.

"Oh, oh, ya, I got it, sure. I can do that; what are y'all betting on?"

"Foosball," Arnold says.

"It's a lot of money, so we want you to stay here and hold it, ok?" says one of the wiry guys.

"Yes, I got it; guys have special gloves for this, I see," Slade says, pointing at the two sliding on thin white gloves. "Are y'all like professionals or something? I think I saw some people playing this late at night on ESPN."

"Yes, we play in a traveling league," one of the two replies. His friend then nudges him and adds, "Well, we want to be professionals; not THAT good."

Slade couldn't look at Arnold, who had rolled his eyes.

"Hmm, well, ok, I wonder if anyone bets with me while I hold y'alls money, I might as well since I'm standing here and watching anyway."

"About that time," Lewis pipes in. "I'll take some action. I got fifty a game on my boy here," he says, patting Arnold on the shoulder. "Those two are gonna swap out every so often. It's like practice or some shit, but we don't care, we got this," Lewis says with complete arrogance but with that slow drawl.

Oh, well, hmm, how about twenty? I'm not sure I want to gamble that much, replies Slade.

"Oh, a lightweight, ok. Twenty a game, but so you know, they're betting two hundred a game."

"WOW, this is all pretty exciting, so y'all give me your cash, and I'll scooch over here to this table and wait for my pizza."

The game starts and is back and forth, with Arnold raising the bet as he goes but staying ahead and not beating them by much. Slade stopped betting after losing forty and is watching. A crowd of people has started to form.

Slade had moved over one more table, so he wasn't in earshot of Arnold and the other player. Lewis was sitting at the same table.

And then Slade spotted him: the third member of the foosball crew. He was going through the crowd and headed directly for Slade and Lewis. Slade caught Lewis' eye then motioned at the third guy.

As the third guy approached the table, he asked, "How's the action?"

Lewis quickly answered. "Well, they're betting four hundred a game, but It's back and forth. The two with the gloves are outmatched, but this tag-team thing is interesting; it seems to keep them in the game."

"If one of them were to play, my guy would clean up, I bet."

"I tried to get some rail action, but this guy here is holding the cash and won't bet with me anymore, so from that end, the rail is DEAD!"

"Hmmm," the third guy says, "I'll take that action, but we gotta bet something to make it worth me interrupting them to ask if they'll send in only one player. How about we bump it? Say a dime a game?"

"Interrupt. Have this guy hold ours too since I don't know you," says Lewis.

The third crew member walks over; sure enough, only one player is playing against Arnold.

It's at two thousand dollars a game.

Arnold hits the gas, playing on the fact that a crowd and their egos won't let them quit, even though they're at a disadvantage.

The crew lost twelve thousand before they quit; Arnold saw it right.

As Slade hands the money to Lewis and Arnold, the three head out the door without a word. Slade is picking up his last piece of pizza with a grin and, with full snark, says, "Too easy! Where in the hell did they come from, and how did you spot them?"

"Just blind luck, man, ya know," Arnold replies, then Slade and Arnold say in unison: "Sometimes It's better to be lucky than good!"

"Sweet, well, that is two dimes my end after expenses," says Slade, laughing. "Not bad while drinking beer and slamming some pizza!"

"It has been a good day. I'm gonna hit the hay."

"Oh, fucko, the action was so quick when I got here; I totally forgot to tell you, I'm getting that duplex. I'm meeting at the bank tomorrow to sign the papers."

"Oh, wow, Fatman, that shit's awesome. Dude, let's go out and fuck around tomorrow after you buy it; page me when it's done; beers on me!"

Slade is leaving the Side Pocket with more cash, more excitement, and more hope than he's had in weeks. He's both nervous and excited to go to the bank the next day and somehow, relaxed. He's also going to mend some fences with Ramona tonight. He called her and sent his driver. She should be waiting for him when he gets home.

Slade is more confident that he will make it in this new life he found himself in. He believes that he'll find that groove and return to the game. As Slade walks into his room, sure enough, there's his redhead: fully naked and waiting for him. What a great end to a great day!

Slade wakes up early the next morning and tells Ramona to call his driver when she's ready. He explained he would take her to breakfast, but he had some business today. Providing exactly zero details as to what business he's referring to. With that and a quick peck on her forehead, he's out the door.

Slade pulls up to the bank in his truck, noticing that it's starting to smoke a little more, but he can't worry about this. He grabs his envelope of information to walk into the bank. He has a duplex to buy!

Slade walks up to the teller line arriving a bit early like Phil had suggested. Time to get himself a cashier's check.

The teller asks how she could help and looks at Slade oddly. Slade pulls out thirteen hundred-dollar bills and hands them to her, and a twenty to cover the charges.

"I'd like a cashier's check for thirteen hundred dollars, please. Make it to ABC Mortgage."

Without a word, the teller takes the money and goes to the side. She starts to print out a check.

Slade is looking around the lobby of the bank. Focused on getting the check, he hadn't even looked around for Phil before he went to get in line. It's a large lobby with high ceilings, white marble floors, and offices around the edges behind deeply frosted glass. In the center are several leather couches: two round ones in the center, surrounded by standard full-length sofas. While Slade thought it was supposed to feel inviting and relaxing, all he felt was that they were trying to be intimidating. They were showing off with floors and furniture that only rich assholes have in their houses. And it was sterile and WAY too quiet. This irritated Slade and, for whatever reason, put him ever so slightly on the defensive. It was as if this building was here to say: "Kid, you don't belong here."

As he continued looking around, he noticed that everyone was "dressed up." People wore dress clothes. suits, ties, shiny shoes, skirts, fancy blouses, and high heels; everyone here dressed up, except Slade. He was in his usual winter attire: jeans and a long-sleeved t-shirt. This one, of course, also had a large caricature duck on it which had become a trademark of sorts for Slade.

Just then, Slade spots a friendly face: it's Checkbook, also well-dressed. Just behind him is Phil. To Slade's relief, Phil looks like Phil; wearing his usual track pants and shirt that somehow looks brand new.

"Let's go meet Randy. He should be ready. Do you have everything?" inquires Jimmy.

"I do, right here in the folder," Slade replies.

As they walk past the couch arrangement, they come to a different office. It has wooden walls, a wooden door with a round brass knob, a security lock, a keypad and a brass placard on the door.

RANDY JONES

Executive Vice President

Jimmy knocks once, opens the door, and walks in."Randy, this is Slade, and our friend Phil you know."

Randy is a slight little man who stands up and, in a surprisingly deep voice says, "Hello, nice to meet you. Jimmy here tells me this is your first real estate purchase. We're glad to be your bank for this transaction."

Unlike the teller and other random people who stared at Slade as if trying to decide whether or not to call the cops, Randy was treating Slade with, well, respect.

With that, Randy goes on.

"If you have your documents, I'll take them and get the copies going and we can start signing. This won't take long; just sign everywhere you see the little yellow stickers. His tone had shifted slightly, and Randy was also talking to Slade as if he were a second-rate person. Slade didn't like this place or the fact that everyone here seemed to be judging him.

And then it hit him consciously. This reminded him of church. It was all a fucking show.

In one show, they worshiped a guy from a two-thousand-year-old book. In the other, this one, they worshiped money. If you didn't worship like "they" did, then you were not "one of them" and were looked down upon. Slade shrugged it off and completed the task at hand.

Randy returned with a full folder of documents including copies of what Slade had just signed and a set of keys. Keys to the duplex. He stuck out his hand and returned to the voice he'd used when Slade first walked in.

"Congratulations, you're a property owner."

Slade thanked Randy, Jimmy, and Phil but was ready to leave the bank.

Phil said, "Hey, I have a little business here. Tomorrow, you come around to my house, I want to show you some stuff. You know where it is?"

"Well, no. I know It's out in the hill west somewhere, but not exactly where."

Phil hands Slade one of Randy's business cards. "I borrowed this while you were signing the paperwork and wrote my address on the back, I'm sure you can find it easy enough. I'll see you then. Come early. We'll have breakfast."

As Slade leaves the bank, the enormity of what just happened sinks in. He has a new home. He'll start to move there next week.

He then also realizes he learned a whole new hustle. A thinking man's hustle. A strategic hustle.

He's hustled the bank and all their rules and government regulations.

To get a loan in this country, you need a job that pays a certain amount and a down payment that isn't borrowed or from illegitimate means. Slade had none of these things, yet, as he tossed the keys into the air, he had taken out a loan and owned property right out from under all these privileged, wealthy, square-john assholes.

It felt good.

Slade was a confidence man.

CHAPTER ELEVEN

COMING OUT OF THE FOG

S lade's eyes pop open with the sunlight streaming into his bedroom; he had forgotten to close the blinds when he got home last night.

What is this, some kind of a "Groundhog Day?" For the second time this week, he finds himself awakened to sunshine and hope. He's still in the house he rented with Arnold. This arrangement is about to end as he's become a property owner.

Slade remembers that Phil wanted him to come around for breakfast. He isn't sure what time Phil gets up, so he sends Phil a page: 241130, which is the code for "to your location in thirty minutes."

Without waiting for a reply, he quickly hops in the shower and gets dressed. As he grabs his pager a few minutes later, he feels it buzz and sees 104 from Phil, so he knows he's awake and is good with Slade heading that way. As Slade backs out of his driveway, he notices more smoke from his truck. He's not a car guy, but he knows this is not a good thing.

Slade pulls into Phil's wealthy neighborhood. The yards are all manicured, the likes of which Slade is unfamiliar. They have those tall skinny columnar trees up next to the houses when you can see the house at all; mostly, Slade is looking at large rock walls, and gates with the houses set far back off the streets.

Phil's address is written atop one of these tall rock walls. A gate that usually crosses the driveway has been left open; he assumes this is so he can pull right up into the driveway without using the intercom box mounted on the left wall.

WOW, Slade thinks. *This is big time!* He parks his truck along the circular driveway past the stairs leading up to the front door. As he does, Phil opens the front door and comes down the steps to meet Slade. Slade thinks well, that's lucky timing but quickly reevaluates that thought as he looks around at the driveway. As he is admiring the immaculate landscaping, he hears a slight squeak and notices Phil's gate at the bottom of the driveway is closing. He also notices a camera mounted on the wall above the intercom. Not good timing after all. Phil likely saw me on the camera, Slade decides.

Phil greets Slade. "C'mon in, little buddy. I hope you came hungry. Toni makes some mean breakfast tacos!" As Phil is leading Slade into his home and to the kitchen table, it's all Slade can do to take it in.

"THIS IS the next level," Slade manages to say to Phil.

"We'll eat at the little table if that's ok," says Phil with a slight grin, playing on his observation that Slade is impressed with his home. This brings Phil great joy. "Little table?" replies Slade. "That's cute, Phil; this thing wouldn't even fit in the duplex."

A tiny, elderly Hispanic woman brings out a large platter of breakfast tacos and a small bowl of homemade salsa and sets it on the table where Phil and Slade are seated.

"I am telling you, you are in for a treat. Toni here makes the best-damned breakfast tacos in central Texas," Phil says as he touches the lady on her shoulder. He then turns to her directly and asks, "Can I get a coffee?" Then, looking back at Slade, "What would you like to drink? We have fresh squeezed orange juice. Coffee? Apple juice, name it," Phil continues.

Slade replies, almost embarrassed and not knowing how to deal with people waiting on you inside of a home, "That orange juice sounds great, thank you, ma'am."

"Well...so what do you think of the place?" Phil asks rhetorically with a broad grin, fully knowing the answer.

"Damn, I mean, this place is next fucking level. I mean, awesome." Slade kind of stammers repeating himself.

167

Phil smiles with pride and changes the subject. "Look, I didn't bring you here to show off my house, though I'll admit I enjoy doing it. I want to talk to you about some stuff. You're a smart kid, one of the smartest I've seen. And I don't want you to waste your talent."

Slade cuts Phil off. "Look Phil, I know where you're going here. I left college and I'm not going back. That was my parents' dream and shit, I don't want that life; fuck it, I'd rather live in my truck before I go back to that life!"

"No, no, little buddy, hear me out. I'm, not telling you what to do, nothing like that. I want to give you some ideas, real shit to think about. Sure I'm doing well, no doubt, but I started off well. That's a story for another day, but the point is, you're even better and smarter than me."

Phil continued with his pep talk to encourage Slade to grow even further than his imagination let him. "There are two kinds of us rounders. There are the hustlers, and in some ways we all are, but then there is another kind, the rare kind. The people who are IN the business of hustling. We never do anything without reason, we think about what we're doing and have a base stream of income somewhere that isn't a gamble. We are, in every way, businessmen.

"You have it; I've seen it. You're a thinker, and you get bored doing the hustle. If you tell me I'm wrong, we stop talking here and now. We can change the subject, and you can tell me all about your plans to move into the duplex and what kind of car you'll get to replace that damned truck before it dies. You know, I do want to know all of that, too. I do care about what is going on with you."

"You're not wrong, Phil," Slade said with shy pride. "That's why I went to LD's game to start with. That seemed like a thinking game and way more than a hustle. But fuck, I lost my ass, so, hustle it is."

"No," said Phil emphatically, "you're still not quite getting it. It's not the game you're playing that matters; it's HOW you're doing it.

Stay with me on this and answer quickly. Do you know how to play pool?" Phil wanted Slade to see how his strategy played out.

"Hell ya, I do. I'm one of the best in town," Slade says instantly and with authority.

"OK. Do you know how to play poker?"

"Well, I mean, sure, I know the rules and the odds and.... "Phil cuts him off.

"NO, you don't. Look, when you answered me on the topic of pool, there was no stutter, no hesitation, you're among the best, and you know it. When I saw you at the bowling alley, it was clear; you were a winner. In the square john world, you'd be a professional bowler. How many three hundred have you bowled?

"Only eight," Slade replies.

Phil is shaking his head. "ONLY! The odds of bowling a three hundred are the same as sinking a hole-in-one in golf, so I'm gonna go with, you know how to play. But you're not there in poker, and yet you risked more money in that one night than I've seen you risk any other time! Again, tell me I'm wrong."

"Well, no, you're right, I guess I don't know much about poker," says Slade with his head slightly down.

"Ok, now we're getting somewhere. "Look, I'm not saying poker is the be-all and end-all but whatever it IS, you need to do two things." Phil says in a teacher's voice. "One, set up a regular income off of whatever the hustle is so that it won't matter if you make a mistake or not. And two, manage your bankroll.

"Notice what I did not say because that is JUST as important. And before you argue with me, think it through. Do you think I'm an expert sports gambler? Don't answer, but you should see what I'm talking about. I know HOW to run a sportsbook, which isn't the same as betting on sports.

"This shit's simple but not easy. Don't overthink this part; just do it." Phil says firmly. Then he adds, "My sports book is my base, and I ensure the odds are in my favor. It's as good as flipping a quarter at eleven to ten odds. The only way I lose is to violate the second rule and stop managing my money. It takes a LOT of money to run a sports book AND manage a bankroll correctly.

"Again, learning the sports book business isn't why you're here. Finding and learning YOUR business is."

Phil then offers a little tip for the next time Slade plays poker.

"Here, listen to this. "A's and K's, and Q's and J's. No nines no tens, nor none of their friends. A pair in the hand and one on the flop[72]. Play these cards to come out on top."

"What the fuck, a rhyme? says Slade.

"You laugh, but I know I suck at poker. I don't have the concentration for it, and I can't keep all that shit in my head. But I can remember this. These are the starting hands to play if you want NOT TO LOSE.

And this is the only other lesson I've had on playing poker. You're playing not to lose. As soon as you take aim at one player[73] or try to win, you're sunk. When you understand that, THEN and only then will you be on the path to being a poker player for real.

Toni comes to the table. "Hello, Mr. Phil, can I get you more coffee," then looking at Slade, "or more orange juice for you?"

"Oh, no, ma'am," Slade replies, "I need to get moving, but thank you very much. Those breakfast tacos were some of the best I've ever had, so thank you again!"

Phil and Slade make their way back to the front of the house and to Slade's truck.

"Ok, little buddy, think about some things we talked about and know I'm here to help, whatever you need," Phil says.

"Thank you, Phil; I want you to know how I appreciate you getting me up and at it again. I am lucky to have folks looking after me, but you were in the center of it and gave me that push, and didn't have to.

---

[72] This represents the best starting hands in Texas hold 'em
[73] Try to beat one particular player at the table instead of trying to play your best hands.

I want you to know I will never forget it." Then with a little reflective grin, Slade added, "I noticed the cameras and security system my duplex has are not "kind of" like yours, but are exactly like yours. I am guessing you also had something to do with my new kitchen upgrades. Again, it does not go unnoticed or unappreciated."

"Well, you got me, little buddy; should know that I can't move past you. Let's call it a housewarming gift and be done with it, ok?"

"For sure, Phil." Slade sticks out his fit for a fist bump.

Phil walks closer and gives Slade a bear hug as a father would his son. They're past that fist bump shit. As Slade is climbing in his truck, Phil spins and walks straight over to him.

"Hey, I almost forgot to tell you. If you like that little Honda sports car, that CRX Si, see my buddy Frank at The Honda dealership in South Austin. Remind him Phil sent you. He has a few with low miles that he might make you a sweet deal on. As in, you won almost that much at the bowling alley from those rednecks," Phil says with a grin and a wink.

"Damn, Phil, you have this town wired, don't you?" Slade gathers his thoughts, admiring the stretch and pull of Phil's influence.

As Phil walks back to his house he waves and gives Slade a "See you out there little buddy."

Slade drives away. His mind is racing. Talking rapidly to himself, he's making a spreadsheet in his head. He continues to think aloud.

"I need to set up a spreadsheet on my computer to see what I've coming in and going out and set aside some throwing around money."

The next six months are filled with rapid-fire and focused hustles. Slade is fully focused on earning and has cut personal spending to a minimum. Then there's the upheaval of moving from the rental where Arnold and he have been living for the last eighteen months into his new duplex.

Slade is back in the groove and grind, literally on a mission. He has fully realized and accepted that he needs a real bankroll for any kind of business to be real. And that every dime of it needed to be accounted for and have a use: Phil's second rule to manage your bankroll. Even though Phil had given Slade the info for a new car, Slade took the bankroll conversation to heart and decided he wanted to have the cash fully in place before he even thought about buying a new car.

With this new focus and absolute tracking of what money was coming in and what money was going out. Slade knew with certainty; that day had arrived.

The first bedroom is Slade's office, where his computer is and where he goes daily to keep a tally of all his cash. He pauses at the whirring machine with two large twenty-one-inch monitors on his desk. He's proud that he built this from a few parts that had "fallen off of a truck." This system would be the envy of almost any geek out there. In addition to it being a top-end machine, Slade has it connected to the Internet via the newly-released DUAL ISDN protocol.

On one side of the desk, there are several books: all on poker, statistics, and gambling. These are the newly-acquired prize possessions Slade uses to study in his spare time. Although new, they seem worn and dog-eared. Slade is dedicated to exploring the basics of the math behind poker. It's been that way since he left Phil's house and stopped at a local bookstore.

Just to verify one more time that all the cash is in order, Slade opens his spreadsheet. As he flips between tabs, he sees the one marked VACATION and makes a mental note to talk to Arnold about a quick trip to Vegas. It's been a few months, and Slade's learned the value of letting it all go from time to time, even at this young age, even if only for a short while. A mental note made, he flips to the tab that reads CRX. The total at the top says $12,385.00, enough for the car and the modifications he wants to make: a stash box for cash, a badass stereo, and a custom-mounted holster for his Glock.

He walks over to the closet in the bedroom, a standard squeaky bifold door. At first glance, it seems to be an essential closet of stuff, a few hanging clothes, some golf clubs to one side, and some bowling stuff to the other.

But something is off a bit.

Slade slides the clothes to each side, which reveals a small latch underneath the shelf; one would miss it if they were not explicitly looking for it, as it was painted to match the shelf and set right beside the shelf bracket. Using another of his talents of being handy at building things, Slade built a faux wall inside the closet. As he pulled the latch, a thin piece of wood covered with sheetrock fell forward. Slade pulled it out and set it aside.

Behind the faux wall, he sees a stack of about ten VANS shoe boxes. Each is labeled with a sticker indicating the denomination within the box: $5, $10, $20, or $100. Slade reaches for one of the hundreds of boxes and puts it on the desk. Inside are rolls of hundred-dollar bills, pre-bundled in rolls of five thousand dollars. He quickly shoves three of them in his pocket, then puts the box back and secures the faux wall, sliding the clothes back to the center. He slams the door shut as if to tell the world: *case closed.*

"Let's do this! Where the hell is Arnold?" Slade says out loud.

About that time, Arnold's familiar knock is heard at the door: one short; three long. "It's open!" Slade shouts, and Arnold lets himself in.

"Hey, Fatman, ready to go get a car?"

"Hell ya. Phil says his guy will hook me up; cool, huh? And you can meet him too if you want to get the hook up at some point."

"Thanks, man, I appreciate it. Let's get moving, and hit The Side Hole afterward." Arnold is in a happy-go-lucky mood.

The two hop in Slade's truck and head to the south side of town. "Hey, I have been thinkin': We need a fuckin' vacation," Slade says to Arnold. "Let's hit Vegas!" Slade's mind briefly returns to his spreadsheet tab marked VEGAS with $5,000 at the top.

"Man, Vegas is wired. You know the saying, 'Those lights don't burn on winners,'" Arnold pushes back.

"No man, I know that; I said VACATION. Not work," Slade presses on. "We'll hit the cheap shrimp buffets and the fully naked strip clubs and drink like a fish. Let's blow some dough without thinking about making it for thirty-six hours," he coaxes Arnold. And since he's already checked out flights and hotel rooms at the Tropicana, he's raring to go. "Five dimes apiece, and we go nuts. Red-eye out and back, we're gone less than two days. Then, back to the restaurant for you and back to earning for me."

Arnold stammers, "Hmmm, look, Fatman..." he starts.

"C'mon, don't be a pussy, come to Vegas with me," Slade pleads, then adds "Dude. Look, if you don't wanna, I'll see if Phil, Checkbook, or someone—" Arnold cuts him off; this comment gets him riled up. Slade has successfully triggered Arnold into agreeing to come to Vegas.

"I'm fucking with you, Fatman," Arnold replies. He leans across the front seat and shakes Slade's arm. "It's Vegas, BABY!!"

Slade knows Arnold's not that enthusiastic. As they settle into the tighter space of the truck, Slade catches a whiff of alcohol just "seeping" from Arnold's skin. This isn't the first time. But it's not something that one mentions.

The two pull up to the Honda car lot and head to where the sign reads USED CARS. Slade is walking up and is met by a sales guy. He indicates he's there to see Frank.

"Sure thing," says the salesman and leads him to a glass building, with various cars and several desks separated by cubicle walls. A thin balding guy about Slade's height walks up with his hand out and introduces himself as Frank, asking how he can help. "Well, I'm a friend of Phil's, and a few months ago, he told me that you might have a good low-mileage CRX Si around. So I thought I would give it a shot and see what you might have," Slade ventures.

"Oh, ya, Phil told me you might be stopping in." He pauses and looks at the sales guy thanking him, shooing him away because he wants this one solo. Look, I got this sweet little number right out back. It has seven hundred and fifty miles on it. It was a demo, and I've been sitting on it for you if you want to check it out.

Slade was thinking damn; it will probably be closer to the total price of ninety-five hundred dollars than I had planned. His mind again goes to the spreadsheet as he thinks he might have to slow roll the stereo. "This will be all cash, is that right?" asks Frank. "If I like it", says Slade, never giving too much away. As he opens the door, Slade sees the all Black little sports car. It's super clean and sleek, like the pictures in the magazines.

That's a pretty nice ride, Slade says. "Leather inside?"

"Oh ya, this one has all the upgrades possible. It's prewired for subwoofers and an amp that can go under the passenger seat if you want to get the stereo pumped up, replies Frank. Phil said to take care of whatever you needed, so consider this a one-stop shop. And I do mean anything. Phil mentioned you might want some customizations as he has in his truck"

"Ok, good, I have a list of things I will need to be built to my specs."

Just as the words spill from his mouth, Arnold steps in close to him and says, "Dude, what are you doin'?" in a quiet tone but not quite enough; it's clear that Frank can hear him too. Slade steps back and holds up one finger to Arnold, then turns back to Frank.

"Ok, let me drive it, and if we are good, we can talk price and customizations and go from there. Frank tosses Slade the keys and nods in agreement. Arnold starts. "Do you need insurance or a driver's license or anything like that from us, Frank? Slade glares at Arnold. "No, man, any friend of Phil is solid business here. We're good. Drive as much as y'all want," Frank replies.

Slade hops in the front seat and adjusts it, starting it up and sliding back the sunroof. "Super cool," says Arnold, as he plops down in the passenger side of the two-seater. Slade eases out of the parking bay and rolls onto the street, then looks at Arnold, and says. "Watch this!". Slade punches it and quickly shifts from first to second as the two feel the front tires slip and screech as they spin a second gear "scratch"[74].

"Wow, front-wheel drive?" asks Arnold.

"Yep, and this baby will do zero to sixty in eight seconds and tops out at one-twenty!!"

"Shit, this is a little rocket," Fatman.

"Let's see what this guy is gonna do for us. The new price on these things is ninety-five hundred dollars."

"Well, it won't be much cheaper from a dealer since it has less than a thousand miles on it," Arnold says.

"We'll see; Phil says. He has the hookup, let's find out—and one more thing. Look, I know you think you are looking out for me, but I got this, let me deal with Frank alone."

Arnold nods and says, whatever you need Fatman I am backing off.

As they pull back into the parking bay, Frank awaits them.

Well, what do you think he says with a grin.

"I like it. What can you do for me? Will you take that truck in the trade too?" Asks Slade. "Let me hear about your upgrades and I will give you all one price," replies Frank.

"No," says Slade, "I want the car price first, then I'll decide what to do on upgrades. We'll keep it separate."

Arnold is observing his friend. He's noticed a change over the last six months, but this is the first time he's seen this kind of thing from Slade outside the pool hall. Slade's in control here. Arnold briefly remembers when he helped Slade buy his truck a couple of years back and how nervous Slade had been. This was a whole new Slade.

"Ok, no problem, we can do this," replies Frank. "How about seventy-five hundred dollars on the car?"

---

[74] When the tires spin from over acceleration and make a noise on the pavement

"Well, I was thinking more along the lines of sixty-five hundred; we all know that a car drops forty percent of its new value the instant you drive it off the lot. That should still give you some gravy, ya?"

"Hey, I want to do you right here, but I've got some things to hold up, too." Frank is looking around. "How about we meet in the middle? Seven thousand including Tax, Title, and License."

Slade's mind flashes to his spreadsheet and the cell for the car, including TT&L: it reads $8,000.00 "That'll do." Then he adds, "And I'll let Phil know you took good care of me. Let's talk upgrades."

Frank's relieved "Great, yes, let me know what you're thinking." Easy. First, let's do a top-notch stereo, at least four tweeters, two mids, and full bass Cerwin Vega sub-woofers in the back. Also, drop the best amp that fits and won't overheat under the passenger seat, and I want one of the new CD player stereos; I'm not brand conscious other than the sub-woofers Slade continues.

"Next easy is a tint, as dark as it comes, and let me worry about street legal or not. You can go one step back from dark limo tint on the front two, but damn near black out on the back. Are we good?

Yes, Frank replies taking notes.

"Now the custom stuff." Slade continues on. "I need a lockbox here behind the center console somewhere, carpeted in and concealed. It needs to be a numeric lock, on a quarter-inch thick aluminum box. I want the lock also covered with Velcro that I can pull back but's not obvious. The box should be about four inches deep, six inches wide, and ten inches long. I would like the inside covered with felt or something similar that won't come loose off the aluminum, I'll leave that to your guy, but I want it to be a light gray." Slade rattles off requests in rapid succession with little room for anything but a yes from Frank.

"Then, under the front dash, I'll need a holster with a single snap button for a Glock 22, .40 caliber. Your guy should have the specs. I want a molded holster, not a soft side. And I want it pointed down to the floorboard, not at the wheel."

"Sure, this is all doable," says Frank.

Let me go talk to Jimmy and make sure we have everything you need so you can pick this up in the morning. Slade frowns slightly when Frank suddenly changes his mind and says, "How about we deliver it to you tonight wherever you're at?"

"That would be splendid," Slade replies using a "proper" word to let Frank know it was expected all along. Frank wanders off out the back of the bay towards the garage section of the dealership. Arnold turns to Slade in disbelief, "Damn Fatman, cut the guy some slack, he made you a hell of a deal, and you needled him down another five hundred for nothing."

"Just chill, Arnold," Slade says, using his friend's name to show dominance and seriousness. I told you already, I got this handled, so don't worry. He'll get his five dollars back, I'm giving it, and it didn't cost me a thing. See how that works?"

The student has fully become the master. The two friends will never speak of this role reversal, but Arnold is aware of who's boss is. They both accept this new arrangement. Arnold admiringly lets on, "Ok, I gotcha. I should have known you had all the angles; you're back in the grove, brother."

"All the way in" Slade beams. They shake hands and pull in for a hug and a back slap to remove any tension Arnold might have felt when Slade calls him by his formal first name.

Frank returns and says, "ok, we can do the full set up, cash price is three thousand dollars even. I don't—"

Slade interrupts, "Don't sweat this part, Frank. The three dimes is good."

Slade reaches into his pocket and pulls out a couple rolls of cash, opens them and counts out seven thousand dollars.

"Here's seven for the car. I'll drop the other three on you when you deliver and sign whatever paperwork you need."

"Ok," says Frank, "I'll need to get a copy of your driver's license for our files if that's ok."

"Sure, man," says Slade and hands it to Frank. "Hey, do you have a loaner?" Slade asks as he tosses Frank the keys to his truck. "I'll leave the truck, I already cleaned it out."

"How about one of these LXi Accords? They're not sporty, but a smooth ride, top of the line."

"That's great," Slade replies.

Frank returns with Slade's license and hands it to him. "It was great doing business with you; I'm your guy any time." He then turns and hands Arnold a card, adding, "And you too, anything you need, let me know. I'll get you a good deal with whatever little extras you might need." Arnold smiles, and thanks Frank, telling him he's a good dude to know!

"We'll probably be at The Side Hole when the car is ready, Page me, you have it," Slade asks.

"Yes, I do, thank you and I will as soon as we are done, sir," Frank replies.

Arnold and Slade head out and back north to The Side Hole.

"Well Fatman, let's talk Vegas BABY!!!"

"Not this week but next?"

"Done, I'll get us the tickets and book a room. You can square me later. Red eye in and out. It's gonna be a thirty-six-hour trip. You good with that?"

"For sure, Vegas is always open," Arnold replies. "Sleep when we're dead!"

"VEGAS BABY!!!" The two say together as they fist bump and laugh. They get out of the loaner Honda and head into The Side Hole. Slade is smirking. "I guess that wasn't a bad ride, then a slight pause; when I'm old, like forty or something, I'll get one !!"

They walk in, and the usual hustle ensues. Slade's found himself a mark within thirty minutes, and Arnold is hanging out at the bar drinking a beer and chatting with Johnny.A little after midnight,

Slade's pager buzzes. He recognizes the number: Frank at the dealership. Slade holds up his pager so Arnold can see it as he's walking to the pay phone on the wall.

"It's Frank from the car dealership. I'm guessing the car will be ready tomorrow. I'm giving him a call," Slade shouts out.

We're all done if it's not too late, tell me where you are, and I can get it to you right away," Frank says. "Wow, pretty impressive there, Frank, I didn't expect you to get all my customization done and delivered so soon. I'm at the Side Hole. It's a pool hall in northeast Austin; you know it?"

"Oh, ya, I got it. I can be there in thirty. I have a few things for you to sign."

"Sure thing, Frank, and I've got your dough. Just tell the bartender you're here to see me if I'm not upfront when you get here."

About forty minutes later, Frank comes in with a folder and a set of keys. He sees Slade walking up and notices Arnold leaning up against the bar.

"Hey, how's it going?" he says to Arnold as Slade crosses the pool hall.

"Good. Man, y'all knocked that shit out quick," Arnold replies.

"Hey, Frank," says Slade, sticking out his hand to shake Frank's. "Let's get this done."

Frank lays out the papers on the bar all marked up for Slade to sign, "Just three places, and it's done. He hands Slade the keys and a little card with some tiny writing and a number on it. "This is for the custom box."

Slade nods and replies, "Thanks, I'll play with that later. Ok, Frank, thanks for everything," Slade says as he passes Frank the keys to the Accord and five hundred dollar bills.

Frank looks at Slade. "Oh, no, I'm good, I'm all taken care of."

"No Frank, I know Phil set this up and we're tight and that is all good but," Slade says firmly, "I want you to remember that I take care of those who take care of me,."

"Oh, you got it, boss," Frank replies in deference. "I'm your guy, whatever you need, you let me know. If any of that's not right, you come to see me, we'll fix it up johnny-on-the-spot."

With that, Frank heads out.

"What, did you finally get a new ride?" asks Johnny.

"Ya, I picked up one of those Honda CRX Si's (pronounced cracks sighs), loaded and blacked out."

"Sweet, those things are quick. like zero to sixty in eight point five seconds right?"

"Ya, this year's model is eight flat; they freaking get it!"

"Nice, well, it's about time you ditched that smokin' ass truck of yours," Johnny says, laughing.

"I think I'll call it a night," Slade says to Johnny and Arnold. "I cleared just under two dimes tonight," he continues as he drops a s bill in Johnny's jar. "That's enough for today and it's been a good week, no reason to push it."

Slade has been back to school.

Business school.

Phil's business school.

Now it is time for some research disguised as vacation...

Chapter Twelve

VEGAS BABY!

S lade pulls into his duplex driveway and sits for a moment in his new car reviewing how good the last few months have been. He's proud that his bankroll is almost where he needs it to be.

As he walks into his office, he takes the cash out of his pocket and puts it away in the little shoe boxes behind the faux wall in the closet. He then walks to his desk, turns on his computer, and opens the spreadsheet he's been diligently working on

He flips to the tab marked dailies and scrolls down to the current date:

Daily Cash	IN	OUT
September 12, 1987	$1,900	$200

New Ride	
NET	$1,500
Target	$12,000
Actual	$10,500
Car with TT&L	$7,000
Upgrades	$3,000
Other	$500

He then scrolls past the vacation tab and others like house, monthly and entertainment then stops on the one labeled BUSINESS

TARGET	$25,000
Cash to Target	$2,000

One-Time / Setup	$5,000
Operating Cash	$20,000
Cash on Hand	$23,000

Man, I'm close. *ALL* I need to do is figure out what business I'm gonna be in, he thinks as he laughs aloud. I have been to school, but it will have been a waste if I do not put it to use!

He glances at the poker books at the end of his desk, sure that the answer to his nagging question, 'What type of business should I create' will magically appear somewhere in one of them. Slade's staring at the spreadsheet, and his heart sinks a little. He's still unsure how to get that "base of regular income" Phil mentioned. Slade is finished *ONLY* earning income from being a player since shit can happen. Even the best can lose from time to time as Slade knows first-hand. He's missing something, some angle or advantage. He goes to bed with these concerns but not in a wrong way and quickly drifts off to sleep.

A few weeks later, Arnold is knocking hard at Slade's door.

"C'mon Fatman, I don't want to be late for the fucking plane; you know it will take us at least ten to fifteen minutes to get parked and boarded, even with just our carry-on luggage. You're cutting shit close!" he whines.

"Damn, when did you get to be so fucking uptight? I'm ready; let's go," Slade replies openly, irritated at being rushed. "Vacations are to fucking relax." With that statement, it occurs to Slade that this will be his first vacation without his parents. That's why Arnold's rushing irritates him: it's how his parents took vacations. Every single minute was planned out. No time to chill. . With that in mind, Slade takes a deep breath and decides he needs to back off on his friend a little; he probably didn't deserve that snarky response. He also reflects that he is not being fully transparent with his friend; this trip is as much about research and investigation as a vacation. Surely there will be some kind of inspiration; As Arnold says, Vegas is wired, so why not take an idea of theirs and make it my own, he thinks.

The two hop in Slade's CRX, and as usual, Slade does about eighty-five miles an hour to the airport. They have plenty of time to spare, as Slade planned it. Exacting, not late, not too early. Thinking back to his earlier realization, he doesn't mention this to Arnold and heads to the gate.

Once on board, Slade decides to nap. "Arnold, wake me when we land. Let's grab a cab when we get there, and then we can hit the buffet after checking out the scene a bit. "Nap? What the fuck, Fatman? Don't be snoring and shit. Now I know why you wanted the window."

"Ya, so I've got a place to lean without snuggling up with your sweet little ass" Slade says, poking Arnold in the ribs with his elbow. "Get off me, Fatman, that shit ain't funny. I'm going to be bored to tears all the way there."

Slade is asleep even before the plane has taken off and awakens, abruptly as it touches down. "Damn, you went out, Fatman so I ate all your fucking peanuts. They were the good kind with the sugar on them!"

They exit the airport and head to the long line of cabs waiting outside. In unison, they look at each other and, in unison, say, "It's a dry heat!" and laugh heartily.

"Tropicana," Slade tells the driver, and they're at the hotel in no time.

As they're checking in, Slade hands the concierge a credit card. "I know you want it, but we'll pay out in cash," he tells her.

"Yes, sir, thank you. Are you planning on enjoying our casino in the hotel on your visit?"

What an odd question, Slade thinks, as in, what the fuck else were they gonna be here for, but he does not say what he's thinking. Instead, he replies, "Yes, we'll play a little here and there. We might check out the shows too and grab a buffet or two."

"Great," she says, "we have this new program with these gamblers cards." She hands one to Slade and slides another toward Arnold. "There are different levels related to the amount you play. You get redeemable points at our gift shops and discounts on future stays with us or any of our affiliated hotels. There are many perks listed here in this brochure," she continues as she slides it to Slade.

"Ya, whatever; we'll sign up; it's free, right?" Slade is ready to be done talking to her as he is itching to get his stuff stowed in the room and back down to the casino floor.

"Oh, yes, sir, no fees whatsoever. Make sure you insert your card if you play our slots or hand it to any of our dealers as you play our table games. Good luck."

She hands them their cards and keys to the tower room they've booked.

As the two walk to the elevators, Slade turns to Arnold and asks, "What are we going to do? Four dimes max in, save a dime for booze and strippers, and fifty-fifty winnings?"

"Hell ya, I brought five dimes, so that works," Arnold chimes in.

"Same!" replies Slade.

As with all casinos, you can't get to any of the rooms or other "non-gambling" areas without passing rows and rows of slot machines. The dollar slots are positioned conveniently between the check-in counter and the elevators at the Tropicana.

"Let's get this shit rolling," says Slade as he stops at one of the dollar slots. "I read about this in one of my books. Always play the max amount on these things because the top payout is twenty percent more than what you get if you play a single dollar or anything less than max."

"Damn, three grocery dollars a pull. Fuck, we should set one of these up at home," Arnold says. For a moment, Slade considers what he said. Damn, this is automatic money. I win whether I fuck up or not. It's a base, a house advantage. Then he snaps back and replies to Arnold. Sure thing, idiot boy, if you want to do time in a federal lock-up. This shit is big time, we aren't risking that.

"I know, Fatman, pull the fucking lever and let's go; I wanna drop this shit and wander around."

Slade inserts his little card in the slot that reads TOP TROP POINTS, drops three dollars into the machine, and pulls the handle. The mechanism starts whirring, the light on top starts to spin, and it's twice as loud as it had been. Arnold looks at Slade asking if he broke it. "Dude, I think you pulled the handle too hard or something." They both look at the machine again, and they see it: three in a row. MAX | MAX | MAX. The machine's not broken, they hit the jackpot. Twenty-five thousand dollars!!!!

"Dude, it's not broke; we broke the fuckin' bank," Slade replies.

"Then why isn't the cash coming out? " Arnold asks quizzically, adding, "Maybe you did break it."

Suddenly a little man in a black vest and white shirt followed by a cocktail waitress appeared. "Congratulations sir, you have won the MAX slot prize. For winnings of this size, we'll need to get some information for tax purposes and then I'll present you with a check that you can deposit in any bank. Or we'll be happy to exchange it for cash or chips at any of our bank cages around the casino floor."

"Seriously, the man, Uncle fuckin' Sam, right here to get his fuckin'slice before I even get to taste it. That is some straight-up square-john shit right there," says Slade to no one in particular. "It's bad enough that you are taking on "the house" here, but you gotta take on the man, too." He continues to rant to the air.

The waitress steps closer, asking if she can get the gentlemen anything at all, cigars, cigarettes or drinks while Slade's filling out the paperwork.

"Sure, honey," Slade replies, "I'll take vodka and seven, Stoli or something decent, not rotgut." Arnold adds, "Same for me," and the waitress heads out to get the drinks.

"Right this way, sir," the little guy in the vest motions Slade to a small round table and has basic IRS forms to be filled out.

Slade quickly signs and sees the cashier's check sitting on the table. "Damn, ole uncle sam takes a bite. That's thirty percent!" The check reads $17,500.00.

"Here you go, gentlemen! The waitress is back with the drinks, complimentary of course." The little man in the vest then reviews the documents Slade's signed and thanks him. "We want you to enjoy your time here with us at the Tropicana, so here are four vouchers good at any of our buffets, plus some complimentary casino chips. This is one hundred dollars' worth of roulette chips and two hundred dollars worth of standard chips you may use on any of our table games. We do hope you enjoy your stay."

Arnold and Slade leave the slot machine pit and continue on their way to the elevators. "Well, that don't t suck," Slade says, "we comped out everything: free food for half our stay and nine dimes a piece to throw around. Let's drop this shit in the room and get to the cage and cash in. I'm sayin' we can make this a break-even trip. No reason to even go into the five dimes each we brought, we live on house money. I'll throw you your half at the cage and we don't have to worry about splitting shit up after that, Slade says, giving Arnold a fist-bump. Slade is ensuring his win right here. He's seen what his friend does sometimes when he's ahead; he'll blow it all on silly shit, then turn right back around and gamble with his original stake.

That works if you are not a "real" rounder Slade thinks, but thinking back to what Phil has said, Slade is always managing his bankroll, even if he gets an unexpected windfall like today on the slots. Arnold bumps his fist back and does not seem to care one way or the other about the split that Slade mentioned.

After tossing their bags in the room, the two head right for the cage to cash in the check, still riding the adrenaline rush from the unexpected win.

Once at the cage, they cash in the check for two trays of chips, each with a bounty of eight thousand seven hundred and fifty dollars.

"Where to first, Fatman? Hell, your luck is running hot. You get to pick!"

"Let's hit the roulette wheel, next to betting the Pass Line and three Come Bets[75] on the craps table; this is as close as it gets to fifty-fifty odds." Slade smiles broadly, proud of himself for reading up on the odds of the various table games over the past few months. Slade and Arnold wander around the casino playing this table game and that and grabbing as many free drinks as possible as they go.

The goal is to have a good time, and that's what they're doing! Arnold does seem to be getting a few more drinks in. Slade notices, but again, this is not something one mentions in the rounder world.

As they leave the blackjack tables, Slade sees a sign that reads Poker Room and nudges Arnold, saying, "Let's go play some."

Arnold looks at Slade with a frown. "Nah, go ahead if you want. Vegas poker is for grinders[76], they play limit too[77] not even pot limit

---

[75] On the dice table game commonly known as Craps.

– Pass Line

An even money bet, made on the first roll of the dice (known as the "come out roll"). You win if a seven or eleven roll, or lose if two, three, or twelve roll (known as "craps"). Any other number that rolls becomes the "point" and the point must roll again before a seven to win.

– Come Bets

Made anytime after the first roll when a shooter has a point to make. You win on a seven or eleven and lose on a two, three or twelve. Any other number becomes your "come point" and must be repeated for you to win before a seven rolls

[76] Poker players who sit and "grind" hand after hand and only play the best odds while folding the rest. It's a low risk low reward way to play poker.

[77] Limit poker refers to the maximum limit a player may bet in a given round of poker. Pot limit means that a player may bet up to the amount of money in the current pot. No limit means that there are no restrictions on the amount a player may bet at any time.

on the main floor. That shit's boring, I'm gonna hit the bar and play some Keno and video poker and drink like a fish!"

"Cool, I will come back around after I play a few hands. I want to see what it's like since I am all read up on all the rules and etiquette of casino poker. Let's see how many rules I can break and get away with." He laughs and once again bumps fists with Arnold as the two part ways.

Slade walks to the poker pit and watches, considering that he's back at school and needs to learn the ins and outs of the actual game to win. He wasn't kidding about breaking the etiquette as he wanted to see what was and what was not "a big deal."

One of the pit bosses wearing a black vest walks up to Slade. "Can I help you sir, would you like a seat?" She's looking at Slade's tray of chips and as Slade is saying "Yes, but I have a question first," she "clicks" this little device she has in her hand three times.

"Yes sir, what can I answer for you?" she continued.

Slade notices that a waitress has appeared and is offering Slade a drink. This is the first mental note Slade makes: This place is all about customer service. Then Slade replies, Stoli and seven please, at my table?

"Oh yes sir, right away," she replies. "Would you care for a cigar or cigarettes as well?"

"I'm good," Slade replies.

Then, turning back to the pit boss, Slade says, "Look, I'm pretty much an idiot about poker. Tell me about the little signs by the table and why the dealers seem to be taking chips and putting them in those little slots?"

"Oh, sir, I am sure that's not true, and I'm happy to review any of the rules or signage with you." Man, she is slick, Slade thinks as she continues.

"The signs tell the stakes of the table. For example, this one right here next to the front is a lower-limit game. On the sign, when it reads two-dollar and five-dollar limit, the wagers are two dollars pre-flop and on the flop and five dollars on the fourth street and the river. Limit means that these are the maximum bets allowed. Here at the Tropicana, it's also the minimum. The next line on the sign is one dollar/two dollar blinds. The small blind or first person seated to the left of the dealer is automatically required to bet one dollar, and the big or second player to the left of the dealer is automatically required to bet two dollars. The last line tells the max raises for any one round. Here at the Tropicana, we set this at three for all of our limit poker games and have it listed here as a reminder."

"To your other question of the dealer removing the chip from the field of play each hand. This is the rake or the amount we charge the table for each hand. We do it this way so that the only players incurring this charge would be the pot winners. Here at the Tropicana, we rake ten percent to a maximum of five dollars per pot for our limit games." Slade knew all of this as he had been reading and studying the ins and outs of the game for months.

"Oh, cool, see, I can learn stuff. I would like a seat, please. Do you have a ten/twenty seat open?"

"Yes, we do, sir. The buy-in is one thousand dollars, but you may play the entire tray as you wish," she says, pointing to Slade's chip tray with a grin.

Slade isn't that gullible and buys in ten black chips and hands the tray to the pit boss, asking (but already knowing the answer), "Can you hold this for me here, or do I need to go to the cage?" Before the pit boss can answer, the waitress arrives with his drink. He hands her a green twenty-five dollar chip and as he motions and says, "the ten/twenty table please." Then he turns back to the pit as she is filling out a voucher for his chip tray.

"Oh, yes, sir, we're happy to help; let's get a count. I count eight thousand, eight hundred and seventy-five dollars; is that your count as well?"

"Yes," Slade says with a grin at the fact that he is earning more "on the house money." As the pit boss hands Slade his voucher, he thanks her and hands her a green twenty-five dollar chip.

Slade sits to play but is paying little attention to the game, folding every hand and counting how many hands are being played per hour. He can feel an idea forming around the rake. While the rake isn't news, it was in all of the casino poker books; Slade had not considered it something HE could leverage.

His thoughts are interrupted by one of the other players who thinks he's somebody.

The guy is constantly playing with his chips. He has two stacks of them that he grabs each side of, then pulls up and makes into one stack. It's a constant click-click-click noise, and it's annoying as shit. Slade knows this is the point of it.

He looks at Slade and says, "Man, why are you here? Do you play or just fold? You know you can get free drinks anywhere; you don't have to take up a seat that a gambler could be sitting in and wasting our time." The table laughs.

"Oh, sorry, I'm new to the game, so I was kind of watching; I'll play one." Slade looks back at his hand as if he has forgotten what he had: two jacks, a trouble hand and Slade knows it.

"Ok, so I say raise here, right?" and with that, Slade tosses a green chip to the center of the table, knowing he is breaking a rule of etiquette.

"Sir, please don't splash the pot," the dealer warns Slade. "That is your only warning, you forfeit next time and leave the table after that, ok?"

"Oh, yes, sorry. So, I knew I had to announce something, so I push chips out and let you pull them in; sorry again, I'll be better," says Slade, continuing to play the part of a total newbie.

Slade had a flashback to the game at LD's when he was yelled at for splashing the pot. He *WAS* a newbie then and didn't even know it. The dealer slides the green twenty-five dollar chip back in front of Slade and says to the table, "It is now ten to call."

Most players fold, but the chip clicker guy re-raises. The rest of the table folds and the dealer is looking at Slade. "Ten to call, sir."

Slade looks at his cards again and appears to be thinking when the chip clicker mouths off again. They're not gonna change by staring at them, you in or what?

Slade looks at the dealer and says, "I'll raise," and he places another green chip in front of him. The chip clicker calls.

The dealer now slides Slade's two green chips to the pot and returns two five-dollar red chips. Just as Slade had read in his books, the dealer keeps things going and makes the change as needed.

The flop comes a seven of hearts, a four of diamonds, and a jack of hearts. Slade knows he should bet here and does. The chip clicker quickie raises, as does Slade. But then the chip clicker calls instead of taking the third raise.

Fourth Street is a two of diamonds, and Slade certainly has the dominant hand. He quickly calls out, "I check" to see what is going on with the other player, and in this case, it works. The chip clicker bets and Slade insta-raises to see if he can throw him on his heels. When the chip clicker instead re-raises, Slade caps the round and maxes out the third raise.

Fifth street is a nothing card; a two of clubs, and Salde hold the best hand which in this case is a set of Jacks[78]. Slade insta-bets and the chip clicker insta-raises and back and forth until three raises are made. Chip Clicker flips over his pair of Aces and says, "Hope you don't think your pair of queens was good?" as if he knew what Slade was holding.

"Nah, but, I got the nuts, not queens," Slade says with a smile as the table laughs. Slade's use of poker lingo plus his distinct change in

---

[78] A set is a specific "three of a kind" in Texas Hold 'em. To have "a set" one must hold a pair in one's hand while the third card of the set in on the table and part of the community cards.

mannerisms show that he's not a newbie.. "Cash out please", he calls to the dealer.

"What, one hand and you're leaving, what is that shit, are you scared or something?" the chip clicker says.

Slade turns and looks at him. "Hey, ya know, man, there's a name for people who get up and leave a table after winning. You know what it is?" The guy rolls his eyes and is about to say something when Slade butts in. "They call those people WINNERS," and taps his chest with a black chip that he then slides carefully to the dealer. "For your patience with me today. I appreciate it."

Slade walks away grinning from ear to ear. The casual observer would think he was proud of himself for taking out a loud mouth at the poker table, but this was the furthest thing from his mind. One-off hustling a chump like that was an everyday thing to Slade; this just happened to be at a poker table. Slade learned there was business to be made from poker; it was right there all the time.

This *WAS IT*. This was the steady business he'd been looking to set up. And it had in fact been in those books all the time. It took seeing it in action, and learning how many hands were being played, which is something past what one could learn from a book, to have it sink in.

The table makes money. Slade had been counting and the tables were averaging thirty-five hands an hour on the very conservative end. That's one hundred seventy-five dollars an hour with no risk. *THAT* is a base I can build Slade thinks as his mind races with numbers. He couldn't wait to share this revelation with Phil. Hell, Slade was done with vacation! Building a business was all of a sudden WAY more enticing!

But, he had come to Vegas and all but cornered Arnold into coming along, so he would honor that. Phil wasn't going anywhere. Slade heads to the bar area where he last saw Arnold and starts to look for his friend.

It's not long until he spots Arnold at the bar talking to a tall thin young woman with dark skin and the deepest brown eyes Slade's seen. Simply put, she's gorgeous.

Slurring his words, Arnold says, "Hey, Fatman, meet my new friend, Tatiana. She's from Costa Rica. I was gonna come find you and tell you that we're gonna go eat and stuff," Arnold winks at Slade.

"Hey, you two go have some fun,' Slade says. Looking at Arnold's chip tray he can see that Arnold has gone through a thousand dollars or so. "Hey, I'll get your tray all secured away in the room vault for you." Reaching into his friend's tray, Slade pulls out five hundred dollars worth of chips. "Here's five dollars you can fuck around with," Slade says as he holds Arnold's hand open and drops five black chips in one at a time, clink, clink, clink, clink, clink.

"Thanks. You're my brother and I love you, man," Arnold says, hugging Slade. Arnold is drunk and Slade is glad he got there to hold the cash.

"You stay in the hotel to eat and stuff ya," Slade says.

"Oh ya, Tatiana is staying here too, we're not going outside. It's hotter than hell out there man, why would we leave?" Arnold is off to get laid, and this is what vacation is all about!

Slade hits the room, puts away his friend's chips, and realizes he hasn't had anything to eat in a while. Damn, he wonders what a twelve-dollar cheeseburger tastes like, as he looks over the room service menu. The food arrives, and Slade scarfs it down in record time. Damn, that is a tasty burger, he thinks to himself. With his stomach full; thoughts and plans of a new business are forming, then, Slade falls fast asleep.

He is startled awake by a VERY hungover Arnold. Slade looks at the clock and realizes the plane is leaving in three hours. Vegas operates on a different set of time rules; he can barely believe it's almost time to leave. Thirty-six hours fly by!

"Well," says Slade to Arnold, "Aren't you gonna tell me you should have your dick bronzed (borrowing the line from Eddie Murphy in the movie *48 Hours*) or something?"

"Ya, I should," Arnold replies, seeming distracted. "Hey, you got my chips last night, right?" Arnold asks.

"For sure, they're in the safe like I said, all *safe* and sound."

Arnold shows a real sign of relief; it's clear he isn't sure what happened. This bothers Slade, but true to form, this is not something one discusses.

"C'mon Fatman, let's grab some food before the flight home. I'm hittin' the shower."

The two make their way to check out and as they do, they hand the counter person their little Trop reward cards. She perks up a little and says, "We thank you for your stay, gentlemen. With the reward points you have accumulated, you're now a platinum member. This makes you eligible for room upgrades and complimentary VIP buffet seating. Make sure to give us your card numbers anytime you're booking a stay with us or our affiliate hotels. Today I can offer you a complimentary buffet if you have the time before your flight leaves," she continues as she hands Slade the bill and the buffet vouchers.

"Thank you," Slade says as he pulls out cash to take care of the bill. He then turns to Arnold. "I did good last night, I got the room brother." Arnold starts to protest, then Slade continues, "I added almost two dimes to the house money."

"Shit brother, you the man, I'll take you up on it. Hell, I dropped fifteen hundred on something but still left Vegas a winner. Who would have thought!"

In the cab to the airport, Slade can pick up the distinct smell of alcohol coming from Arnold's skin, even after his shower. Damn, he thinks, that must have been some serious drinking! Just as with the plane ride to Vegas, Slade is fast asleep on the plane ride home. Arnold, not having any quality sleep for the last thirty-six hours, quickly follows suit. Once Slade is back home at the duplex and has told Arnold his goodbyes, he pages Phil to set up a lunch and talk things through. It's baseball season, and Phil has to go out of town a lot, to take care of customers.

Phil calls Slade back, and they set up to meet up after the regular baseball season is over. "I want a clear head and no distractions for something "this important" and if you need to rush it, it's wrong," Phil says as he tells Slade the timing. "Baseball takes a lot of time and focus for me, so I need it mostly done. Let's meet in mid-November at the alley for those enchiladas," he adds.

Slade doesn't appreciate the delay, but he also wants this to be right. He also knows he can play more games around town and see what the "local rake" looks like versus what he saw in Vegas, so he sets out looking for local limit games, not sure what he would find.

Slade knows what Arnold thinks of limit games, so decides it's best to go look on his own. While the two have been separating their hustles more and more with Slade opting to win regularly rather than with excitement, this would be the first thing in the rounder world Slade had done without Arnold being involved at all. Somehow, this felt REALLY good.

Slade heads out and decides to start the hunt for limit poker from his comfort zone of The Side Hole.

He arrives and says his hellos to the mid-day regulars, then walks back to the bar. Hey, Johnny, I need to make some calls, mind if I stretch the phone over here beside the bar and set up Slade asks?

Sure thing man, make sure and answer like you work here in case it isn't someone calling you back replies Johnny as he slides Slade the phone. Got it replies Slade, then adds, can I get a diet coke too please and slides a hundred dollar bill in the tip jar.

Slade settles in and pages Tex O'Sullivan first, then quickly orders a pizza for lunch. He decides to start with Tex if for no other reason than he already has his pager number. No sooner than Slade can click the phone back into the cradle, it rings. Slade answers, "Side Hole."

"Hello, someone paged me," Tex says from the other end.

"Oh, hey Tex, this is Slade Garrick. Not sure if you remember me, but I met you with Phil a couple of times and sat around a table with you for a while at LDs." All of this is carefully worded so as not to say anything about gambling at any time.

Oh, ya, I remember you for sure, how are things?" Tex asks.

"Good. Hey, I've heard you play games sometimes. Do you think we could meet up somewhere and talk about it? I'm hanging out at The Side Hole snagging me some lunch, but I can meet up with you wherever, say the word," Slade continues.

"No man, all good stuff, I'll swing by up there, I am not far, we can talk about what's what." Again, all a vague conversation as you never know who might be listening. "I'll see you in thirty," Tex says and hangs up the phone.

Tex walks in as Slade's pizza is being delivered. "Hey Tex, wanna slice? I have plenty."

"No, I'm good, just finished up some burritos," replies Tex. "Let's talk cards, shall we?" he continues.

"For sure, I'm looking to play in some regular games and see if I can keep from losing all I steal from these chumps at the pool table," Slade laughs with the same arrogance Tex had seen at LD's game.

"Ok, well, I run a limit game once a week. I have one tonight, as a matter of fact. cards are in the air at seven It's two dollar buy-in, dollar rebuys five/ten with one / two blinds. We cap three raises, but if it gets to heads up, it's pot limit. I seat twelve max," Tex explains.

"Wow, twelve, that must be a hell of a table. That pot limit on the end adds a twist. I think I like that," Slade adds.

"Yes, that makes it interesting, and the fact that you even picked that out says you might know a little more than you did at LD. If you don't mind me sayin', you were a little out of your depth that night," Tex adds with candor. Slade likes Tex; better to have someone who tells you like it is!

"Yes, I was for sure," Slade replies. "I'm trying to change that, learn while you earn and all that. Do you mind if I ask some questions?"

"Fire away," says Tex, "what do you need to know?"

"Well, how do you rake, and what is the typical buy-in?"

"Solid questions. If it makes it to the flop, I pull a nickel a hand and another nickel if the pot is over five dollars. Most players buy-in for three hundred or so. I also provide drinks and chips, dips, and snacks. If we're full, I order pizza, don't want anyone starving."

"Cool setup, count me in. I won't be going off like I did at LD's but I will be a regular," Slade replies.

"I want to play more than one night a week, so if you know of other limit games, hook me up, I would appreciate it."

"Sure thing," Tex says. "You'll see Victor and Evelyn there tonight. They also run games; make sure you say hello.

"Well, cool shit, man. I'm gonna play here a bit and earn up a buy-in or two, but I'll swing by for sure."

"Great," says Tex as he slides Slade a napkin with an address on it, "see you tonight."

Slade arrives at Tex's place and observes a large round poker table. Clearly custom-made. He also sees a slot in the felt next to where Tex is sitting, like the tables in Vegas. Slade can't help it: He looks under the table and sees the lockbox mounted beneath the slot. He'ss impressed. This is a much cleaner setup than other games he's played, a professional feel similar to Vegas.

As the play starts, he notices that Tex is also the only dealer and that they pass the dealer button[79] like Vegas. This feels like home, like other hustles Slade does. There's no chip on his shoulder; he doesn't feel he's out to prove anything, he's doing the math and playing the game. Nothing cute, play. Just like playing pool, better to make the

---

[79] A dealer button is a marker used to indicate the player who is dealing or, in this case the player who acts last on that deal.

easy shots and play safe than to look like a player and make a bunch of trick shots. Flash does not pay the bills.

At the first break, Slade walks up and introduces himself to Evelyn and Vicktor, who are both getting a fresh beer. Soon he's secured two more invites and will go check out their games as well. He learns that there are slight variations like both of their games seat eight players maximum, and at their games, the deal passes between the players. Victor has games like Omaha and seven-card stud available, while Evelyn also has low-card wild as a possible game in what they both call Dealer's Choice. Neither of them has the heads-up rule that Tex does.

Over the next few months, Slade makes the rounds and rarely misses any of these three games. He occasionally will hit up a "pick-up" game, but He avoids what he refers to as "the silly games". Games like the garage game that Arnold used to take him to. He has taken note that Evelyn's game with the occasional low-card wild twist is close to silly sometimes. It's also a game where he will see Arnold from time to time.

"Hey Fatman, you're branching out, I hear," Arnold says to Slade at Evelyn's game one night.

"Ya, I'm makin' the rounds here and there, trying my luck at poker. Why not?" says Slade.

"Ya, whatever, don't hustle me up, I taught you that shit, remember? Word is you are a player; most of these guys are afraid of you."

"Ya. better to be lucky than good as they say. I'm playing around a bit," Slade says, holding on to the facade of another guy at the table.

"It's all good my brother, good to see you out and about. I hope you lose your ass tonight," Arnold jokes as he pours himself a double and heads for the table.

With poker added to his regular routine, time flies by, and Slade finds himself once again at the bowling alley cafe with Phil whom he's seeing more and more as a mentor.

Phil walks into the bowling alley where Slade is already waiting. "I think I've found "my business," but I want to run it by you to see what you think." Slade starts right in with excitement. "Ya know, to see what I might need to do to get it going the right way."

"Well, you are certainly excited," says Phil, "let's get us some food ordered and chat."

"Oh, my bad, ya, I am excited. Man, Phil, how are you, things are good?" Slade says as the two head to the cafe counter for enchiladas. They order and take their seats.

Phil then reopens the conversation. "Fire away little buddy, I can see you're excited, so that's already a good thing. And that you waited means you're serious and not onto the next thing," Phil states with a sense of pride in his voice.

"No, not even, I've been working on some aspects of it, but just doing the hustle, not running a business or even talking about it yet before talking with you. Waiting IS the right answer as it's also given me more time to tweak how I want to run this particular business.

"I want to run a poker room, or multiples at some point. That's the short of it," Slade says as their enchiladas are being delivered. Slade pauses while he starts to cut the steaming enchiladas. His fork makes that little scraping noise against the thick plate, causing him and Phil to flinch a bit, then chuckle as Slade repeats, "Ya, I am excited I guess, even more than I have let myself think."

"So, you're good enough to win every night, is that it?" Phil inquires with a slight tone of cynicism.

"No, and I was listening to you. No one is ever gonna be that good. That's being a good hustler, no different than pool or foosball," pointing at the bowling lanes, "or even bowling. This isn't about me winning at poker, although I'll win some. It's about the poker room making money. This is about the rake." Slade is speaking in rapid succession; the excitement in his voice is building again.

"I can run limit games and the occasional no-limit or pot-limit game. If my math is right, even with slow players I'll average one-hundred seventy-five an hour per table. With two tables, five nights a week, and assuming six-hour games I am looking at forty large a month. Regular expenses will run about five dimes a month. That is four hundred large[80] a year if I don't hustle a cent. And, that is if I don't win anything playin'. That won't happen either. I've been playing the past few months at least three nights a week. Net up 7 dimes a month three months in a row," Slade brags a little. "But, that is NOT where the real money comes from.

"I also know that I'll not start with that many games, hell I'm not even sure if this town will support that much poker, but I wanted to start with potential. Hell, just adding 10% of that amount to my hustle is still a base to build from.

"Here is some shorter-term and realistic math today," Slade continues as Phil evidenced the smallest little smile.

"One table, the average game is eight hours, eight games a month. That is eight dimes a month. I keep the costs low to start. I want this to be a "place to go to" Nothing against the other poker games I have been playing, but I want people to come for the "place" as much as the "game" if that makes sense. Anybody can have a game, I will provide an experience that will be a draw other than the possibility of playing with Wild Phil from Liberty Hill in go-off mode," Slade says, teasing his mentor.

"I have Arnold catering, and I will set Ramona up to be hostess and my end should still be an easy four dimes a month. It's a place to start.

"When we spoke at your house, you said I needed to understand WHY I lost my ass at LD's game. I do. And, I know that limit poker which I will be mostly running and no-limit poker are not even the

---

[80] Large is $1,000; so, 300 large is $300,000

same game. At the end of the day, my dumb ass missed it all. Just like everything else, the GAME of poker has shit little to do with being a poker player. I'm also starting to get a reputation since I get regular invites. People WANT to beat me and sometimes I let them."

The two say in unison: "Sometimes you gotta lose to win!"

Then Phil adds, "You do have a rep; it's gotten back to me, so I'm not a hundred percent surprised with your news today. You'll add draw by being there, at least in the beginning."

"Well, that's good news. How I start is important. I need to remember, nothing happens in this fucking town without you knowing!

"Back to the game itself and make IT a draw. I also want to run a straight-up game. This along with always serving GOOD food and HOT waitresses are differences that will make my games stand out," Slade says in a flat tone.

Slade then gives his mentor some props and continues. "I see how you take the few extra minutes to talk to your customers, and you treat them like that, customers, not marks or targets. People like you come back. It's not the fair lines and prompt payments, it's, well, I dunno, customer service. I want my players to feel that too."

Slade pauses as he realizes he has been almost ranting and hasn't even taken a bit of his food.

"Well, that's what I got. What do you think? Is this silly, too small? I mean, I know four dimes a month is rattling change for you and the book?"

"Well, Slade, my friend, you have graduated. you're fully in the rounder business if you make this idea a reality."

Phil, staying with a serious tone, delivers some starting advice. "You need to start leaking the word out for your first game. Nothing fancy, not a grand opening or anything. Just simply that you're gonna host a game. This way, if the first night goes to shit, you can wait a bit and do it until it does not. THEN announce another. Then let the players DEMAND that you have a regular game, then a second night, and so on. Are we on the same page? SLOW and steady to start, you need to keep hustling to keep the cash up." Phil is saying in full teacher voice.

"I gotcha," Slade replies.

Phil continues, "And you need a location if at all possible, not your house. This will also set up the feeling that this is a REAL game, not another house game. You need to set yourself apart in as many ways as possible. Let them feel like customers and not like friends. It's a fine line, but an important one."

"Hmmm, ok, that gives me an idea.

"My tenant's lease is ending soon. She's not renewing. Since It's Section Eight, the government has to give me six months' notice on this lease and they have. This is a cool story. She was getting assistance at eighty percent when she moved in. Since then, she has been paying more and more. She's only getting twenty percent and she pays the big end. The reason she's leaving is because she's been able to pull herself out of debt and get the down payment on a house rounded up. That is doing something, a single mom of three, too. Her husband drove a cab and got stopped by the cops and shot for basically, well, being black. It started as a sad story and this woman has pulled her shit together. Very impressive.

"Anyway, I could use that half of the duplex for this. It's also a good timeline to get my shit together. I can target her exit plus a couple of weeks for carpet and paint or so for the first game."

Phil grins broadly. "You're thinking like a business person. This is where you're much better than me, little buddy. I'm so proud. Now stop banging that fork and start eating before your enchiladas get any colder," Phil says, shifting to a fatherly tone of affection.

Slade then pulls out a wrinkled flier he had stuffed in his pocket.

"Ok, one more thing. What do you think about this stuff? I've looked around town and I can't find anything like it at prices anywhere near this cheap," Slade says as he's showing Phil the flier from a casino supply company in Vegas. "Table and chairs, that's easy, but this stuff, damn, I can find it but It's twice the price!"

"Oh, good, I was gonna ask if you'd thought about fitting out the place. You should for sure go back and fly as much home as you can. All cash, no paper. You want to leave Johnny-Law in the dark."

"Cool, I have a list made on my computer so I could set the budget," Slade says, as his mind's eye looks at the spreadsheet. I'm gonna get some of this stuff in bulk to get good prices. I'll start with ten setups, but I'll buy one table and chair set.

Item	Cost
10,000 Chips	$3,500
10 custom chip cases	$1,000
10 Drop Boxes	$200
8 Chairs (one table only)	$800
1 Table	$1,500

"Solid plan little buddy, keep at it. You're doing this right!"

"Thanks, Phil, I'm gonna keep playing and start to mention here and there that I might have a game, then as I am closer, I'll start throwing dates out. I can count on you for opening night, yes?"

"C'mon little buddy, you know I wouldn't miss it, I'll have my ass in a seat all night!"

Slade walks out the door somehow a little lighter and plops down in his CRX, rolling the sunroof back. It's still warm in central Texas in October and Slade likes the breeze when he drives.

Slade heads for the strip club as he pulls out. I should let Ramona know what is up in case she's not up for it, he thinks to himself. Damn, that would suck for her to say no and leave me without a waitress for the first night!

Slade walks in slowly to allow his eyes to adjust, then quickly spots his favorite red-head fuck buddy on the pole. He takes a seat near the stage and as she saunters over he slides a hundred in her g-string pulling it way out as he does. "When do you get off, hottie," he says to her. "If I am lucky about forty-five minutes after my shift is up," she says then moves away quickly to the pole throwing her top back at Slade as she does.

Sure enough, about an hour and a half later, the two roll onto their backs in Slade's bed breathing heavily but fully satisfied after an afternoon hook-up. Slade quickly rolls two joints and passes Romona one as he says, "Hey, I want to run something by you."

Ramona perks up, thinking person, not business; it's clear as day on her face. Slade quells any silly thoughts she might be having. "This is a business idea and, I want to keep it on the DL (fully knowing that she will leak the word as soon as she hits the club). I am going to run a poker game from time to time, and I want you to run waitress. I will give you a flat rate of two dollars and you keep one hundred percent of the tips."

A disappointed Ramona replies. "Ya, all business, for sure sounds like an easy gig. you going to have the games here?"

"No, but not sure where yet, I'll make sure you have a ride and such," replies Slade.

"Fine," replies Romona. "Happy to help you out," as flatly as a person can speak as she gets out of bed.

"Where you going?" inquires Slade, all but oblivious that he's crushed her hopes of taking the relationship a bit past purely superficial. "I thought we could burn one and go a couple more rounds."

"I need to get some things done. I have to work again tomorrow," she says as she sets the joint on the dresser. As she pulls her flex dress over her bare body, she snags her shoes and coat and continues, "Don't get up, I know the way out.

Hmm, Slade thinks, I need to keep her happy at least until I get the game going. I'll smooth it over later. Slade decides he'll chill, lights up his joint, and flips on the TV in the bedroom. Calls up for Chinese take-out. *Time to head back to Vegas, I should see if Arnold wants to go back sometime after Christmas.*

Arnold's pager is buzzing as he's getting out of bed about noon just after New Year: It's Slade.

Arnold grabs the phone and calls Slade. "What's up Fatman, It's fuckin'early.

By the way, when are you gonna clue me in on your grinder house game? I've been hearing about it from everyone. Are you gonna run a game or what?"

"Hilarious and well, yes that is kind of what I am calling about. And don't get snippy, you hate plain ole hold 'em" Slade adds with snark in his tone.

"Let's go back to Vegas, another thirty-six-hour quick trip. I need to get some stuff for the poker game and I can only get it from there. I ordered the stuff from them and they'll have it ready for pickup on the twenty-third. I figured with the luck we had last time you might be itchin' to go back!"

"You moron, that is the day after the fucking Super Bowl. Do you know what the fucking odds are of us getting in then, we're literally calling up three weeks before the game and looking for a room," Arnold says, seeming to take great joy in scolding his friend.

"Shit.

Fuck.

I forgot," says Slade. "Ok, well, that little trop reward thing says if they can't accommodate us, They'll find us a room even if not on one of their properties, I read the fine print."

"Well hell, that's cool," says Arnold with a new tone. "If you can get us booked, I'm in. Super Bowl in Vegas is the NUTS!"

"Cool, let me get it set. Let's meet up at The Side Hole tonight and I'll give you the scoop."

A few hours later, Slade walks into The Side Hole and sees Arnold leaning up against the bar, drinking a seven-up.

"What the fuck are they out of beer or what?" Slade asks. "No, man, having a cocktail instead," Arnold replies as he pulls out a flask and adds to the glass.

"You need to slow up on the hard stuff, man," says Slade. "What if a mark walked in?" Slade is finally finding a way to say something acceptable about Arnold's drinking.

"What, are you my mother, tell me about Vegas BABY!!"

"Dude, I call them up and They're all like, well, that is Super Bowl weekend you know, we're booked up.

Then I say, hey, I've one of those trop number things and it says if we're gold level or higher you'll help find us something. we're Platinum so can you help us?

I'm on hold like ten minutes, I figure the bitch ditched me, then she comes back on and says: 'Mr Garrick? Funny shit right there. Anyway," she then goes, "would you like the Tower or the main hall? we have a suite in either for you and can we assume Mr. Cabrasie is traveling with you?'"

"Dude, we got the hookup and we're IN."

In unison, the two say: "VEGAS BABY!!!!"

Over the next few months after the trip, Slade has what he needs to set up the room with the exception of the table and chairs. The tenants have moved out and the duplex has fresh carpet and paint and looks crisp. The morning before the poker game is scheduled to start, Slade wanders into his office and sits down at his computer to validate what he already knows: he's running short on cash for the setup. It was an error in the first calculation: he'd set aside five dimes for flat-rate setup and he had missed correcting it until last week.

The friend Slade used to count on to set up hustles has been slipping away over the last six months. Arnold has been drinking more and winning less. While it's mostly a break-even event for Arnold, whose restaurant provides a steady income, breaking even isn't an option for Slade, who relies on winning for income.

The spreadsheet tells the story clearly. Slade is eighteen hundred dollars short for the table and chairs to finish out the room. And while Slade could over-extend with a trip to "the closet" to get the table he wants, he holds firm to his decision to make money first and then bankroll the things he wants. He understands the value of risk-taking and when not to blow money on "things." He'll go over a little and get the good chairs, but decided to build a table with some used felt and some of the padding left over from the new carpet in the duplex.

When Slade mentioned this idea to Arnold yesterday, his friend didn't understand...at all. "Just get the table Fatman. You know you have the cash, don't be a tight ass," he said. It strikes Slade as odd since Arnold's plan is to run the family restaurant one day, but Arnold doesn't seem to have basic business sense. He doesn't understand Slade's thinking or what he's building. It's not some rinky-dink side gig. From here on in, things HAVE to follow a plan and a budget, or else It's another hustle.

The game is set for tomorrow, so this is the plan. Put the table together in the morning and keep the game day set. Phil is coming as are all of the folks who want to play wherever Phil is. If people don't like the table, then like Phil said from the beginning, wait and run another one. It's the game that matters, not the table.

Slade calls the local supply store and says, "Hello, this is Slade Garrick. I'll take the chairs today, but I'll hold off on the table. The down payment I left should cover the chairs, including delivery."

"Yes sir," the voice says, "we'll have those to you shortly and we're delivering to the B Side at this address, is that correct?"

"It is," Slade replies. Slade tips the driver who brought the chairs. He lays the leftover padding from recarpeting the duplex and the felt he snagged from Johnny at The Side Hole last week in the middle of the living room floor next to a large black leather sofa.

Tonight will be the inaugural game of Bird–Man Poker.

Or not...

CHAPTER THIRTEEN

NOPE

THIS CHAPTER IS INTENTIONALLY LEFT BLANK

CHAPTER FOURTEEN

THE HOUSE ADVANTAGE

S lade comes fully back to the present hearing a knock at the door. Nothing special, a regular knock, so Slade knows it's not a "usual" player.

"Y'all keep it going, I'll hit the camera and see who it is," Slade says, hopping up from the couch and heading to his office. On the screen, he notices LD's girlfriend, Charlene. Slade remembers seeing her around, but he's never met her.

Slade comes out of the office, walks over to the poker table, and leans in close to Arnold. "You invite Charlene?"

"Oh, ya, I did mention it to her but I never figured she would show."

"Well, she's here," Slade informs him.

Slade opens the door and greets her with a warm hello as if he knows her. They smile at one another. "Arnold told me y'all are playin' a limit game tonight - is that right?" she asks casually.

"C'mon in, save us some AC," Slade says with a little chuckle as he invites her in. "We're full, but you're first on the rail. Becky here will get you whatever you need. Let Becky know what you prefer to drink and smoke, and next time we'll have it for sure if we don't already. Oh, and smoke all you want, but if you need to burn one, not here. No drugs at all, even though weed ain't really drugs, ya know how it is."

Charlene took the generous plate of food from Becky along with a beer, saying, wow, you do it up nice!.

Slade started explaining the game, which was pretty straightforward. "It's five / ten limit with two / five blinds. Easy buy-in two hundred and rebuys are the same. Standard ten percent rake to a max nickel per hand, and the deal rotates. It's all Hold 'em."

"Sounds like the perfect game for me," Charlene replies.

Slade isn't quite at ease. Things look like they're going well, but something feels off.

On the one hand, a full table and two on the rail is a good thing, but on the other hand, no one has made a rebuy. He ponders if he should loosen up the action, as the game is looking like it will break in two hours, and that will be that.

All of his work over the years, since he was a scared little boy in eighth grade, was coming down to this moment. He couldn't accept the thought of "just hustling" for another six months. He needed to focus on building a business.

He listens to what's happening at the table, trying to focus when he hears Arnold sounding like he's half lecturing and criticizing someone. Slade realizes Arnold is criticizing him and, worse, the game!

"Ya, I tried to tell Fatman not to run a limit game; everyone knows those are house games, and the only people that do well are those IN the house."

Slade's ears ring with the sound of his voice in his head, screaming to Arnold to shut the fuck up. That idiot is going to screw the game. Goddamnit, he has to do something, Slade thinks. This is about to be over before it fucking starts. I've been about action, not sitting back and waiting for things to happen. I make things happen. I've scratched and clawed and paid my dues. I've lost, and it's time to win. I *HAVE* to *DO* something. I have to step in.

Arnold's friend from the garage game is getting grumbly too. "Ya, and what is this only Hold 'em rule? This shit gets boring, and I like action!!"

Slade looks at Charlene, who's all ears and listening to Arnold as well.

Slade is furious but draws on his skills to stay calm. An opening appears, and Slade takes it. With a light tone so smooth that not one person in the room would detect anger, Slade says to Arnold. "Hey, fucko, let a Fatman sit in a few; let's swap for a bit."

About that time, he hears, "I need to hit the head," from Jimmy, "Where's the little boys' room?"

Slade reacts quickly and adds, "Hey y'all, let's break five, grab some more food and freshen up drinks." He follows on and asks Becky to help out the players. He reminds them, "And y'all take care of her. Hot chicks gotta eat too!

"Hey, Fatman, I think I might jump early. You got plus one on the rail, so you should be good?" Arnold asks Slade.

Again, not showing emotion, Slade replies, "Sure, man, that works." In reality, Slade feels as if a huge weight has been lifted. He didn't want an awkward confrontation with his friend, but he knew he could not let Arnold stay and continue to talk down the game. Arnold's dislike for the game and desire to be anywhere but here "putting in the work" had worked in Slade's favor. Sometimes It's better to be lucky than good, Slade thinks.

Arnold leaves the table. Slade pulls him aside and talks in lowered tones. "How you stand? Up? Down. Even?"

"I'm down right at a dollar," Arnold replies.

"Cool, come on, I'll cash your chips out."

Back at the table, Slade counts the chips, and sure enough, Arnold has right at ninety-five dollars in chips.

Here you go, sir; Slade says formally. Thank you for coming to the opening night of Bird-Man's Poker. The room breaks into laughter at the two goofing around to cause enough of a distraction that no one except Arnold notices Slade sliding him six hundred and fifty dollars.

Slade leans in close again and tells Aronold "That will square us on the rake and the food. Thanks for running the game to kick things off. I appreciate the support, brother". Slade speaks the word brother as smooth as silk, hoping Arnold's exit moves along without confrontation.

Slade isn't happy with his friend and believes he jeopardized the game; the future business!

Slade decides at this moment that from now on, Arnold won't be part of the game or the future business. He is just another player.

Just as Arnold walks away, the guy from the garage game pipes up. I think I'll call it a night as well, I have I've got a quarter left, and I'll cut a high card with the house for it." Action taken," says Slade as he fans the deck across the felt; guests choose first.

The guy pulls a nine of hearts; a respectable card.

"Hey, Becky, come pull a card for the house," Slade beckons.

Becky slinks over and, with a broad grin as Slade ever so slightly cups her ass, turns up a card. The queen of hearts.

"Well, I guess that fits," says Slade as he slides the green chip off the table and hands it to Becky.

Looking at Charlene, Slade motions to the table and declares, "Seat open!"

She gives Slade three hundred dollars, and Slade quickly stacks out her chips about as Checkbook is returning from the restroom.

"Hey brother, be safe out there, and if you two start that power-drinking and shit, call my guy, He'll take you anywhere." Slade hollers to Arnold as he is heading out the door.

"Ya, thanks, Mom," Arnold replies sarcastically, as he and the garage game guy are heading out.

Slade has the oddest feeling, and Checkbook sees it on his face. In a serious and somber tone, he says, "He's been drinking more lately; we should keep an eye on him, this could be a bad road." Checkbook has broken the unspoken rule as only a part-time square-john, part-time rounder can.

Danny chimes in, "Ya, I have a brother-in-law that this shit happened too. All of a sudden, like in six months, three DWIs and two totaled cars, the fool is lucky he hasn't hurt himself or anyone else."

"Ya, he's slippin', I think, but he gets super pissy if I even mention it," Slade says as he stops shuffling and starts to deal around the table for high cards. He then announces, "First Ace deals."

Charlene gets the first Ace, and Slade slides her the deck. Jimmy then continues.

"Look, I wasn't gonna say anything, but I know other people noticed, too, so I am."

"Ok, hold up a second, Charlene, let's hear Jimmy out; this sounds a bit serious."

"Look, not for nothin', but Arnold was hitting the rake hard like I know he pulled fifteen in on one of the big pots, that's more than even Tex, no offense Tex, pulls back. I mean, he was drinking pretty hard here at the table, but that shit's not cool," Jimmy says.

"Fuck," says Slade, shaking his head slowly back and forth. He then takes a deep breath and exhales slowly, and proposes, "I tell you what, I'll make it right; I'll always make it right, please remember that. If shit is ever wrong, it will be made right in THIS house."

Slade opens the box and slides everyone at the table a green chip.

"That should cover any over-rake to this point, *AND*, I'll not pull any more for the next hour. Is that fair?" Slade asks the table.

"Whoa, I wasn't asking for anything, man, that is way past fair. You don't need to do that, I just wanted you to know," Checkbook says appreciatively and a bit surprised.

"Nope, I need it right, and this feels right. So, let's get the cards back in the air so I can clean all you motherfuckers out!" Slade adds, trying to get the room back into the swing of things.

It worked.

The table is alive again. Check raises, out-of-position moves, and of course, Danny the Drain, in his signature move, throws a deck of cards into the kitchen, and one starts to melt under the warming plate. The table loved it and Danny threw the house two green chips saying, "I'll pay double, sorry to make a mess for you, Miss Becky."

The game is starting to wind down but after almost eleven hours, It's time. The sun will be coming up soon, and It's time to break.

Slade looks over, and the kitchen is clean. Slade noticed that Becky was gone about three hours ago, but had been so caught up with the game he hadn't tipped her out or walked her to her car. His mind wanders a bit, thinking Damn, I should have taken better care of that, I might need her to play hostess again. Not to mention I was hoping to go a round or two.

They're down to five players and Jimmy says, "Let's racehorse one time and call it a night, I'm beat."

"Ok, we can do that. This is purely optional, anyone who wants to cash out can."

Tex pipes up, "I'll take my little win and hit the road. He then adds, "Ya know, you run a tight game, and I'm looking forward to the next one. Count me a regular to any five / ten up to thirty / sixty limit you ever decide to run. I do have one little suggestion, though."

"Yes sir, I'm all ears," Slade listened intently.

"You might want to get a different table, this one is a tad tall for the chairs, and us old folks get a sore neck after a while, catch my drift?"

"Man, consider it done, I'll get one delivered tomorrow!" Slade is on board with pleasing the customers.

Tex stands up and extends his hand to Slade, adding, "Seriously, it was a tight game, and nice to see."

Next to cash out is Sam Lorenzo. "I'm out, too. I didn't grind all night to give it up on Racehorse," he says, sort of making fun of himself as one of the tightest players in the game. "And since you're taking suggestions, may I give one?"

"Absolutely," Slade replies with a big grin.

"Given your set-up, it looks like you might be gearing up to expand, or am I off base here?" Sam asks.

"Well, it can be a consideration, but I don't have anything solid set yet," Slade answers, not wanting to give anything away. Sam then continues: "Well, I would love to see a non-smoking night. I've got several friends from church who would like a good clean game. If you let people smoke outside, that'd work. Give it some thought. I'll help you fill the table, we all have to make a living," Sam says as he stands up to shake Slade's hand. Slade slides him his cash, and he's a happy camper.

Sam added for good measure, "Tex is right, this is one of the most solid and straight-up games I've seen in a while, so count me in as a regular. Good food, good drinks, and an honest cut which is rare these days."

Slade thanks Sam and promises to talk more about the non-smoking night to see if he can wrangle it.

Just Charlene, Slade, and Jimmy were left at the table for Racehorse. "Two dollars good?" Slade says.

Jimmy and Charlene, at almost the same time, reply, "Sold," then start to do that little giggle laugh one does when they have been awake for too many hours.

Slade deals each player seven cards. He points to Charlene, who flips over an Ace. "Damn," says Slade, "this shit might be done."

The three are aware there's absolutely no skill involved in this game. It's a pure gamble.

"Beat the ace," Slade says to Jimmy, who starts flipping his cards. As he turns the fifth card Slade recaps "damn, that's the fourth heart, you might have a winner there my man." The sixth card is a club, and there's nothing higher than the ace. He flips the last card. It's a diamond, and it makes a pair of nines.

"Pair, says Slade, let me see if I can take that out."

One by one Slade starts to flip his cards, and the sixth card makes a pair of jacks.

"Well, that takes you out, my man, let's cash you."

Slade quickly counts out Jimmy's chips and cashes him out. "Pretty sure you came out a winner my friend," says Slade.

"I did, thank you for a good game. I want to add some of my input as well. Bit of a rough start, but Tex and Lorenzo are right, this is a good game. Hit me up, and you can count on me most of the time," Jimmy promises.

"My suggestion is to get some TVs going, I'm gonna want to see the scores during football season for sure and probably basketball season, too," Jimmy adds as he grabs his cash.

"Consider it done, my man, we'll get this going on the regular," Jimmy goes for the fist bump and is out the door, leaving Slade and Charlene alone at the table to finish out the hand.

Slade points out to her, "you have six cards to take out my jacks".

Charlene flips three cards and has a pair of queens and an ace showing. Slade flips his last card which doesn't help his hand and slides Charlene the six hundred bucks. "Nice way to finish up," Slade says. Then pulls her chips in and counts her out.

"Damn, you only had one buy, right?" Slade asks her.

"Yes," she replies a little sheepishly.

"Fuck me, you did well and quietly racked up tonight," Slade says trying to provoke Charlene a bit. Then quickly adds: "You think you'll make it back if we get this game on the regular?" Charlene nods in agreement, but her face shows a question.

At once, she asks, "Can LD play here?

"Well, hell ya he can. Why would anyone think he wasn't welcome?"

"Well, she replies, looking at the floor. Most people know you went to go off mode at LD's game and never went back. He thinks you're pissed at him or something. You've been playing all over town. Word is that you are a serious player."

"Man, I hit other games and have been focusing on limit and pot limit most of the time so I hadn't rotated into his game yet; that's it, I'm telling you."

"Ok, awesome, I'll pass it on to him. Count me as a regular, hit me up anytime you're running the game and I'll make it around," says Charlene; "I prefer limit games."

As Slade locked the door and set the alarm, a broad smile came across his face.

This shit had worked. Even with the payback and not raking for an hour the house advantage had pulled in thirteen hundred dollars.

Add to that the overwhelming support. These people all knew there was a rake and were happy to pay it, as long as it was "fair."

Bird-Man Poker was born.

The End

EPILOGUE

Slade closes his faux closet after stashing away the cash for the night and thinks to himself. Things are going to be smooth and predictable. I've set the groundwork for a new business. I can't wait to tell Phil!

As Slade shuts off the light, the morning sun is starting to light up the duplex. Slade reaches and clicks the office light off and then hears what sounds like his waterbed sloshing. Slade is fully alert, and in the moment, his mind is rushing at the thought of an intruder.

Quietly but quickly, Slade backtracks into the office and retrieves his spare pistol from under his desk; his mind is shaking and racing, but his hands are steady and sure. He makes his way down the hall hugging the wall to glimpse the mirror in his bedroom that will let him have an almost complete view of his bed. Seeing the bed, he relaxes fully as a broad smile crosses his face, and he breathes an enormous sigh of relief while uncocking the pistol and tucking it into his pants.

In the mirror, he sees Becky sprawled across his bed, waiting for him. The bed's still moving as she rolls over and reveals her fully naked body to him. Slade walks in, and she leans up to kiss him. Lightly at first, then hard and with passion. She stands, takes Slade's hand, and silently pulls him toward the walk-in shower; Slade drops his clothes on the way. Sometimes you have to lose to win, Slade thinks. This, he muses, is when it's better to be lucky than good. As they exit the shower, still glowing passionately after a round of standing sex, Slade decides not to send this one packing straight away.

Lightly drying her off and leading her back to the bed, Slade asks without a stutter. "Well, word at the club is that you play for the other team. What up with that?"

"I play on whatever team suits me at the moment. There's nothing like the thrill of watching the inner thighs of my dancer play things tremble at just the right touch. But I also enjoy the heated release from men like you. Men who know exactly how to take care of me!"

"Well, alright then. I got zero issues with that; I just like to know the score. Best to have things down up front."

"How did you do tonight? I know it was a rocky start, but once you calmed everyone down, things seemed to go well," Becky said, smoothly changing the subject.

Slade is thinking, damn, brains too, and I had better be careful here. "The game went fine. I want to make this a cornerstone and add more games as I go," he spills, instantly realizing he's revealed more than he intended. The two fall into bed, this time thinking about actual sleep.

Just then, as if on cue to keep Slade from revealing even more, the phone rings. "What the hell," he says, "at this fucking hour."

"Hello, this is Slade," he answers.

"Hello, sir. Is this Slade Garrick?"

"Yes," Slade replies.

"This is The WILCO Sheriff's Office, and we are calling to inform you that Arnold Cabraise has been in a serious car incident."

"What!? Is he OK?" Slades ask in quick succession.

"Yes sir," the voice says from the other end.

"Oh, good," Slade interrupts.

"Sir, he will be taken to the county jail after we see to his minor injuries. His car, which is almost certainly totaled, has been impounded." The official continues. "He has requested that we call you and said you would take care of obtaining his representation in his DWI case and setting up a bond to post bail once set."

II

"OH, I see, well fuck! I mean, I apologize, yes, ma'am. I will get it all handled; please let Arnold know."

"Yes, sir, we will. Please have his attorney contact our offices for details; it will be at least twenty-four hours before he can see a judge."

The bed sloshes as Slade is fully sitting up. And he replies. "Ok, I understand; at least twenty-four hours, I got it." He hangs up the phone.

Becky sits up in bed, holding the sheet to cover her breasts, and says, "Well, that sounded less than good."

As Slade's mind drifts, wondering why a woman he has seen naked in every sense of the word would hold a sheet to cover herself, he also tries to make sense of what he has heard on the phone.

"Ya, that was Williamson County," Slade starts to answer. "It seems Arnold got in a wreck and..." but trails off and abruptly snags his buzzing pager, instantly recognizing the number is Phil's.

"Damn, he does have this town wired. I can't believe he already knows and is calling me," he says to Becky while holding up the pager. "It's Phil." Once again, Slade is WAY more revealing with Becky than ever with any of his playthings; typically, he would silence them and send them packing with this turn of events.

Brushing that thought aside, he immediately starts to dial numbers as Becky slides back down into bed slightly, scratching Slade's back with her fingernails.

"Hey Phil, what's up? Are you calling about Arnold?

"No, what about Arnold, little buddy? I haven't heard a thing," Phil replies with genuine concern.

"Oh, I thought. Not important." Slade stammers. "We can catch up on that later. You have something important, or you would not be paging at this hour; tell me what you need, and I'm on it."

"I'll get to that in a minute; tell me about the game. You sound awake, so I'm guessing it went long, so that's a good thing," Phil says with pride in his voice.

III

"Oh, ya, the game went well; we finished up about an hour ago. I've been doing a little employee moral work since then, if you get me," Slade says with a snark.

Becky pinches him, leans close to the phone, and says, "Hi Phil," in a super sexy voice.

"To be a young man and winner; you enjoy these moments, little buddy," Phil says to his mentee.

"Thanks, Phil; for real, what can I get done for you?"

"Well, I am back from the Colonial; some folks wanted to talk about the greens, so I made a quick trip."

Slade knows this is code, as Phil knows absolutely nothing about golf. Slade is sure that some members of the Colonial Golf Club have something to do with the sportsbook business. If you have to talk to them, it's usually not a good thing.

"Oh. I didn't know you went to the Colonial, fuck, I understand for sure why you couldn't make it to the game."

"Yes, I figured you'd get it. There are some brown spots on the greens, and I'll need to get that handled pretty quickly. I am going to need you to help me; I mean, I'm asking if you will."

"Done. I'm in one hundred percent. Let's meet for breakfast and plan on how to get those brown spots back to green. I can catch you up on the Arnold shit too." Slade says without hesitation.

"Breakfast sounds good; Pancake House Westside, ten o'clock?" Phil asks.

"Solid," replies Slade as he hangs up the phone.

"Well, so much for grabbing a long nap. I'm sure you heard. I have some business to take care of. Look, I'm not sure what's up with me, maybe I'm dead tired on my feet, but normally I do not even let people listen in while I talk business. We need to make sure we have this shit straight. This is MY business. It is NOT to be shared with anyone. I know how you little girls cluck, cluck, cluck up there at the club, but this shit is for fucking real. We good?" Slade asks.

"I understand. Look, I know who you are, and yes, Ramona ran her mouth sometimes, but she didn't know much. I am not her; I get it. That is business. This," as she grabs Slade's ass, "is fun."

"Damn, I am gonna have to watch out for you. You catch on too fucking quick and say all the right shit. Now bring that sweet little ass over here, and let's go another round or two."

Becky inches in closer and starts to grind into Slade. The waterbed really starts to slosh as she pushes the covers away and climbs on top of him. Always good to take a moment of escape from what promises to be a long day ahead...

About the Author

Will Simpson is a change agent who has served as a senior executive in the Austin technology and services sectors for 25-plus years. He

currently serves as Co-Founder and CEO of Ten Eleven Twelve, an Executive Consulting and Coaching organization.

Will is a husband and partner to his wife, Caroline, and father to his three children, Sam, Hannah, and Madeline. An Austin native, Will loves to hike the local trails, play terrible rounds of golf and sneak down to the coast whenever he can for some redfish action.

Will is now fully embracing his new career, writing fiction, and as the saying goes, the best is yet to come!

Links:
https://amazon.com/author/willsimpson
https://www.goodreads.com/author/show/19516967.Will_Simpson
https://www.instagram.com/willrsimpson_author/
https://www.facebook.com/Will.Simpson.Writer

Made in the USA
Columbia, SC
09 August 2023

6c34099e-50be-40b0-9648-7db0f8ef4843R01